OMEGA RUMOR

Book 1

Cody R. Tucker

For Jerry & Minerva McGregor.

"You can do anything you set your mind to."

Thank you, Pappaw. Thank you, Drammaw. I love you.

"In all her dealings goodness is her guide."

FROM "THE CANTERBURY TALES" BY GEOFFREY CHAUCER

MAP

Omega Rumor

By Cody R. Tucker

PROLOGUE: THE FIRST VERSES OF THE HOLY VOLUME:

It began when the God and Goddess worked together. They made the universe as mortals make children. They are the Father and Mother of all living things. They are Alpha and Omega. Now and forever. Know their names and revere the fruit of their work for all eternity.

When the world was first made, it was but a great pool of water. They bathed and delighted in it happily. Then they began to work on how their children would dwell upon the earth. They took the rocks of space and planted them in the sea. But the Father feared that his creations were more likely to drown- being so close to the waves. So, they took those rocks and formed masses of land that could float in the sky. Omega playfully called them orbs as she stroked them warmly. The lovers embraced as they looked upon what they had created thus far. They saw that it was good.

But wherever good is, evil also dwells close at hand to strike out at it. That is the truth that pervaded even the Gods in the beginning. The question of how to govern their children was introduced. The Goddess, full of deceit, wished to rule with a hard fist ready to wipe out freedom so that all the world would bow down to her. The gracious God disagreed. He wanted his people to be free, safe, and happy. He left it in the hands of his children to worship him for what he hath done. God knew that his greatness neither increased nor decreased with man's praises. The Goddess would not listen to his divine reasoning. She wanted to take precious free-will so that she would be lifted up on high. Being the Goddess was not enough for her.

The Goddess struck out against her God. They battled across the universe. The force of their blows broke many of the asteroids that they were going to use as orbs to hold humanity over the waters. The Goddess tried many ways to overcome her lover-turned-foe. She tried to beat him and strangle him. But he managed to overcome her until finally he had to kill her. He sorrowed for this loss, though she was evil. To honor her, he encased her body into molten rock. But then he saw that he did not have enough orbs to hold every creation over the waves. He'd have to make some land on the water after all. So, with a heavy heart, he broke the Goddess into pieces and made each end of her body into the very lands upon the face of the sea that are dwelt on even today.

That was how it all began. The world may have had death before it had life, but Alpha showered his blessings upon us all. Therefore, shalt thou shun the past deeds of evil and instead overcome them with goodness.

CHAPTER 1 PRINCESS ILENE OF PANGEA

Ilene put the book back into the pile. She considered these holy writings that her parents pushed on her since childhood.

The God may be great, but I still don't understand a few things. If he were able to encase the Goddess in rocks, why couldn't he have simply created more orbs? Why not just make her body parts into floating isles as well?

Ilene shrugged and merely chalked it up to the indiscernible mysteries of religion. She had nothing to fear of it. That sort of consideration was for Alphite priests and prayer maidens, not for an already blessed princess such as herself. Speaking of her life, she looked up to hear that a praising song about it was being played before her throne.

Here was a life that began as nothing more than something for happy violins to sing of. The ballad had lyrics that boast of a sweet girl's happy existence before her major step into womanhood.

Ilene! The King's daughter!
Ilene! There's no one greater than her!
There was never one like Ilene
She is beautiful, the finest face ever seen

Unmatched in beauty, yet she does not have pride,
For kindness is her guide
She showers all her subjects with courtesy
No hand could be raised against her sweet charms
She can make the strongest soldier lay down his arms
If she were a prince, we'd call her lord
Ilene, we know you can conquer without a sword
Ilene is our kingdom's greatest light
Her blue eyes, her maroon-golden locks are all so bright
So pretty she is that artists beg to paint her from about the earth
It is how the Prince of Ur first knew her worth
They say he has been a bored royal in his kingdom
He first knew joy when he saw her face, and then some
Further gossip finds that he grew sick with grief without Ilene
For he knew that he lived squalidly without a face so serene
Word got back that Ilene was the boy's only chance
Soon, a Pangean and Ursian will be joined in a lover's dance
So wedding bells ring for this meeting of states
In the name of Pangea, she'll make a happy mate!

The royal ship seemed rocked by applause. The quartet singers bowed. As these fellows went back to work, the ship also proceeded back to its usual activities. The captain put his mountainous hat back upon his head. He had taken it off out of respect for his country. He combed his wind-torn mustache and beard back as he went up the steps to inspect the helmsman.

As for Ilene herself, she was at the other end of the ship. The fine girl sat near the men muscling all their might to shift the ropes of the sails. They lowered the sails into half capacity to slow the power of the wind upon the vessel. Ilene sat upon a carpenter's masterful representation of her throne back home.

From her seat, she listened appreciatively to the quartet's song. Watching them play in the middle of the deck made the ship seem more like the much-missed royal court to Ilene. It was a fine tune that she was happy to hear as opposed to the half-melodious grunts of sea shanties.

Ilene was even more beautiful than the song proclaimed. They failed to mention that her "maroon-golden locks" were as smooth as fine silk, while also forgetting to chime on these locks woven into a series of curls in a pattern so symmetrically perfect that her head's top seemed like an image for a family crest. Ilene wore a fine dress that made a playful contest at being brighter than her own beauteous features. The violet dress sparkled as if it were a rare jewel shining out for all to see. Her smile, even, was as wide as the mighty ship in-route to her marriage with the Ursian prince.

Ilene got up. She turned to her old servant, Marlene. "I am a little dizzy from sitting on this rocky deck, Marlene. Perhaps we could walk around a bit?"

Marlene got up from the bench by the stairs. The servant picked up her raggedy, finely cleaned gown as she waddled over the rickety deck towards her lady. "Not a bad idea, little Ilene. Would you prefer to walk about the deck or below?"

"Certainly **on** the deck. I might as well get used to it. I hear that the Prince of Ur loves sailing."

"Now, now, Ilene. Can't you see that the rocky foundation of this vessel is keeping my poor, old feet off-balance?"

As if to illustrate, Marlene thudded about with every step she made. If not for her long black hair and fine features becoming of a nearly middle-aged maid, one would take her burly build for that of one of the tight-fisted shipmates. She was rather tall and muscular.

Ilene looked upon the state of her maid's body. Though it was strong, it still needed to earn its sea legs. "You'll manage. Now come walk with me. Sitting tires me out."

"Very inconsiderate of you, my lady. Don't mind me if I fall overboard as these rocky waves hurl me to my demise."

"That's the spirit," said Ilene. "Now let's race up the stairs." They rounded a corner on the deck to a small flight of steps heading to the upper reaches of the ship's stern.

Seeing Marlene out of breath half-way up, the princess slowed down for her maid's benefit. Marlene heaved some words. "You, little Ilene," she huffed, "are harder to chase after since you grew up." Breath finally revived- Marlene continued with regular speech as they began to walk together. "That reminds me, wasn't that a lovely song that those boys wrote in honor of your wedding?"

Ilene agreed. "Yes, indeed. Although, I think that they could have sung a few more lines on my wonderful hair design. I happen to pride myself on its craftsmanship."

The ship rocked over a slight wave like the hump of a small hill. Marlene bobbed her head back in a chortle. "Really now? I should like to take some of that pride on your hair's fine craftsmanship. I am, after all, the starving artist at work braiding it each morning while all you do is sit there."

"And read…!" Ilene said insistently.

On the way up, the two ladies made an opening for two half-hurried shipmates to go past them.

Ilene playfully quipped back, "I also refer to it as my own pride because I have to endure hearing you sing each morning as you fiddle with my hair. Not only do you crack my lovely mirror as you sing off-key, but you fiddle too harshly with my hair and hurt me. Any other girl of lesser willpower could not endure your tortures for a minute, let alone all morning. So, my dear Marlene, I've surely earned the pride that comes with my hair's beauty."

Ilene brushed a handful of her locks up as if to present them as her own accomplishment's trophy. Upon the stern was little activity. Not many people came up here. Only the two men at work on some broken section of railing towards the back were seen next to a man standing off to the side on a self-appointed smoke break. They walked about on this generous space of ship and chatted on.

"You know, maybe that song isn't perfect. Some could say it was attempting to act as your biographical ballad. If that is the song's case, I'd be the first to vote that it didn't capture every facet of your life."

Ilene snapped back curiously, "What do you mean?"

"Well, although it was fine to listen to, it didn't offer a complete history of Pangea's dear princess to be wed. It didn't even mention her faults, especially the ones from her naughty childhood days."

Fanatical hushes giggled from the girl as she tried to wipe away the rest of the words from her maid's mouth. Marlene spoke on as she dodged the covering hands. "Why, I remember that our perfect little princess was so ill-behaved that she would not admit to her faults even after I smacked her bottom red. Because of her tight lips, we've still yet to decipher who was throwing bad fruit at the guardsmen over the castle walls."

Ilene laughed, "Come on, Marlene. I was only six."

"Ah-ha! You admit it after all these years. I knew I would get through to you."

Ilene smiled and blushed red while spying to see if anyone was listening to these embarrassing memories. "But Marlene, you were only my nanny then. Now you're my servant. You've no place to humble a woman of my estate in public like this."

Marlene, speaking more soberly said, "An elder always has a place to lecture on the faults of the young, no matter their estate. You remember that, my little Ilene."

"Yes, ma'am," assented the girl.

"Now that I've embarrassed you enough with a past fault, let's see if I can think of another. Oh, yes. I remember when I taught my little Ilene some proper manners. I thought it was the end of her spanking days. Then a party for the nations came to Pangea. The Duke of one of the revolving orb states (I forget which) arrived a little drunk. In greeting Ilene's parents, she heard the Duke let slip a curse word that got her spanked once. Thinking herself an authority liken unto nanny, she came behind the Duke and spanked his bottom for his potty mouth. This incident made you two the laughingstock of the ball."

Ilene mused, "I still don't know why you spanked me again later that night. I did no harm. The man **did** act very rude."

"Still," said Marlene, "it was not your place to chide him."

Ilene got smart-mouthed again, "If only **his** nanny were with him that night."

"My point is that there are so many interesting things about our dear Ilene that would make good songs other than her beauty and her grace. I should really talk to those musical mates and help them write a ballad of Ilene's childhood days. Would you happen to know any words that rhyme with: 'She wet the bed until she was six?'"

"How about: 'She then gave her disrespectful maid many kicks?'"

Marlene grunted, "It doesn't quite have the melody that those boys had. Perhaps we'll stick to the royal life of marrying abroad and leave the songs to the professionals."

"It's agreed, partner." They shook hands roughly as if they were business accomplices. "Now be a good servant, or nanny, or whatever you are and go fetch my ball. I'd fancy another game of catch."

Already walking toward the stairs, Marlene groaned, "Do I have to? This is the hundredth time we have played. We are both too old for these childish games. You're about to be married and I'm fixed to retire."

"We've got to pass the time somehow. The captain told me that even though we're riding a strong current, the Ursian Sea is still a long trip."

Turning back, Marlene implored, "It would be healthier for your mind to read the many books you've brought."

"I'm sorry to disappoint you, but I've already had my fair fill of fairy tales. I had to pass the time while you were on my hair somehow."

"You're a brat."

"You're so understanding."

While her maid was gone, Ilene went for a better look over the railing. There were no mountains or floating isles to behold. All she could see was a pure blue vista. The sea, the sky, and even the clouds looked blue. The sight seemed like the farthest she could be from home, from anything.

"I got the ball, Ilene. What say we get some of these boys to join-"

Ilene did not turn around. She still stared into the blue.

"What's wrong, sweety?" Ilene still did not turn back.

Ilene spoke slowly. Ilene only spoke seriously when she spoke slowly. "Sometimes I look out here trying to get one last glimpse of home, even if it's a dot in the distance. I pretend to wave and imagine my parents waving back."

Marlene said nothing as she cradled the ball at her side. Ilene made a pretend smile. It didn't work on Marlene.

"Not that I'm complaining. It's every girl's dream to grow up in a castle, be a princess, and marry a prince. I guess the part that I can't figure out is why mom and dad just shipped me away. Why didn't they come with me for my special day? It's hard to not assume that they don't care about me."

Marlene raised her mouth.

Ilene put a stop to that. "Please don't give me that stuff about them being busy on government business. Please. You always taught me to say please if I wanted something, Marlene. I want you to not use that excuse again. Please. I mean, you've been harping on that since I was a kid. The closest thing I had to a loving parent was you. All they ever did was trade me off to teachers or to your care. They never thought that more than four dinners together a year were appropriate. They were always too busy running the kingdom or meeting with other leaders. Honestly, I think a lot of that was just an excuse to ignore me. I don't even remember the last time she gave me a birthday gift. How sick is that? A mother that won't even give her child a gift? Am I such a stranger?"

Marlene said, "Well, the queen **did** announce your coming engagement during last year's celebration if that counts."

"Oh really? Well, I guess it's better than nothing. At least **you** always get me a new dress or book each year, Marlene. Queen

Barda couldn't be bothered to turn from her precious kingdom to even acknowledge my existence. I've heard the rumors. They tried for another child. They wanted a son- a proper heir. When it turned out to be a girl, do you know what they did with her? Do you know what my own mother did with her? Let's just say that nobody has to remember any birthday gifts for her."

"Please," whispered Marlene, "don't be upset. You don't even have a sister."

"Exactly."

The wind sighed as it careened the vessel onward.

"I guess I should just be grateful that they didn't get rid of me too. They only kept me around for diplomatic measures, though."

"No. That's not-"

"Ur is expanding- planting more of their bases on neutral or Pangean territory. They've had their eye on Pangea: 'the head of Omega, the head of the world.' So, they offer me as a token of good will- an alliance. Pangea's trading wealth and Ur's mighty military will soon be brought together in holy matrimony along with their heirs in order to settle these land disputes. Not as sweet and simple as the song makes it out to be, huh? But like I said, at least I get the prince out of it. I get the prince just like you said good little princesses do after you read me those romances that mother had no time for."

Ilene scoffed again. "I really hope romance is everything that you said it was, Marlene. I brought all those old story books with me to recapture those wonderful feelings that they used to give me. All they did was make me feel hollow. Because none of those fabled princesses felt as badly as I did unless a dragon, or witch, was around. Things got happy again when the prince arrived. I got my prince. So why do I still feel this way? I really hope it's better in Ur. I hope he is wonderful. Because I don't know if I belong at home anymore."

Marlene put her arm around Ilene's shoulders. The girl's gaze finally snapped back to her companion.

"Maybe your parents didn't think the most of you. But I did. Maybe it hurts to think of being alone. But I'm here. Maybe you **will** be happy over there. If not, guess what?"

"**You'll** be there?"

"You're smarter than you look. Now let's play catch before I make you walk the plank."

Ilene smiled as she went to the other end of the deck. "Aye-aye, captain."

CHAPTER 2 SHIP LIFE

A shadow loomed over the ship. One of the revolving orb isles was above the vessel. These isles are one of the great wonders of nature. They rotate around the planet, high above the world like asteroids. They are inhabited by traders, travelers, and merchants. These isles are also used as communities. They are a means for trading on a well-scheduled orbit cycle. When the isles hover over shipping routes, cities, or pre-scheduled locations; a large conveyor pulley descends a wooden platform that holds the traders and their goods. Such relations are short. The isles quickly pass on in their orbit like a large cloud crawling past the horizon within every hour. So, the ship had to work fast.

As the chains cranked down to align the platform over the vessel, Ilene and Marlene were roused from their game. "I wonder what they're selling," said Marlene. "Is this really even the best time for trade?"

"It's no wonder, my dear," said a smoking shipmate, "we're a ship on the go after all. We need to keep on the up and up with food, water, and other necessities."

As those on the upper deck looked on, they saw the captain march before the colorfully dressed merchants. The captain slapped the pudgiest one- knocking off his red hat.

As the merchant slinked his billowy red hat back atop his curly-wheat of clumpy hair he squawked, "What was that for?"

The captain, Amadeus Crock, became a decorated naval leader of Pangea for his no-nonsense loyalty to protocol.

He said, "Your supply of goods was short last time. We only got less than half of what we paid for. The rest of the food was either partially eaten or fully spoiled. I lost a man because of you!"

The merchant flinched and winced. "Heavens! He's dead?"

The captain glared. "No. He quit because I didn't have enough food for lunch."

The pudgy man looked to his partner. This other man was guiltily slurping up a cookie in fear. Turning back, the head merchant said, "I wasn't around for that run, sir. It must have been Jake who was in charge."

Crock looked to his captivated crew in frustrated disbelief. He looked back. His hairy, hard hands were suddenly like small swords. "I distinctly remember a man in such a hat," said Crock as he whipped the red cap off again, only to be followed by the merchant trying to pick it up.

"I also remember this idiotic cape," said Crock as he swished it around the merchant's neck to hold him in place.

"I even remember the same green blouse, and yellow boots," said Crock as he used his leg to sweep his leg behind the yellow stockings to trip the tradesman on to the wooden floor.

"I remember all of these same tacky trappings on the same fat man whose stomach poked out of it. I **distinctly** remember who deals with me. This conman was most easy to recall because he was color-coated," said Crock as he suspended the culprit up by the throat with his own cape.

"Now the question is: will this same man claim responsibility for his actions?"

The man tried to painfully speak and breathe. "Prrhpsh... we... cnnn... mkkkk... uh... comprmshsh...?"

The captain let go of the leverage of the cape, releasing the merchant's throat, and spilling the gasping trout upon the hard floor. "Repeat."

A dramatic sigh sounded. "Sweet air! Her kiss was missed!"

"Repeat."

The merchant sighed, happy to feel oxygen again. "Anyway, I said: Perhaps we can make a compromise. Then I think I died there for a second. I do apologize for our unfortunate dealings last time. *Royal Services* is an enterprise that prides on excellent service. But you have to remember the words of the Prophetess Ada: 'We come from an imperfect race. We make mistakes. There is no need for shame in this.' There is also no need for stone-hearted murder as I like to also add."

Crock sternly asked, "Enough of that, whelp. You were in no danger. I also happen to recall the Prophet Sygar saying: 'Sometimes you have to prick the mule to get it to stand up straight.' Now what of this compromise you speak of?"

"Suppose we only charge you half of what is normally charged for this present order, that way it is all even."

The captain flipped the cape back behind the merchant. "Only a fourth. Now load us up."

The merchant snapped to an orange suited mate. "You heard the man, Jake. Get the stuff moved."

Jake replied, "Why? So that you can blame me for another order you miscounted as you push me around like a pack-mule?"

Red rage splotched the leader's face as he retorted, "It's like the captain said. If you don't straighten up, I'll prick you for all your stubborn whining. Now go."

Transfixed by the small drama, Ilene whispered to Marlene as if they were commenting on a play. "Seems that this little pack of mules has appointed a king-ass. Don't you think that they look a trifle familiar?"

Marlene only smiled as she began to stare more intently at the merchants.

The merchants proceeded with carrying the goods to the lower quarters of the ship with little to no help from Crock's crew. Most of the goods were in crates. Ilene noticed an hourglass and a medium-sized mirror held precariously by Jake, who gave a sour look to the main merchant via its reflection. While they made these trips, Ilene had some of the mates bring up lunch: a nice sandwich and glass of milk to go with the show.

When they were done, Crock approached the pudgy one. "What is your name? I wish to contact your supervisor about your unsavory behavior."

"Name's Isaac Inklewood. But I'm afraid that I don't have a supervisor. *Royal Services* is a co-op business. We don't just transport goods. We also do many other jobs, including entertainment. Sir Jake, despite his less than cheery moods, was once a fine jester for the King of Pangea himself."

As Ilene washed her chicken sandwich down with milk, she

turned to Marlene. "Oh, now I remember that man. He was the one who pretended to fall down a lot."

Marlene said nothing to this as she abruptly got up. She couldn't keep her eyes off the jester.

Jake turned upon hearing his name. This sudden motion caused him to lose balance and fall down for real. The ship, including Isaac, erupted in snickers at this.

"Hm. It appears that not a lot has changed."

At last, Isaac was about to receive his payment when his platform started slowly cranking upward. It gradually went higher and faster. The time for the orbiting sphere to go out of alignment was upon them. With a cry of curses, Isaac ran to the rising platform using mightily chugging legs. Before the platform went out of range, Isaac made a leap. His chin, and then his arms managed to clop on to the platform.

"Help me up," he begged. Jake stood over him.

Jake crossed his arms as he stared down upon his fellow merchant. "All right," gruffly said Isaac. "I'm sorry! Now: up! Or I'll pull you down with me."

The jester bent down to retrieve poor Isaac. After standing up straight again, Isaac implored the captain to throw him his payment. The captain tossed a small bag of coins. Instead of landing in Isaac's hands, the bag hit the panel's edge. The finances plopped into the water.

As Isaac rose above the crow's nest, he asked the man there with crowing concern, "Tell the captain to give me double on the next delivery."

The request was mimicked to the captain below. "I will do no such thing," was the indignant reply of the naval leader. But the chain had pulled the merchants well out of ear shot.

The jester caught sight of Marlene. He kept his gaze fixated on her as well.

The captain paced back to his position by the steering. "Blood licking merchants. They live on those isles because no one wants them down here." The sails were then ordered back to full capacity. "Come on now. No more shows. We still must get the princess to her wedding."

Ilene touched Marlene as the maid was still staring at the orb floating off into the distance. "Marlene? Are you okay?"

As the sails were whipped back into shape, Marlene turned to Ilene and said, "It's my obligation as your maid to tell you that her ladyship has had enough excitement for one day. But as your friend, I know that you'll disagree and beg to toss the ball about some more."

Marlene was hiding something, but Ilene was respectful enough to discretely ignore it.

Their lunch's table was cleared by some mates. The waves seemed less active and gentler in their swishes. The sun was beginning to wane. Though Ilene's eyes were beginning to wane too, she agreed with Marlene's statement and wished to play some more. The ship would reach Ur the next day. As foolish as it may seem to some, Ilene wanted to make her last free day last.

As the two friends threw the ball, one of the two men by the back railing exclaimed, "There! We've finally sanded down the crack in the bloody thing."

"Now you're sure that it is secure, nephew?"

"Of course, uncle. I'm just glad that we're finally done with it."

The two men were about to leave when Marlene called them. "Ahoy, mates. Do you fancy a game of catch?"

The biggest, and apparently oldest, had long blonde hair and an even longer beard. The other one had red hair nearly shaved down to the round of his head. He also had scruffs of red hair in the attempt of a beard. The blonde said, "I don't believe our captain would like that. We may have more work to do now that we are done with the busted railing."

The red snickered, but the blonde jabbed him fast enough to silence him. "Besides," the blonde continued, "I'm no master of regal protocol, but I don't believe that we lay-folk are worthy to be in her ladyship's presence, even for a... game of catch."

Ilene replied, "Don't fret. For 'her ladyship' has more authority on this ship than your captain. Thus, it is my royal, regal, and-er, Marlene? Do you have another synonym with 'R' that you can think of?"

"Hm... 'righteous?'"

"-And my **righteous** will that you boys can have a break."

The two men looked to one another, shrugging in confusion as to what they should do. Ilene then ceased their quibbles by asking, "What are your names, boys?"

The blonde said, "I'm Osiris."

The red said, "I'm Marius. You may not remember, but we were part of that quartet that played you that song just now."

Marlene gasped for joy. "Her grace just adored it. We were just talking about it not so long ago." The two knowingly sneered at each other with affection.

Marius began to boast with his hands contentedly crossed over his chest. "I wrote that whole thing. Your world-renowned beauty was my muse. And may I say that I came short of fully representing it, Ilene."

Ilene blushed and looked down a bit. No one had ever called her simply 'Ilene' outside of Marlene. It was always: 'majesty,' or, 'ladyship.'

Osiris stirred the pride of Marius away. "You didn't write that song. Mr. Hound did. You only added in that last line."

Osiris then said something that was less outspoken as he drew closer to Marius. "And do not make familiar advances to the lady. She is to be married, you flirtatious goon."

Marius disputed. "But, Osiris, I made quite the closing line, eh?"

Osiris turned to Ilene and said, "I beg your ladyship's pardon for my nephew. He likes to stand tall for show."

Marius quipped, "It's better than standing small for a foe."

"Sounds as though we are both collaborating lyrics to a new song, little one," returned Osiris.

Hearing this, Ilene noted that she was a hair taller than Marius. "Well, now that we've all gotten to know each other better, can we play a bit? I promise not to tell the captain. And if he does find out and say anything, I'll feed him a verse about how you lads were just serving my need for... personal entertainment, or something like that."

Marlene agreed. "I'm sure he'll understand. He wouldn't punish Mr. Marius, the greatest song writer of the sea."

With this, the men laughed their fears away and played.

Each player went to their own corner of the stern's deck. For fear of dropping the ball, Osiris merely rolled it to Ilene across the way.

Marius, always ready to tease, said, "What do you call that?"

As Ilene threw it back to Marius, Osiris said, "A precaution. I don't want to accidently throw the ball overboard."

Marius mocked on as he threw it to his uncle. "Weren't you listening to Ilene? There is no need to fret. You worry too much, uncle."

Osiris began one of his stern lectures as he rolled the ball back to Ilene.

"My boy, you would do well to be more cautious in life. Take the nation of Ur that you're about to enter. I need you to be extra alert, for your own safety... It was once a land of giants, you know."

Ilene threw the ball to Marlene, who looked curiously at Osiris. Marius swiped his hand at Osiris's words as he caught the ball thrown by Marlene. "Those are just fairy tales. There are no giants in Ur."

Marius threw the ball back to Osiris. "That's because they were all killed off."

Osiris did not throw the ball this time. He held it as he told of the legend.

"Once, Ur was where the giants dwelt. They say that they were the children of Alpha and Omega. Smaller humans like us were the children of the giants. These children grew insubordinate of their masters, like Omega was when she turned on Alpha. A war started. The brutality, not the size, of the people against the giants won the land for the humans. The giants were enslaved into building Ur's cities. They were tortured if they refused. It's why Ur has such big buildings despite being one of the poorer nations. Those were prisons once. They were made with the bones of other giants. When you hear thunder, that is the cry of giants echoing from the past. Some men found the treatment of the giants terrible and tried to fight the new rulers. But they were defeated and cast out. This is how the other nations, such as Pangea, formed over the centuries. Over these same centuries, the giants began to die off. The remaining few of their endangered race revolted and now they wander the ocean as one would wade through an endless swamp- surviving off of even the largest leviathan sea beasts for food. Now, I'm not saying that the legend is true. I'm saying that I've seen how the Ursians hunt and kill leviathan sea monsters for food as well. The sheer fury and effort they put into their naval battles with those terrifying behemoths makes me believe that these are people that can conquer giants. If not for their current lack of wealth, allies, and total ambition; I believe that Ur could take on the greatest giant of all: the world. I just want you to know what kind of place we're going to, Marius. Take caution. Please."

Osiris looked to Ilene. "I wish the same to you, Ilene. I pray that your marriage to the prince of Ur will mark a unifying of all nations into one body at peace. The wealth of Pangea is exactly what Ur needs after all these years if its ambitions are growing again. That could mean dark times if we're not careful."

Osiris rolled the ball to Marius.

Marius then held the ball as if considering his uncle's story. Then he stretched out a cocky grin. "They probably just made that stuff up to sound tough. I know a boaster's tall tale when I hear one."

Marius beamed the ball to Marlene. The ball fumbled in her hands. She tried to lock her fingers around it. She backed a few paces to get her footing. Then she lost her footing, slamming into the railing where the crack was. It wasn't repaired strong enough to keep from breaking under her weight. Before any gasps were let out, the maid fell overboard with the ball.

CHAPTER 3
OVERBOARD

Ilene sprang for Marlene first. She didn't scream out her name. She was mute with shock. Ilene's shoes did the crying out as they bolted her towards her beloved nanny. Ilene didn't quite know what she would have done had she reached Marlene on time. Jumping after her seemed to be a foolish choice. Still, Ilene had to see if she could do something- anything. Most of all, she had to see if Marlene survived the fall.

Before the voyage began, the captain gave the two ladies a quick course on ship safety. "Remember: do not fall in the water while out here. It's not a refreshing dip. It is icy cold, like hell's own frozen waters. The fall from the ship on its own could kill you."

In her youth, Ilene always believed that bodies of water were the softest of pillows. Because of the captain, she realized that they could be the cruelest of killers.

The opportunity to prevent this fate for Marlene was seized by Osiris as he dived in. Marius seized Ilene before she could reach that same edge. Her elbows battered the young shipmate's face.

Ilene finally rang out, "Let me go! By the bloodline of Pangea, I command you! Please! I need to see if she's okay!"

Not released, Ilene's arms still hit Marius from behind as the mate's weighty arms coiled around the rest of the girl. Ilene resorted to heavy biting. She drew a little blood. She let her mouth go as she began to taste it. She finally managed to kick and squirm free.

Cries of, "Man overboard!" engulfed the ship. A great multitude gathered on the stern where once only stood four people engaged in a simple game of catch. Everyone seemed gathered. Even the captain appeared after commanding an end to the sails. Everyone tried to leer over the edge for a sign of the stragglers.

"Here! Here!"

It was Osiris. He was a fine distance off. The ship's momentum before the sails were lowered left Osiris a nearly invisible dot. Ilene could only make out Osiris, and another dot stamped near him. Ilene's heart halted often between wondering if that other dot was clinging to Osiris or being torn from him by the waves.

Orders were then made to raise half sail and turn around. Ilene suddenly felt the vessel leaning into its abrupt steering. She and a few others tripped on to the floor. The world felt like it was spinning all around her. Until the ship was close enough, Ilene did not know what to do. All she could do was pray.

"Merciful Alpha..." she began to whisper.

Then Captain Crock's thunder boomed over her timid prayer, "Double-time, mates! Once we're turned around, we'll go at full sail again and we'll be close enough before you know it! We can't just stand here and pray that they'll make it. Mr. Hound, you and the other men get the biggest rope we have. Tie it to the mast, lower it into the water, and prepare to heave it back with all your might. Connor, you boil some water. They are going to be half-frozen once aboard. Marius, you round up some blankets. Let them hang in the same room where Connor's water is heating. When the time comes, I want every man on that rope."

Ilene could not help but ask, "What can I do?"

Forgetting that he was in the presence of royalty, Crock said, "Just say some prayers, miss. We'll need them."

Ilene disputed. "No. What can I **physically** do?"

The captain grew agitated as all the other men had cleared the deck to go about their jobs. "I don't know. What **can** you physically do? You've never worked on a ship before. You'd just get in the way of the other men."

The world stopped spinning. Ilene's face looked out in desperation. The ship was at full sail- full speed again. The wind was whipping her hair at the captain.

"But captain, that's my maid out there- my friend! I want to do everything I can."

The captain saw that the sails were lowering, the ship was slowing to a stop, and the rope was secured. He rushed down to help with the pulling.

Ilene followed him. "At least let me help with the rope."

The captain quickly said, "You're welcome to. I've no time to debate it. Just don't get in our way."

As Ilene sprinted down the steps, she saw Osiris and Marlene more clearly as they were closer to the ship. She saw Osiris muscling each stroke with one arm. Ilene could hear him breathing gusts of air each time they moved. The other arm was trying to keep Marlene's limp form afloat next to him.

Ilene had to look away. She had to tell herself: *She'll be okay. Alpha won't allow her to die this way. He is merciful and loving. She'll be okay. I just need to do everything I can to save her.*

Ilene held fast to these thoughts as she held the rope tightly. It was rippling with ridges now stretched out at the seams thanks to the tying by the men and their collective hold on it. Two of the ship's biggest mates were last in this great line upon the rope that spanned almost all of the crew. Ilene took her place in front of these two. Ilene didn't have much room to fit herself in. She slithered by a shirtless mate with a back that was as big as it was sweaty. She got her pink fists around the rope along with the other white-hot knuckles.

A small shout from below was heard. It had to be Osiris confirming that he had grabbed the rope. All at once, the rope became a thin string of steel as it tightened in each fist. The force of this shift in the rope's leverage scared Ilene. Then she remembered those fingers that eased over the bookshelf to find a story to read the young princess every night by the fire. Ilene then clenched her hold along with the others.

Everyone's grunt for the great pull seemed to be a wolf pack's howl. Ilene could barely sound a whimper as the rope felt as though it were ready to slice through her fingers like a knife. She stamped her feet down, constantly trying to restore balance to her stance. No progress seemed to be made. As Ilene's eyes locked on to the rope's end for a sign that someone was coming up, she considered Osiris's climb. Then she realized that holding on to an... unconscious woman while climbing may have been too much for Osiris.

The captain crowed, "Harder! Pull harder!" Everyone's pull

seemed to simultaneously surge with new energy. Ilene tried to make the same effort, but she slipped and fell into one of the bigger men. She felt the sweat and ache that had been growing upon her body rain down all at once. This onslaught washed hotly upon her as she cracked her head on the deck. The pain seemed to be but a prompt to get back up.

The larger man's brief loss in the line was felt as most of the crew faltered forward to the edge as they struggled to hang on. Ilene saw the larger man blast back to his place with an angry resolve. She heard him growl, "Stupid!" as he beamed hatefully at her. Ilene took her place again.

The aches on her joints cranked her arms like bent wooden sticks- ready to snap. Her sweat was drowning her. Her fingers were re-introduced to the rope's biting vise. It was like hanging for dear life on a serpent's fang. The pain could no longer be endured. Ilene closed her eyes to numb it. Yet this only seemed to increase her sense of misery. The eyes were slammed open when she heard another bellow from the captain. "WAVE!"

The wave towered over the ship and was prepared to hit the edge wherein Marlene and Osiris were still making their slow, painful procession up. They were barely out of the water. Marlene regained consciousness to climb back up, but she still needed one of the mate's arms to get up the ship.

It was the weight of an uphill battle piled on both of Osiris's arms, red from the strain. The ship was tall enough to stand the wave, but not for those out in the water. Already discouraged, Ilene turned away and laid her head aside in preparation for the greatest loss of her life. Her despairing neck led her eyes to the pulley system for the sails.

The words that blasted over the murmur of the on-coming current sounded like another one of Crock's commands. Ilene could not believe that they were coming from her mouth. Yet the words still raced out. "You two! See that pulley to the sails? Secure our rope on to it and it will pull them out."

The two larger men were stunned by the girl's sudden tenacity. The one who had cursed Ilene for her earlier mistake disputed, "But I can't pull this any harder."

Ilene again found herself talking with a fortitude born of one desperate to save a friend. "Then give it all you've got or..." Ilene saw a knife in the man's sash. The wave was almost upon the fearful eyes of Marlene. Without hesitation, Ilene snatched the knife from the sash as she pointed it into the man's stomach. "I-I'll stab you if you don't pull harder right now. I mean it!"

Afraid of the blade, the man hurled all of his muscle's veins back like the force of a thousand meteors. His sweat flew off him like frightened birds until he and his comrade attached the rope to the pulley.

Swiftly letting it go, the lever was activated. It sprang with a zipping sound that expounded with enough power to immediately floor each man still holding on. Full sail was set again as a result. This moved the ship away from the wave's impact while the sail's attached rope pulled the two swimmers back on to the ship. Rising up was Osiris holding on to Marlene, crumpled in one of his arms as his other limb had the rope wrapped about it. They sprawled on to the deck like a pair of freshly caught fish.

As howls of joy replaced those howls of struggle, Connor and Marius helped them into the hot blankets and slowly poured the steaming water over the covered parts of their limp bodies. Both were gasping loudly like wild beasts. Ilene dropped the knife and knelt before her beloved friend to hug her neck.

After Ilene kissed Marlene's cheek, her eyes tilted to see the large man picking up his knife and sternly nod as if he understood Ilene's passion behind the terrible threat. It was a silent contract between their eyes that established that they would not tell anyone of what occurred. Ilene got a better look at him. Before, all that she could note of this figure was that he was big.

He wore no shirt. His back turned from Ilene to reveal a tattooed map of the world. Its nations were shaped like the body parts from the story of the fallen Goddess. The ancient nation of Ur in the southern seas represents Omega's chest and torso. To Ur's north is the mountain filled land of Vaalbara, the arm-continent. Its 'fingers' were broken off to the east by volcanic bursts- creating islands that are now under Ur's control. To the northeast is the tropical continent of Kenorland as one of her legs. Almost at the core of it all is the head colonial trading power of the world: Pangea as Omega's head. To the far north is the tundra continent of Pannotia making up the other arm. And the northwestern nation of Rodinia is her other leg.

The other large man from before approached him. The other man was censored by the larger man's mapped back. "Atlas! We can't let what she did go unsaid. We must report her mutiny to the captain."

Ilene expected a threat from Atlas. But he merely laid hands upon his shipmate in a brotherly manner and said, "Let her be, Ferrio. She simply did what had to be done. She was trying to save a loved one, you know."

Ilene turned back to Marlene. Marlene was awake, coughing wildly, but very alive. Marlene squinted her eyes to see Ilene under the sunlight and whispered, "Oh, drat. Is this hell? I can see the dreaded Omega! Forgive my sins, dear Alpha!"

They laughed together again.

Their laughter ceased when Osiris roared out in pain. Marius snarled at Connor. "Don't pick him up by his arms! Can't you see that he broke one of them holding on to the rope?"

Osiris's face was red from exhaustion. "Slowly now," muttered Marius as he and Connor maneuvered their hold on to Osiris before carrying him into his cabin to heal. While they were gone, the ship was in an uproar of celebration. Each man puffed out their chests while asserting that their own individual part in the great pull won the rescue. They did not know the truth.

The ship proceeded back to usual business when Crock superseded their joys so that they could get back to their duties. Marius and Connor returned to help Marlene into her cabin that she shared with Ilene. Ilene could not help but scowl coldly at Marius when he arrived. It was his fault after all. He was too busy helping Marlene to look back.

CHAPTER 4
RECOVERY

Ilene sat by Marlene's bedside in the cabin. Ilene remained by her maid for the rest of the voyage. Marlene faded to sleep. Ilene grew tired of watching Marlene, so she read an old romance book. Ilene knew each of its collected short tales by heart, best recalled under the gentle voice of Marlene who read these stories to the young princess whenever she was sleepy or sick. Now an educated woman, Ilene wished to read them for herself on this journey. She considered this the farewell to her childhood days before getting married. The last tale for Ilene to re-explore was: "The Three Noble Bachelors."

A beautiful princess, "like you," Marlene would add to the younger Ilene, was of age to marry. Three men had been taken by her beauty. One was a foreign soldier in prison. His name was Allen. "Short for alien," supposed Marlene. The other bachelor was a rich man. His name was Stanford. Marlene noted, "I've found the one that I would choose." The final bachelor was a servant for the princess. His name was Franz. Marlene chuckled, "Fine aspirations for that one."

Stanford proposed to the princess, and she accepted as he was a handsome and respectable gentleman. The other two bachelors never confessed their love to the lady for fear of rejection. But a war began. Stanford had to leave his love. The narrator then spent a long time bemoaning the status of each man in relation to their lady love. Allen was imprisoned and could only see the princess from afar past his cell's window. Yet he had the longest view of her beauty as he could gaze upon her while she rode her horse in the field, her lofty hair dancing in the breeze.

Franz could only bring her food. Yet he got to be closest to her angelic voice as a reward. Stanford could no longer do either of these things while at war. Yet he had her vow in the depths of his heart to stir a comforted spirit within him. Each man was blessed to be close to the princess in their own way, but none could have all of her.

One day, Allen escaped from jail. He could have left the country. But his heart was still chained to the princess. So, he stayed hidden as the soldiers searched for him. Allen spied upon her near the castle. He planned to approach her and express the depths of his love. But Franz saw the spy and attacked him. They both learned that they each loved the princess during this struggle. The princess suddenly appeared and asked what the meaning of their fighting was. The two confessed their love for her. They explained that this was the basis of their feud.

The princess tried to express to them that her heart belonged to another. Since Stanford did not yet return, both men wished to prove their love for her. Both reasoned that they could win her over should Stanford not return alive. If not, both honored Stanford's claim. They simply wanted to let their feelings go free.

Allen proposed a jousting contest in the forest away from those that would capture him. Franz never had a violent encounter in all his life. He knew that he could not survive such a contest without dying. Yet when he saw her finally noticing him, he decided to compete anyway if only to risk it all for her. The contest began an hour later in the woods. The war-tested Allen easily bested Franz. The princess was so touched by the final dying gaze from the ruined servant that she utterly refused to have Allen as Stanford's substitute. Allen could not convince her that he too risked so much for her hand. Then one of the soldiers in search of Allen found him in the woods. He fired an arrow and killed the fugitive. The princess flew back to her castle in tears.

Stanford returned. The princess told him everything that happened. Stanford was touched by the story. In honor of their valiant sacrifices, the princess said that she couldn't marry another- not even her betrothed. Stanford agreed with her choice. He proposed a law to the king that forbade her from marrying another. For the princess's heart was already heavy with the chivalrous works of three lovers. With the story finished, the narrator proposed a riddle for the reader.

"Which bachelor was most deserving of the lady's love if they could have had it? Was this Allen, who forsook refuge from enemy territory at the cost of his life? Was this Franz, who broke from his timid mold to stand and die a martyr for her heart? Was this Stanford, who honored each man's sacrifice by abstaining from the lady's hand?"

"So, princess," began Marlene after finishing the story for little Ilene, "which bachelor was most honorable to you? Personally, I would have picked the rich one."

Young Ilene cast a serious glance at her fireplace, whose flames were waning away. "I don't know. I couldn't have either one. And even if I could, they were too nice to decide from. I don't know..."

Seeing the child confused by such a heavy question, Marlene kindly patted her head. "Now, now. You don't have to worry. It was just a story. Now get some rest."

Marlene stopped the fire and cast the room into darkness.

It was the most interesting story that she had heard. It bested all the others about knights, dragons, and wizards. This one felt personal to Ilene as the princess in it didn't have a name. Ilene stayed up many a childhood night pretending that this story was a prophecy for a future in which she had to make the right choice. The story literally asked her for the answer. How could her young mind comprehend it all? It faded as she grew older and wiser, yet the immediacy of the question jumped back into her heart as she re-read it by Marlene's bed. It was as if she was approaching a crossroads to choose from.

"What are you reading?" It was Marius at the open door. Ilene slapped the personal book up with a whip.

Feeling as though she seemed too nervous when he came in, she tried to speak gently. "May we help you?"

But her voice betrayed her. Her response was curt. "I didn't scare you, now did I?" Marius asked this as he sat on the end of the bed.

"Don't sit there. You might sit on her legs. Give her room." Despite Ilene's sharp attitude, Marius could only grin playfully at her.

"Don't worry. She's got plenty of room. And I got to have a place to sit after the wild time we just had on deck."

A silence stemmed from Ilene as she stared at the book for lack of better things to distract from her sick nanny, the growing night sky out the window, and the obnoxious shipmate that was trying her last nerve.

"Uncle Osiris will live to nag me another day, thanks for asking. Last time he'll probably play catch with me on deck. Anyway," he sighed, "I really just came in to see how she was."

Ilene snapped back, "She's fine."

Marius continued with his own snap over hers. "**And** I wanted to apologize for somewhat being the cause of your maid's fall."

44

Ilene slowly turned away with each of his words. Marius moved in closer. "Please, Ilene. It was just an accident."

Ilene turned back. "She's everything I have. **Everything.** Understood? I almost lost her because of your..."

She stopped and turned her eyes back down to her book.

Marius squinted at her. "Because of my what? Look, I know that I can appear to be a bit-"

Ilene jumped in. "Boastful?"

She did not smile, though this reply did cluck a laughing affirmative out of the young mate. "Yes. That. 'Boastful.' It's just that... being a teenager, no older than you in fact- I just got to build myself up around these big, old men who are full of stories and rough housing. Do you understand?"

Marlene began to cough herself awake. Ilene turned speedily back to her, casting the book to the other side of the bed. "Are you okay?" Ilene did not get a reply, only more coughs.

Marius jolted to the door. "I'll get some water."

Ilene yowled back, "No. We brought our own supply."

Marius outstretched his hands in confusion. "Well, is there anything that I can do?"

Ilene's patience jumped over the edge. "She just needs some water. Why don't you go out there and look boastful without throwing women overboard?"

Marius stiffened before his exit. "I also wanted to tell you that Osiris fished your ball out of the water during the chaos."

Marius gently rolled it to Ilene's chair and left. Ilene kicked it aside as she got a canteen of water out of one of the cases.

Before getting it to Marlene's lips her coughs ceased, and her normal voice began to return perfectly. "If I weren't almost dead, I'd get up from this bed and smack you as I did when you used to forget such basic manners."

Ilene stopped. "What?"

Marlene shook her head. "I mean, really. The lad was just trying to make up for his mistake."

Ilene tried to give Marlene the drink. "You were awake this whole time?"

Marlene patted the canteen away from her mouth. "That's alright. I think that I've had enough water for one day. Let me just get my breath back."

Ilene put the canteen down. Marlene laid her hands up comfortably and sighed with her hungry lungs. "Anyway," began Marlene, "I wanted to say that I **was** actually asleep until you started screeching at him. It's fundamental manners, little Ilene. If you want love, give it. If you want forgiveness, give that a try with others."

Ilene stung back, "Even to those who do me wrong? Marlene... I didn't want to lose you."

Marlene said, "Sometimes you have to let things go. Even me."

They later went to sleep. Ilene was weighed down by thoughts of choices, marriages, the mysteries of Alpha's will, her future husband, how she'll get along in Ur, her country, her parents, Marius, forgiveness, and everything else that covered her small world that seemed so huge. All these thoughts that she tried to understand and organize finally weighed down on her eyelids and she slept.

CHAPTER 5 THE NATION OF UR

A sailor's favorite morning alarm flung Ilene awake. "LAND!"

Ilene jumped to the window to see land. It was a jagged rock formation. It was almost flattened to nothing by the distance of the horizon. The jagged formations peaked the Ursian island-head into complete view. On a map, the nation of Ur looks like what remains of Omega's upper torso and chest. This has allowed the country to boast itself as the largest though not the richest.

Ilene realized that the ship must have already passed through the crevice of the mountainous land mass that blocks Ur off from direct travel: Vaalbara, Omega's arm. Vaalbara has a few Ursian settlements while mostly serving as a natural sea wall for protecting the proud people from the rest of the world.

The Pangeans were recently informed of the secret crevice by their rival nation so that the journey to the wedding was less of an extended trip circumventing Vaalbara. Ilene thought that she felt the air cool down while she slept. She must have felt the shadows of its mountains pass over her.

Ilene felt Marlene's head pressing on her shoulder, looking out the window with her. Ilene didn't even hear her get up. "We made it," Marlene said with a sense of finality sighing out.

To prepare, Ilene picked out her favorite dress to wear. Marlene found it fitting as it would be Ilene's last day as a maiden girl. It was of the lightest blue. It almost looked white. Some bands on her collar, waist, hem, and sleeves were of a darker blue. Her buttons were of that same dark shade. It flowed to her ankles. Herein, she wore dark blue heels with light blue stockings. Ilene loved the blue of that special day's sky, the blue of the waving sea, and her dear blue dress. She felt that this gave her the subtle visual cue that this was going to be a good day.

Marlene began to work on re-braiding Ilene's hair before the mirror, as was her custom. As Marlene tamed the knotted curls into submission, the maid said, "You're a fine and beautiful young woman. You're certainly not my little Ilene anymore."

Ilene saw Marlene propped behind her shoulder. Ilene smiled at Marlene via the mirror as the young woman tried to knock back a tear while whispering, "Thank you for all you've done."

Marlene got the first strand into the pattern. Marlene coughed a bit. Ilene asked, "Are you sure you're okay to do this? I can just comb it straight today. I've done it before."

Marlene refused. "According to an uppity young miss that I talked to on the deck yesterday, this braiding is an easy job. It's listening to my haggish singing that is the real labor."

Both smiled largely before letting off laughter just as they did yesterday.

"Besides," said Marlene over her last chortle, "I want to do something special for your hair today, given the occasion. I figured that instead of the same old pattern, I'd tie each braided end into a spiraled link. It'd be akin to a ponytail, but it would appear far more artistic. It'd be my finest work yet. Not that any husband would pay attention to it."

Marlene touched Ilene's hand. Ilene touched it back. Both eyes were anticipating a new future before them as the morning light from the window glimmered into the mirror. A knock at the door sounded. "We're almost ashore, ladies."

Ilene said, "Almost done," as Marlene tied the last of the links together.

"Ready?" Ilene nodded. They both sniffled away their tears as they went to the deck. All the crew was lined to the edges of the ship in royal salute. The men were in their official navy blue Pangean uniforms. The golden ornaments, tassels, and medals shined greatly. Marlene held Ilene's hand as they slowly made their way to the dock.

As they made their way off the main deck Marlene gave a sincere look of appreciation to Osiris, whose arm was in a sling, but still able to proudly salute with the other one. He gazed back at her and smiled. Ilene thanked Osiris with her eyes too. Yet regulations kept the two ladies of the Pangean court from stopping their procession to engage with Osiris. So, they marched on.

A pre-selected company from the crew showered in step behind the two as they began to march along the pier. This harbor was populated with surprisingly few boats. Ur has always had a poor history of trade with other nations. Some of the crew stayed behind, including Osiris and Marius amongst others that had to tend to the ship's upkeep. The captain led the parade of Pangean men as he trailed respectfully behind the Pangean ladies. Ilene saw her nation's flag, with its spherical swirl of light blue and white over a background of darker blue, held proudly by Atlas at the band's rear.

As the group neared the city of Patricho, Ur's capital, Ilene took in the severe enormity of the walls enveloping it. They were of old and eroding marble yellowed by centuries. They gave no hint of a city behind them due to their sky-scratching height. Birds were seen flying above, but barely able to pass over. Even the metal doors seemed overly large.

Osiris makes a lot of sense. This really does seem like a land meant for giants, Ilene thought to herself. As the meeting was pre-arranged, the captain had one of the men blow a horn to herald their arrival. The door cranked awake like the gnawing groan of a resurrected behemoth.

The city was home to mighty obelisks that rivaled the ziggurat towers from Ilene's own country. Yet these marbled structures seemed worn, shapeless, and beyond repair. There were smaller buildings. Unlike the bigger ones, these were more appropriately sized as there were stretches of landscape for collections of businesses and homes. All were made of bronze, rather than dying marble.

Within Patricho's city square near the entrance was another paralleled arch of standing soldiers. They were lined all the way to the palace. The palace was the nicest looking of the buildings. It was of the smoothest material like that of a maroon bronze that matched the greater, yet grimier structures of the city. It possessed a huge width while also complimented by many columns. The royal family of Ur stood at the end of the line. Ilene had to walk closer to get a better look at them.

The company marched by each Ursian soldier that stood at statue-like attention. It was rather quiet and uneasy at first. Ilene looked at their uniforms. They looked more like ancient warriors of old. They wore bronze helmets whose sharp edges over-shadowed their faces. They wore bronze chest plates with woven pants. They had brown sashes tied behind their waists that fluttered in the occasional sneezes of wind. They all had belts that featured a sword. They had a bow and arrow with a musket wrapped about their backs in an X shape. The warriors held none of these weapons, but only a drum for each one.

Their icy silence was blasted away by their methodic tending of the drums that steadily rose to a quaking fruition with each of Ilene's steps. The drums got louder and louder the closer they walked to the family, waiting for the visitors as if standing for a portrait. They stood in front of a bronze statue that was situated before the palace that matched both its color and its great height.

The statue portrayed a naked, life-sized giant falling backward. The cause? A blade descending upon him, just big enough for his throat. The blade was being driven by a much smaller warrior who was swinging from the giant's long locks. This connected the smaller warrior to the rest of the statue- as well as to the very message that Ur's architecture kept echoing. This was the same message that Osiris was talking about. "These are a people that can conquer giants."

Ilene began to look at the mountains and fields outside of the city. This point was suddenly made all the clearer. Upon some mountains she could see several poles that arose from their heights. But they weren't poles. They were towering pikes. Skewered on top of them seemed to be... human skulls- giant skulls. How else could she make them out so clearly from so far? They had been long dead, perhaps since ancient days.

The drums reached a fever pitch. Ilene reached the royal family of the Ursian Empire. She stood before them. The drums stopped.

Ilene expected a group dressed in fine cloth and many jewels. It surprised her to find that the country's family wore sack cloth for their tunics and capes. Yet there was no mistaking that these were the leaders. For the emperor wore a fine, though small, jewel upon his forehead. He had a curly beard of silver with each strand arching wildly back to his face.

He introduced himself first. "Princess Ilene of Pangea: we welcome you with open arms into our country, our home, and our hearts."

His words came from a fierce look that grew into a hospitable smile as he hugged her and kissed her forehead. The rest of the family opened their arms, and ritualistically joined in the father's hug and kiss to welcome her to the family. She saw patches of each relative as they embraced her. It was a quiet and uncomfortable practice for the new girl in Patricho. Ilene stiffened her eyes in appreciation. She looked to Marlene who waved at her with her eyebrows as if to say: 'I think they like you.'

The one who stuck out the most was a young man who seemed very shy. Even as he hugged her, he seemed careful to keep a step back as if afraid of his own family. This is not what initially attracted Ilene's gaze to him though. He wore a black veil over his face except for the bald top of his head that was crowned out by the cloth's upper band on his brow. Unlike the others, he wore no cape and his tunic's shoulder strap was cut loose on one side. Ilene asked no one in her mind: *Could this be the prince that is to marry me?*

The emperor said, "Now we will take you to our main hall to introduce ourselves in the manner befitting our traditions."

With a flourish of the royal family's sack cloth capes they led Ilene and her group into the palace. The main hall was one of the most wonderful that Ilene had ever seen. The floor had a tiled pattern with a snow-white background and was centered by blue illuminations like those of falling flakes. The room was held by four great pillars, swirled by a blend of the blue and white. The tiles' reflection smarted Ilene's eyes as the room had an open ceiling that allowed the sunlight to shoot into the floor's shining surface. Ilene's eyes began to adjust as the royal family disappeared into the shadowed corners of the room behind the pillars.

The voice of the emperor pierced through the darkness. He no longer sounded merry but foreboding. "Men and ladies of Pangea: we present the immortal House of Ahabeus. Each member stands as a great pillar for the nation of Ur."

Ilene was informed about this. A shipmate once told her that the Ursian royal family has this traditional dance that they use to individually introduce themselves to guests. Each dance's music is different for each family member, to best represent their unique personality. This brief description couldn't prepare Ilene for how strange it was to witness the ritual.

A company of instruments were heard from the darkness. Unworldly strings curled softly, but sharply, in repetition that seemed to unfold the body of one family member. It was a woman. She was dancing. She curled her limbs about in seeming obedience to each of the string's notes. Her raven hair was waving like wings. She had a hard stare, but an occasional grin with teeth so brilliant that some of the Pangean company grunted quietly with approval. Ilene noticed that the Ursian royal was wearing a necklace liken unto the jewel on the emperor's forehead.

"I am the Empress Lida Ahabeus. I was born on the eastern isle of Tron within Alpha's holy kingdom of Ur forty years ago. I worked under my father, who was a messenger for the emperor. Our holy leader saw me one day and was satisfied to have me as a wife to replace his first marriage. We gave birth to a child, the first and only heir to the empire: Jacques Ahabeus."

With her introduction finished, she made the traditional A-shaped salute to Alpha with both arms arched- raising them together in the shape of the holy letter. Ilene recognized the salute as the ritual gesture that Alphite priests made back in Pangea.

Lida Ahabeus made a final slide to the pillar behind her as the sharp notes lightened to a dull point until the cello's sound was replaced by harps. Light horns trumped up bouncily as a young boy hopped on to the floor. He stared blankly with the shadow of his fierce-faced father. His smile flashed occasionally. His dance was clearly pre-choreographed as he hopped at certain marked beats of the horns while ducking and turning to the melody of the harps. He wore a headband without a jewel. All the crew smiled to see the good boy. He then introduced himself with an adorable whimper miming the words that were plainly scribed on his arm beforehand.

"I am Jacques Ahabeus. I am heir to the throne. That is all you need to know. My legacy has not been written yet."

When finished, he sloppily raised his arms into the traditional arch and impatiently scurried to Lida. "Okay. I said the thing. Can I have a cookie now?"

Lida hushed Jacques and directed him to stand by the other pillar as she affirmed, "Later."

Then drums thundered triumphantly. They were equal parts made up of the players from the outside and some on the inside. The emperor himself stepped slowly out of the dark with heroic bounds over each percussion's thud. He did not necessarily dance but walked slowly to the center of the room to each beat as he expounded, "I am Emperor Hailus Ahabeus. I am part of the first man's lineage who took up these lands for the good of Alpha's people. My reign is eternal. My will is law. My labors are to the blessings of all. I am the center of all that was, is, and shall ever be... never to be killed by another's hand least the last days of creation be upon us."

With these words, he stopped in the center of the room to a deafening silence that seemed somehow more powerful after the echo of his voice and the drums. He then raised his wiry limbs into the A-shaped arch with regal resolve.

Ilene thought that the presentation was missing one more. She was right. Ilene was horrified to learn the reason that the young man was dressed so strangely. No instruments were played when he stepped out of the shadows. There was the sound of whips instead.

As Hailus stepped to the space between the pillars, the veiled man walked with a stiff march. Some of the crew quivered and gasped fearfully as he seemed like a dark spirit in this dismal setting. He had no dance. He did not even have words. The whips methodically slinked from the shadows in many directions as they cracked closer, just inches from his flesh.

The emperor once again spoke in the ominous tone from his introduction. "This is the spoiled fruit of my last woman's womb. She was a whore who had her way with every man that she could seduce. In truth, this is not my son. When I learned of her treachery, I divorced her and banished her from my home. I was a fool to be so merciful. When I learned of this spoiled fruit that she bore because of her treachery, I had her hung by the neck from the cliff overlooking the merciless Ursian Sea so that its biting waters could eat away at her foul body wave by wave. I kept the child for pity's sake. But know this: he is still an abomination- a bastard. He is not worthy of the empire. Thus, in accord with Alphite law, he shall never marry under our house's name. He has been accepted into the royal family as a servant. He is a tool, a thing to be used- no longer a true heir. He is no more than a symbol of sin's evil that we keep under submission, like a savage beast made a pet. He has been taught to be grateful that he isn't whipped for his misbegotten existence even now. The mongrel's name is Monote."

As Monote slowly raised his arms to salute the Alphite sign, the whips cracked on. Unlike the others, he planted both knees on the ground as he did this. He looked more like he was surrendering to an oppression rather than honoring a tradition. Ilene's eyes nearly popped out of her head as she realized that this meant that her intended husband was to be the child. Ilene exchanged this look of surprise with Marlene.

After this ceremony, Monote walked out of the light, leaving the family standing before the company. "Now that you know us better, visitors of Pangea," boomed Hailus, "we offer you our hospitality as quarters have been prepared for each of you. You may rest until our dinner is ready. We shall celebrate our union of nations that is to commence tomorrow."

Hailus then spoke directly to Ilene. "Dear princess, we shall pray to Alpha that our son, Jacques, will bring you as much joy and happiness as he has brought to us. Pray equally hard that you shall give him his deserved joy as well."

A chorus erupted out that sounded joyfully freed from the sands of time. They sang a hymn in a dead language that, translated, echoed Ur's belief in being the first and last great nation and how its leaders were to bless the world for eternity. They seemed to fade away in the shadows. The crew departed from their military stance to scratch their heads and turn to each other, inquiring where exactly their rooms were.

Some more Ursian soldiers appeared from the shadows. One said, "This way to your rooms, everyone."

The Ursians walked into the dark. The captain was the first to follow without a flinch. Marlene tagged along with a bit more flinching into the unknown. Ilene took Marlene's hand to be at her side. Everyone else surely came next into the darkness.

CHAPTER 6
POWERLESS

Just as the two stepped into the dark, several torches were lit by the soldiers. The rest of the palace did not have any halls nor stairs, but a vast repetition of columns found all around. It was disorientating to see these columns together at once, to be unsure of how many there were, like a cabal of mirrors.

Marlene described them best. "I could see someone getting lost in here."

The soldiers continually lit the spare torches hanging off of these pillars. Each soldier led an even number of Pangeans to their rooms. The rooms were found at the far walls near the end of each column's row.

Navigating through these obelisks, Ilene spoke out. "What is the point of all these pillars? Seems to be a lot of work just to get lost in."

To Ilene's yelp, the soldier leading her turned to answer. She got so close to him by accident that she could see the white of his dull eyes peering from his jagged helmet. He explained these structures to the foreign girl with contempt in his voice.

"The seemingly endless columns, and their designs, represents the literal infinity awaiting all of us when we meet Lord Alpha at the end of this life. Therein he will weigh our virtues and our sins to decide if we are destined for eternal paradise or the frozen depths of hell. To feel overwhelmed is the point, as it is a shadow of the indescribable presence of God. Ur has many such reminders of the unseen world that we live under. Many nations are trying to forget that such a world exists."

They finally reached the door to their room. The soldier left them with a key and a bow. Marlene scoffed after his departure. "I know what he meant by that. He suggests that nations like Pangea have abandoned the old ways over the years. Just because we don't keep as many superstitious traditions does not mean that we've lost our morals. So what if we've abandoned such ornaments for enterprise and trade? That's why our country thrives and theirs is crumbling as far as money goes."

Marlene stopped her words to wipe the hair of the tired girl. "But enough of my political gossip. Let's rest before dinner."

They got the finest room as it was ornamented with great red cushions over-laying the bulk of the floor. The room also had a red curtain laid over the window. The non-cushioned portions of the floor were filled with tiles. By the door was a table and some chairs for reading as well as dining upon. A cabinet

CODYR.TUCKER

was nearby for the stocking of books and clothes. Another design pattern stretched about the wall. The wall's background was yellow and had repeating orange circles within orange octagons.

"Where's the bed?"

Marlene answered, "I suppose we're to use this pile of cushions. After the trip I've had, I could sleep on a rock."

Marlene plopped down to nestle herself into the cushions.

Marlene motioned toward Ilene. "Coming to sleep? You have a grave journey ahead of you, the great misadventure of marriage that is."

Ilene denied her. "No. I'm not tired. Meeting my husband has just been... a lot for me to take in."

Marlene crawled closer to Ilene upon the cushions. "Indeed. I would've never guessed that he'd be so young."

Ilene shook her head. "Neither did I. I would've never guessed that my parents cared so little about me, at least, not to this degree."

Ilene's eyes fell down like the ball and chains used to slow a

63

prisoner. "Is this all that I was meant to do? Be married off? I mean, they might've made me marry their pet growzer if it meant securing an alliance with their military."

Marlene bumbled her way to Ilene's hand as the girl stared out the window while opening the curtains. She reached her dear friend's hand. "I know that it's not a fair world we live in, but what else is there? What do you want exactly?"

Ilene lashed her head at her servant. "I want to be free! I want a life! An adventure! Something that makes sense in the end!"

Marlene returned, "You want your life to be more like one of your story books."

Ilene sounded a sigh that formed the word: "Yes."

Her eyes were attached to the outside of the window- past the city, past its walls, past the sea, and even past the horizon. "I want something with a proper resolution in the end. I don't know, Marlene. I've never tasted it, the world, I mean. Maybe it's not just freedom that I want, but the world itself- to be able to grasp it and make of it what I want, to make it a wonderful joy and experience from cradle to grave, not this endless string of obligations made to please others who can't be pleased."

Marlene removed her hand from Ilene to make a point as she snapped back, "Nothing seems to please you either. You are a princess that grew up in a castle. Now you are to live in a palace with a prince. While it's not exactly what you imagined, can't you at least try to be content for a change?"

Ilene rebuked her, making a raking sign with her arms as her well-patterned hair started to jut out from her upstart. "No! I refuse to accept this lot! I'm better than this! I know it! Those men sang of me conquering the world. What have I conquered exactly? Nothing. Even the princess in the story of the Noble Bachelors at least had a choice in who she could marry."

Marlene noticed Ilene's hair wringing out of place and moved in to help with it. "That's... just a story for little girls, Ilene. This is the real world. Not everyone always gets a choice in life, not even princesses. Believe me: when I was young, I've tried to always have it my way. It hasn't always worked out for the best. But I've learned to be content with what I have, who I have, in life. Someday, you'll find contentedness too. Now please, calm down, dear. Let me fix your hair and we can move on and-"

Ilene ripped herself away and stamped her feet into the corner. "No! You're just like my parents! You hold me down too! Only they don't pretend to be my friend."

Marlene's face stopped. It was frozen with dejection. This commenced a spellbinding pause. Marlene stoically said, "I've never been good at pretending, dear child."

Ilene did nothing but stare at Marlene, neither mad nor upset, but simply caught up in a web of hesitation. For fear of making Marlene snap further, Ilene stood back and waited for the next move.

A knock at the door. The ice between them had not yet thawed. The door was knocked even harder. "Fine," groaned Marlene, "I'll get it. I won't pretend to do it out of love for you. I'm just a servant after all."

Marlene opened the door. It was Empress Lida with Jacques hiding behind her cape. Unprepared for this visit, Marlene blinked and stumbled through the proper words. "Empress! My... what a surprise. Did you... come to visit Ilene for something?"

Lida smiled brightly as she allowed herself in. Jacques trailed behind, trying to stay safely hidden by his mother's cloth. Still shaken by the argument, Ilene did not have time for a sincere greeting before Lida engulfed the girl with conversation. "I do hope you're enjoying your new home, Ilene. My! You're much more beautiful up close. Isn't she, Jacques?"

The young prince's eyes were lost as he took cover under the cape. Lida cooed at her boy's shyness. "Men do not appreciate their blushing ladies as they ought to, hm?" She shifted her tone as she moved upon Ilene to help settle her mussed hair into new order. "Seriously, though, you remind me of myself when I got married. I was so happy."

Lida looked to something unknown above her. "And yet, I felt that something was wrong. I brushed it off of course. But that feeling stayed with me. Do you feel that way?"

Ilene screened her gaze to Marlene, who still stood by the door. Ilene saw that Lida finished fixing her hair. The empress placed Ilene's hair over the front of her shoulder instead of streaming down her back. Ilene liked it. Ilene replied, "There is something… restraining about marriage for women such as us."

Lida reeled Ilene in by the shoulder and patted it happily. "Thou art a woman after my own heart, indeed, Ilene."

Ilene was happy to feel so embraced in a world she thought was so cold. "Don't worry," assured Lida, "if our husbands give us trouble, we'll have each other to rely on. Speaking of which…"

Lida raised her cape away from Jacques. He was crouching-playing with a toy boat. He dropped it out of surprise from being uncovered. The boy scrambled to retrieve it. Lida bent down to him. "Jacques," she said with whimsy, "didn't you have a present for Ilene?"

He straightened up and stared. "Oh, I forgot it."

Lida waved her finger. "Go back to your room and get it. And take Ilene's maid servant with you. You can show her how to navigate the palace."

Jacques moaned. "But sometimes I get lost too. What if we both get lost?"

Lida snickered as if his fears were a joke. "Then you'll at least be lost together. A soldier should be able to help you."

Lida sternly told Marlene, "Keep a good eye on him, woman."

Marlene didn't even say a word as she led the boy out the door without even looking back at Ilene.

"Marlene," said Ilene. "Her name is Marlene."

Lida responded, "You're a better woman than me. I can't even remember the name of my maid."

Ilene looked out the window again. "I suppose."

"Beautiful, isn't it?" Ilene tilted to see that Lida was looking outside too. "I don't refer to this wretched city on the verge of crumbling, and I don't even refer to the sea. I refer to what lies beyond it- the possibilities, the unknown. Anything could happen out there. Anything: good, evil, some valley in between, maybe even a transcendent mountain-top beyond any of it, and all the mysteries found in the cracks of it all.

It pulls you in, doesn't it? Imagine if it could all be ours and we could consider ourselves citizens of the world whose souls embraced an entire universe to make our own. Why must we cling ourselves to nations and families? What's to stop either of us from ripping the chains away and grabbing hold of it all now?"

Ilene flinched when Lida struck the window with an open palm and a covetous look burning in her eyes. Her lustful breath fogged the window enough to shroud the world. Ilene stroked her hair slung over her shoulder in discomfort.

"So tell me, Ilene, what separates us? I see that same look in your eye. Why haven't you done it? Why haven't you tried to break free? Is it fear that stops you? Is it fear that the world isn't as pretty as you imagine it from story books?"

Ilene gulped out, "Why haven't you?"

Lida closed the curtain as the sun began to set. It darkened the room and her features. It made Ilene feel as though she were looking at a stranger. The stranger spoke. "I've got an escape plan for the ages. Don't you worry about me. From what I can tell, you don't seem to have any plans at all."

Ilene sat upon the cushions. She stammered out a confession. "I don't know. I guess I don't. I mean, what can I do? We all know the world's unfair, but is it so wrong to make the best of what one has? It's not like there's anything I can do about it."

Lida sat with Ilene. Her hands sat upon Ilene's shoulders. "Don't worry. I have a means to get you out of this marriage that goes perfectly with my escape plan."

The door flew open. Lida whispered, "I'll tell you about it at the party."

Lida spoke normally when she saw Jacques approaching. "Well, hello there! Is this a dashing prince come to take us away?"

Jacques snorted a laugh as he entered. Marlene trailed behind. Lida said, "Since we heard about you from your family, what we found most interesting was that you love story books. Despite its downfalls, Ur actually boasts the greatest library in the world. It is filled with literature that stretches down many floors. It is kind of a reverse-ziggurat, burrowing underground instead of in the above sky. I wish to give you this book from it. It is one of my old favorites."

Ilene felt the volume's cover as Jacques sheepishly gave it to her. It was of moldy texture, but not dusty from lack of usage. It was dense, yet it was somehow light in Ilene's hands. It was of a dull, and darkish blue. It had red fringes in the binding. It also had a red, ragged, bookmark sewed into it.

"Well, go on," encouraged the empress, "open it. Read only the first line, then close it immediately. I always found that to be a good way to start a story."

Ilene read it. "A man must come to his princess, or neither has hope. Or do they?"

Lida slammed the book closed for Ilene with a smirk. A bell chimed and echoed through the palace.

"Ah, the hour has come. Follow me, everyone."

They left the room. Ilene held the book tightly to her chest, hungry for the rest of it.

CHAPTER 7 THE WEDDING PARTY

Words bounced about the walls and the columns. "Silence, counselor!"

It was the emperor. "I don't care for it! We have necessities enough. I refuse to let our people be spoiled by foreign heathens."

A hallow and weak voice chirped, "Sire, the trading isles rarely orbit over our lands. These isles orbit over other nations far more often, yielding them more trade profits. If we were to expand our fleet more for trade than national defense, our economy could improve."

"No," denied the ruler. "We are going to ally with Pangea via this marriage. That's the plan and we're sticking to it. Their wealth will be boon enough."

"But-"

"Silence! Our party is about to begin. I'll have no more of this-"

A pause. He must have heard the gathering horde of guests. As Ilene returned to the original quad of columns by the entrance under the open ceiling, she saw Emperor Hailus turn from berating a feeble councilman. His eyes locked swiftly into hers. His glee returned. This area now had a circle of tables fencing the men gathered around the ruler. It was the custom of Ur to organize the dance floor in such a way. It seemed to be a stage for the emperor's political debate at the time.

"Welcome, friends. Tonight, we honor the coming union of these two young lovers. Ilene, Jacques: step forward."

Not knowing what to do with the book, Ilene fumbled it into Marlene's hands. Marlene threw a face wiped clean of emotion upon her mistress. Ilene tried to look away in what she wanted to convey as shame. She stood by Jacques' side.

The emperor stood before them as his hands waved in presentation of the youngsters. "Tonight, there will be much merry making. But first, we shall allow the two lovers to have their first dance."

The floor was promptly cleared. With a bow, Hailus was gone as well when the music rose from the echoes of the palace again. As strings fizzled playfully about the room, Ilene reluctantly took Jacques' hand, as was taught to her in the typical dancing position from her childhood. Of course, Ilene expected to be doing this with someone a bit taller. Jacques tried to get in the position with her, but he kept changing where to put his hands. He obviously had minimal training in this art. So, Ilene led.

The music stopped blaring loudly and the strings softened to a light tap that buzzed to each of Ilene's perfectly timed steps. Ilene methodically made sure to lead him in a pattern that placed the two upon every square-inch of the open floor in order to give the illusion that this was a long dance. The music droned on with the same tune that seemed as hollow as Ilene's passion for her partner.

Jacques seemed to care even less as he seemed to be on the verge of falling asleep. His odd odor of what seemed like a raw beef sailed from his ever-hanging mouth as he yawned into her face. Just as Ilene began to yawn too, the music abruptly stopped.

Relief was not to last as the emperor bellowed, "Now let us all join in!"

At least the tempo then picked up. The melody was eerily like the quartet heard on the ship in her honor. Livened again by the happy beat, Ilene reached out to cordially shake Jacques' hand. "You're a fine dancer, Jacques. I thank you."

Jacques seemed half-alive as he yawned again. "You're welcome."

Ilene tried to awkwardly make conversation. "I hear that you like to sail. This true?"

The prince nearly seemed to jump with new life upon this question. "Aye, yes! I hope to sail around the world and then some- maybe even be the first to discover new nations! I love the pretty sea more than anything and-"

Ilene saw Marlene by one of the tables during his praises of sailing. Making a polite curtsy to her fiancé, Ilene asked, "May I go dance with my maid, my lord? I need to talk with her."

With a muffled affirmation deflating his speech about the great sea, the boy hobbled to the dining table for some food. Ilene made her way past each couple, including the emperor and his empress. Marlene sipped the last of a glass as Ilene closed in. Their tension made them one of the few silent people in this den of festivity erupting around them.

Ilene broke the silence. "Would it help if I said I was sorry for how I behaved?"

Marlene put the glass on the table. "It always helps, Ilene. The trick is if the other party accepts such apologies. And I do."

Ilene took Marlene's hand and the two proceeded to the floor.

A rousing, but soothing, cello piece yawned with a perplexing melody that left the Ursian dancers in a state of swaying motion- floating between steps. Ilene and Marlene decided to copy this style.

"I'm surprised by the many dance steps that you remember from my old lessons. You never seemed interested. You always wanted to go outside and play."

"**Explore**," Ilene corrected. "Speaking of which, I'm glad this isn't like the wedding parties that we have at home. For we always have those after the wedding. I have that itch to go explore even now as I think of marrying that... child."

"**You're** not a child anymore, Ilene. You must do what you must- your duty."

"Who says that I must? What higher power other than a mother and father who insist on always having it their way? If everyone could live their life as they pleased, what's so-"

"Please, Ilene. Not again with that debate. Let's simply spend the rest of the evening as friends. There's no way to change the course of things. You'll be married tomorrow. Accept it. Move on. Find some happiness with your lot."

Ilene sighed. "I'll try." Ilene looked around the room at the dancers swaying to the cello's melody. Ilene spotted the veiled bastard Monote roaming behind one of the tables.

Marlene caught Ilene spying. "Curious sight, isn't he? Is he handsome or hideous under that guise? When I was with the boy, other than going on about how he's going to sail around the world someday, he explained to me how his brother was closed off from the politics of this government- though he is still allowed in the palace to be taken care of."

"Like a curtain in a jail house," added Ilene.

Both unsure if the faceless one was looking back at them, Marlene implored, "Let's change the subject. It doesn't feel right to gossip about one of your soon-to-be family in this way. Did Empress Lida give you advice on married life?"

Ilene gazed into the floor. "Only about life in general."

Marlene tilted Ilene's chin back up. "First rule of dancing with a partner: chin up. Don't look so sad. You'd do well to take some of Lida's advice too. She seems like a wise woman."

"I suppose," said Ilene as she gazed down again.

Marlene tilted the chin up again. "I **said**: don't look so sad. It's the night before your wedding. At least be happy during your last moments of freedom."

Ilene looked around the room, past the dancing bodies, the encircling tables of hungry patrons, and even past the ghostly

Monote as she saw the soldiers lined behind this circle of celebration. They seemed to be guarding everyone. They also looked like sentinels of judgement.

"I'm just worried about how much freedom I'll have for the rest of my life."

Marlene gripped her girl's hands tightly. "I'm here. Okay? I'll always be here. Remember? I won't let them treat you the way they treat Monote. I'd die first."

"Make it last and you've got a deal."

The music ended. Everyone clapped. "Let's see if they have anything good to eat here."

They did. A fine chicken was given to each of the seats about the table. Fine water and wine mingled well with the dish. The only shortcoming was the bread. It had a hard shell. Though the inside was soft. "That's how we make it here," explained a nobleman next to Ilene.

It wasn't the finest food that the girl had ever had. But it satisfied her. As night was in full motion, the stars were placed beautifully in the open ceiling above. Ilene wondered why they had the open hole carved into the ceiling. She learned the answer when the torches about the palace were snuffed out at once.

The deep darkness was so sudden. The grand building was seized with cries of panic where once resounded music and laughter. The only light that could be found came from the open ceiling. It was a pillar of light. The stars sprayed a ray through the darkness.

Empress Lida stepped into this open ray. She held out her hands. "Do not be alarmed, everyone. The torches were put out for a special purpose. I was delighted to schedule the celebration before the wedding upon **this** very night. For I've learned from my astrological studies that tonight is one of celestial wonder beyond any sordid sight found on our earth. Tonight, we will see the face of God!"

The panic died. Silent curiosity laid it to rest. "For you see," continued the orator, "just as God brought light to utter darkness, so too does he appear every twenty years in a shining form. He dips his head down through the veil that separates our world and his. Then his features press through the firmament's veil, shaped by our stars above. It is his face piercing out to comfort his chosen people's rulers every twenty years. Since nations collide tonight, I'd ask each of our Pangean visitors to gather with me to see the holy visage of the most-high."

Cautiously, piously, all Pangeans gathered towards Lida's position to look above. Ilene and Marlene joined them. Marlene could only gasp in awe. "The face of God..." she whispered to herself in wonder.

Ilene tried to make out a face from the formation of the stars. Ilene could only see a smile, a wide arc over the world below.

Or was it a frown? Ilene began to doubt if she was even seeing a face at all.

Mere words twisted this company's state of awe. "Cease this blasphemy, wife," commanded the emperor. "No outsiders may take part in the ritual of seeing Alpha's face. Only his appointed ruling family has this right. What madness are you driving at?"

Lida raised her hand over the ray of light- a signal. She hatefully replied, "I'm driving at allowing you to see God's face in person, Hailus."

Without warning, bursts of blood shot out from every direction- drenching the Pangeans in the center of the floor. The Ursian soldier's uniforms and drawn swords were now freshly shining with red as they tossed the still wringing corpse of Hailus over the tables.

Their mass throat slitting of the Ursian politicians, councilmen, and royalty was done. Laid upon the floor, their blood kept streaming out of their mauled necks. The oozing pool of liquid crept closer to the Pangeans.

The Pangeans drew back as they drew their un-used swords and pistols as some others shrieked in horror. Their feet skirted away from the approaching puddles of blood as if the touch of it could poison them from the floor.

Starting with the captain, the Pangeans raised their swords to the neck of Lida, who stood calmly- even smiling sweetly. "Hear me."

The smell overpowered Ilene. She crumbled to her knees. The blood was soaked over her dress and face. She got the brunt of Jacques' blood as he was chopped down like a little tree before her un-closing eyes. When Ilene reached the ground, she had a tug-of-war between her mouth and her stomach to keep the food from vomiting out. She was eye-to-eye with the dead boy. His eyes were endless. He looked like one who had truly seen the face of God.

The men were silent with fear but poised for attack. They held off to hear Lida speak as she requested. She spoke with all the authority that was now, by blood, hers. "For thousands of years, this house has stood on an old, forgotten rock that claimed relation to the beginning of time- to God."

She looked up, her face seeming to challenge the deity to come down and face her.

"It was all lies to give our many poor a sense of security. The real security, the power, goes to the privileged to stabilize the vanity of this regime and its people that followed blindly after it. I saw all manner of foolishness and oppression instituted by the so-called 'servant of God' that you see rotting on the floor over there. I knew what it felt like to lose control to one who only fabricated his authority. So, I believed that I could fabricate my own. Paying off the army with my own secret funds, I have seized Ur as my own. I am the empress supreme of all the land, though it is a poor land as I've admitted. As the new ruler, I am bringing about a change to that. I am humble enough to accept foreign help. I need money. My people need a proper financial foot to stand on. Even Hailus saw this. We needed an alliance with Pangea: the economically greatest of all the nations."

"So, Ilene," started the empress as she held her hand out to the young girl- past the guns and swords still pointed at her. All eyes latched on to Ilene. Ilene clung to Marlene in growing horror. They were both shaking as if it were ice they were covered in, and not blood.

"I offer you that same wonderful alliance without the obligation to marry one that you do not desire. If you join me, I'll help you rip the Pangean Empire from the fingers of your parents- just as I have from my family. Once you've seized power in your own nation's coup, there is nothing that can stop either of us. Combining your nation's wealth and navy along with my country's numbers and strength, we could rule this world like the God and Goddess before us. Only it will be a world in the charge of the Goddess's blood rather than that of the God's- rather than that of man's."

The empress quaked in a passion as if she were a priest possessed by the spirit, shaking her body.

"Women will no longer be held in subjugation. Look above! All of you! You do not even see the God's face, do you?"

Everyone gazed high into the ceiling's open night sky. Only the captain didn't look up. His eyes and his pistol were still aiming at Lida.

"The God's face is no longer up there because he knows that a new era has begun, and he fears to look upon it. Take this chance with me, Ilene. The only way for you to have the freedom you desire is to take control. Take this escape for the ages by conquering this prison of a world that you live in."

When such a decision is presented to someone, a choice must be made. As Ilene stood there, blood covered over her pretty blue dress, her eyes were ready to melt out of her skull from utter disbelief. All she could do was cry. What else can anyone do in the moment between such a decision? No one is made of stone. When unhardened persons such as Ilene break, they scatter like sand. But at least stone does not have to go through the process of putting itself back together.

So Ilene put herself back together between sobs echoing in this hall of soldiers, crewmen, dead bodies, and women that could rule the world. Everyone waited for her reply. Marlene, alone, gave her strength. She hugged her during this entire episode. No words of whether to take this offer were given. None had to be said. Seeing the motherly love coming from this woman made the choice easy.

"I can't, Lida. I am not like you. Yes. I want," a further sob stopped her, "I want to be free. But not in this way. This way…"

Jacques' dead eyes stared further as pus puked from the rest of his neck.

"This way is not me. Let us return and never discuss this again. Please."

The empress pressed closer to the frightened girl. The empress raised her stance over Ilene. With the light of the stars still showering behind Lida, her front looked dark, like the body of a horrible judge sent to execute wrath from above.

"I only wanted to help you, all those like us: the women of this world subjugated by men. And you deny this wonderful gift?"

Lida turned away, her cape flourishing like a heavy curtain. "This wasn't supposed to happen. You weren't supposed to say no."

With less joy gleaming in her eye, she angrily looked up to the sky again and yelled, "This ruins everything!"

A soft, but firm voice sprang out. "Leave her alone."

The cape swung back. "What did you say, wench?"

"I said leave the girl be," challenged Marlene. "She's not doing what you want because I raised her with a sense of morals. Which is more than I can say for you- you…"

Her words wavered. "You child killing bitch!"

"You talk of morals, woman. You do know that those are men's morals, yes? Otherwise, she wouldn't be refusing this obvious key to her freedom."

"Morals are for everyone to live by. You simply choose to ignore them for your own benefit."

"I wish to free women like myself."

Marlene softly scoffed with what sounded like a soft hack. "The only woman you wish to free **is** yourself. You wish to enslave young girls like Ilene with your hateful ways, just as you want to enslave men with a more literal bondage."

Lida moved closer to Ilene, who had hidden herself in the confines of the disheveled tuffs of her hair. "Do you believe what she says, Ilene? Are you happy with following your maid's morals? Or are you willing to cast them aside so that you'll **have** something in this life worth living for?"

Ilene sniffed. The smell of the blood became set in her nostrils. It was salty and sharp. She raised her head. Ilene's melting eyes and stiffened jaw said it all for Lida.

She sternly said, "I've heard enough."

Lida's right hand grabbed Marlene's neck and swung the maid about with a tight chokehold from behind. Swinging around like a new dance, Lida jumped out of the Pangean circle- strangling Marlene's neck. Struggling to squeak out air, Marlene hopelessly gripped her hands upon Lida's vise-like hold. The crew couldn't shoot Lida for fear of killing Marlene. It was all too fast.

"If you won't help me gain the world," hissed Lida, "I'll make sure you lose everything."

Ilene continually pleaded with Lida. "Please. Please. Please." She repeated this plea- hoping it would prick Lida's heart. The stone heart rolled on with its dark deed anyway. Closing into the confines of Lida's crowd of soldiers, she pulled Marlene in with her. Once embraced within the crowd, they were no longer seen. A popping crack and squeak was heard.

"Please... Please..."

Marlene's broken body was tossed over the table like the others were. The collapsing corpse knocked over the table as well as the book that was given as a gift to Ilene. Ilene pleaded on with her shrieking voice rising higher.

CHAPTER 8 EXEUNT

Another voice blasted out. "Everyone, fire!"

The gun barrels rocked with a great howl to trample the many Ursians into dust. The rest of this swarm stumbled back in defense. Ilene stumbled forward, scrambling to get to Marlene's body. Tears littered her every step. She got her book just before Captain Crock wrenched her away. She held it tightly in her arms.

Crock's booming voice pushed into her ear. "We have to go! She's dead, dammit! If we stay, we'll be gone too!"

She kept pleading like an infant as she tried to tear from his grasp. Crock promptly slapped her in the face. It shocked her out of her mania. She glued her eyes, hot with misery, to his eyes veering at her from his bearded face. Tears of pain replaced tears of sorrow as Ilene went limp in his arms. Fully complacent, Ilene let Crock coax her along.

"You can forgive me later. Now let's go!"

The rest of the crew was already racing for the exit. Ilene and Crock tried to catch up. The Ursian soldiers had trouble regrouping past their sudden dead. They pursued the

Pangeans. Some other Ursians took aim with their muskets. They fired. One crewman fell. Ilene just managed to out-pace this man when he was blasted to bits. The shock of this made Ilene falter in her run.

Crock pushed her on. "If you stop, even for a second, I'll knock you out and carry you if I have to."

As they reached the door to the entrance, Lida's voice followed them. "No matter how far you run, Ilene, I'll find a way to bring you to your knees. I declare fiery war on you, your nation, and your family. That old cow's slaughter was only the beginning of your suffering. No one shall escape my reign. 'I am a black curtain that will envelope the universe. Thus saith Alpha.' You'll never-"

The crew shut the door. Atlas said, "That's one way to shut her up."

They ran through the night-time streets of Patricho, past the now dark shadow of the dying giant's statue. The night's empty streets almost seemed peaceful. The peace was shattered by the Ursians bursting from the palace. They made a great noise to get the attention of their soldiers on the outside.

"Get back to the ship, through the wall's gate!" barked the captain.

No noise was greater than a soldier coming to a nearby bell

and ringing it as he yelled, "Enemy troops trying to escape! All bows on them!"

This cry hailed arrows sporadically from the top of the great wall. Men in mid-flight were pinned dead on the spot.

Ilene didn't look back to witness their fate. She couldn't. Each time she tried to turn her head Crock kept slapping it to make her push on. It blistered her feet to run at this unnatural rate. But she had to escape.

As the Pangeans ran closer to the door, it began to slowly slide closed. "Faster!"

Ilene saw Atlas shoot off one of his pistols. It hit a guard rushing to stab them that Ilene did not even see until he was wounded by the shot. Atlas tossed his back-fist into the damaged soldier- out of his way.

Crock hoarsely said, "Don't waste your guns unless they're needed, men. They only gave us one shot each for the ceremony."

Ilene considered how these shots were to be used for a celebratory ritual rather than this soul impaling tableau. Such a thought slowed her down. Seeing another man get shot sped her up again. Ilene knew him. It was the friend of Atlas- the one who wanted to report her for threatening Atlas with a knife. She forgot his name.

"Ferrio!" shouted Atlas. Crock was pushing Atlas along this time.

This brought them to the great door. It was nearly closed. Ilene was practically thrown out by the captain. Everyone else was left to sprint on before it was too late. She slammed past each end of the doors and slid her knees upon the rocks scattered outside. She got up just as the stinging sensation in her knees was felt. The doors were shut up with a deep thud. Ilene was paralyzed with dread when she saw that she was the only one who made it through.

Paralysis turned to surprise when Atlas's fingers dug through the crevice of the door as he used his mast-sized arms to catapult an opening big enough for the rest of the crew to slip through. With each strained, moaning sliver of sweat and popping vein he managed it. The army was nearly upon him before he lunged out as the door was about to eat him up. The captain and the other men helped Atlas up. They ran to the docks.

"We're going to make it," cheered Crock as they made for their ship at the end of the dock.

Somehow, the dark night grew darker. Ilene could not help but look up to see what the cause was. A great twang was heard, like a giant guitar string being tuned. Then she saw a dark cloud. It hurried along at an unearthly speed. It was faster than any cloud, or even any orbiting isle. It was like a vaporous spirit claiming rule over all the stars. Ilene then realized that this cloud was descending upon them. An arrow split the dock's wooden floor. It landed in front of the crew's race to the end. It was a synchronized firing of arrows from the soldiers stationed on the city's wall.

Crock yelled, "Keep going! Don't stop!"

The ship seemed further than ever at the end of the dock. Crock commanded those on board to prepare to set sail. "All hands! On deck! Wake up, boys! We're under attack! Cut the mooring lines and prep the sails! We're coming aboard!"

The arrows rapidly increased their downpour from the cloud. Ilene's heart convulsed nearly out of her chest every time she heard one hit the dock's boards, or even the harbor's water. She feared that one would strike her down. This fear shook Ilene's heart and it wanted to weigh her down. It wasn't a foolish fear. For probability dictated that at least some of the many arrows would eventually hit their marks. The rain killed many of the other crewmen, who turned instantly into obstacles for Ilene to uncomfortably leap over with an unsaid apology in her heart. One arrow hit Ilene too.

Ilene's poor slippers were not made to run in. They were only meant to look pretty, kind of like herself. So, the backs of her ankles arched out of them with each sprinting step. One of those arches opened space for an arrow to jut straight through the bottom of her shoe. This caused Ilene to trip violently down. Her face, already bruised from Crock's slap, pounded upon the hard wood. Ilene slipped her foot from the impaled shoe and hobbled on with the other one.

Everyone that was left made it on to the ship except for Ilene. The heaviest grouping of arrows clamored for her back. She was almost upon the stairs of the deck. She kicked off the other slipper to re-balance her running. The arrows were a second from their target.

If not for Osiris seeing the gathering behind her, and crying, "Jump!" her story would be at an end. Her body hurled itself further than before as it performed a leaping nose-dive upon the staircase- just shy of the arrow's impact. The bolts crackled upon the dock- just missing her feet by an inch.

Beaten by the staircase, Ilene could barely crawl up. Luckily, the book, still in her arms, braced the fall for her. A strong arm bore her up. It was Marius. Upon the relative safety of the deck, Ilene crumbled into a ball shivering with trauma and fatigue. She had seen and suffered so much. But she had to get up. Crock shoved at her head and harshly pulled her up by her hair. Ilene's eyes remained trapped shut and her teeth stayed gnashed down.

"Don't just lie there," ordered Crock. "Most of my crew is dead. We need sails! Help Marius with them over there! GO!"

Not knowing what to do, Ilene's sore feet carried her aching body to Marius. She left the book lying on the deck, forgotten. Marius flinched upon seeing Ilene approach. "What is it?"

Ilene blurted out, "The captain wants me to help."

Marius could not help but shake his head. "My God..." Resentful passion sobbed out loudly. "How many people did we lose?"

Ilene could only think of Marlene. She became dragged down with a new burden as she wondered how it would feel to lose such a close friend many times. So it was with Marius, as he lost multiple friends.

She could not help but say, "Too many..."

Marius clenched his fist and used it to drive away his fears by punching the mast. It brittled his hand with blood wrapped in splinters. He iced out a harsh breath. "Well, let's shut up and get to work. They'll be coming in their own ships soon."

For a second, Ilene really believed that operating the sails would be easy. She was speedily taught the controls to the pulley mechanism. Ilene hated being near them, for they were the same ones used to save Marlene yesterday. Ilene got through it, though she wetted the controls with her sorrow. But it didn't end there. Marius explained that after the pulleys opened the sails, they had to hang on to the base of their ropes to keep them balanced for the cloth to remain aloft in the facing direction.

"Just don't let go! No matter what!"

"For how long?" Ilene asked.

Marius sighed, still holding back his dismay. "Long enough for the rest of our remaining crew to help us tie the ropes down. Until then-"

He motioned Ilene to her designated line that connected to the sail. Ilene knew this would be difficult when she felt the dense rope bite into the tendons of her fingers in retaliation to her grabbing them again. Ilene became sore with worry as she felt the tremors of the ship's sails vibrate through her frail form.

A strong wind had been brewing. The ship was moving free from the moors of the dock. It was lucky for their urgent escape to have such a powerful gust. It also made it harder for the reduced and weaker crew. The wind kicked the sails, and the sails kicked back upon Ilene and Marius below. Before, when saving Marlene, she had to only hang on to lift two people with the help of the entire crew. Now it was only her, Marius, and two other men holding on to the ropes. They all had an entire ship to help carry.

As the ship drifted further, one of the other members called to their partner. "Hold on, Mr. Hound. Do. Not. Let. Go!"

It was said to a pale-faced man with a hat darkly covering most of his eyes. Ilene recognized him from the quartet. She recalled him because he was the only one who did not smile during the performance. His brow was sullen even during the ship's escape attempt. It looked like an old face ready to be peeled away. He had the look of constant, but calm, despair painted over him as if he saw the fate coming to the ship during the song and had accepted it. It was a general despair that he held over life, knowing that we are all dead by the end.

Still in pain, Ilene lost focus on everything but holding on. She tried to imagine that they were going faster the harder she held on. Ilene's ears caught patches of the other crew member's names being ordered about some tasks translated with sea-jargon that was indiscernible to her. The names were: Osiris, Connor, and Atlas.

All of them were names that she had heard barked on the ship before, amongst others. But these names bore into her head as they were the last of the surviving crewmen. They rushed by and went down to the lower deck. When they returned, the captain asked them if the 'deterrents' were ready. They affirmed this. Ilene didn't focus on this, but only on her job's agony.

She felt herself slipping. She couldn't feel her fingers. Ilene felt hours within minutes. A fearful impatience raised her pulse with the same windy buoyancy as the rushing waves while she kept mentally wishing for the ship to finally get out of the harbor. She finally slipped. Her sweat and weariness wiped her straight off the rope. It was an accident. Yet it was a heavenly relief to her hands. With her slip, the ship tottered with sickening imbalance.

"Someone help her!"

The world tattooed on Atlas's back jumped in front of Ilene. The strong man, despite his strain from opening the door, laid fast hold on to the lost rope and the ship was instantly restored to balance. Atlas pulled the rope with the strength of many men until he was able to skillfully tie it down securely. Atlas then began helping the other men tie down their lines. Ilene felt safe until the ship rocked again with greater vehemence. This time, it wasn't because of the sails. The enemy had loaded their 'deterrents' on their ships. They fired. It upset the waves nearby. The enemy set sail after them.

CHAPTER 9
DESPERATE TIMES

Four ships were speeding after the Pangean vessel.

"Damn their souls," bellowed Crock. "With a full crew, we could have easily outpaced those ships."

He tried to say something else more quietly to himself. "I don't know if we could out-fight them, even with a full ship."

Sensing that he was heard, he snapped, "Stop looking at me, maggots!"

Changing the subject, Crock turned to Atlas- still breathing heavily while sitting upon a stool after tying down every sail. "Atlas, are you sure you want to stay on top of sail operation? I know that those doors took a lot out of you. Otherwise, I would've had you tie them down sooner."

Atlas nodded his sweaty brow. "I can handle it, sir. All that matters is getting the princess and the crew out of here."

Crock nodded back. He turned to the princess. "Ilene, join the others on the deterrents."

As the group plunged into the stairs of the lower deck, Ilene felt disturbed as she heard the captain laugh with mock bravado as he darkly said aloud, "If those bastards want to take us to the freezing bowels of hell, we're pulling them down with us!"

Ilene never went below deck before. It smelled like a dog that a younger Ilene once had when it went out into the rain. The dog later died from a cold. In the lower deck was found a long room, framed by moldy boards and small windows with what looked like open attic doors attached to them. Beaming out of these windows were cannons.

Osiris raised his arm that wasn't in the sling. "These are the 'deterrents.'"

The room's center had a long table that ran its length halfway across the floor. This room would have been dead dark if not for the glass lamps that were lit about the table.

Connor the tall mate mumbled, "If we still had our crew, we could let off these cannons in unison, ensuring an enemy ship's destruction. Instead, I got a girly and a cripple to work with. At least the cripple knows how to operate them."

He wasn't being as quiet as he thought he was. Osiris slammed Connor into one of the cannons with his good arm and held him down with his weight.

"Talk dirty about people on your own time, boy. Just show her. And if I hear any more lip from you, I'll attach you to one of these cannons and fire."

Connor rubbed his chest and grunted an affirmative. Connor rushed Ilene through the basics. "Okay, princess," he sneered, "I think the best job for you is to hand the cannon balls to me. I'll set up the mechanism as I'm most qualified. And Osiris: all you have to do is use that one heavy arm of yours to pull the rope that lets it all off. The hard part is that we've got to time it for when we're in range. The captain will signal us when to fire with a bell that he's got next to him on deck. We've got to be ready to fire when it rings."

Ding

"Damn! Ilene! Hand me the ball!" He scrambled impatiently to his spot by the cannon and danced his hands over the apparatus like a wild man.

Ilene waved her hands about in confusion. "But…"

"NOW!" The bell kept ringing.

"But I don't know where they are! You didn't tell-"

"Oh, for Alpha's sake!" Connor snarled with frustration. "**I'll** get it then."

He reached below the table and pulled one ball from the chest. He then put it in the cannon he had set up and Osiris fired it. It flashed a brief spark with smoke as it kicked back slightly, blasting the ball away. A distant splash was heard as Connor yelled, "We missed! You were off the mark, princess. That's why I divided the jobs up- so we could do this faster."

Eyeing Osiris on the side to gauge the properness of his speech to her, he continued on with a heavy sigh. "Just **please** be a little faster next time."

Before Ilene could respond, a cannon ball thundered and split through the ship's side as it knocked Connor into a blur. Ilene seemed to scream forever in that brief instant.

The worst part of Connor's injury was that he lived through it. He bore the orb's weight and it dug into his side after he crashed into the opposite wall. This wooden wall was bruised and most of its structure was disfigured. But it did not break away completely. Connor's body was an even more horrible sight. His rib cage's bones were poking out of his stomach. Profuse bleeding poured from this area. His head was losing blood as well. His eyes, ears, nostrils, and mouth cried red. His arms and legs were strangled worms- barely able to move.

Every word he said was agony.

"No... No... No!"

Osiris did a poor, but earnest, job of trying to calm him. He hesitated in putting his arm upon the mangled body lying on the near-broken ship floor. "It's okay, Connor. We'll..."

Like a braying child, Connor kept crying, "No!"

The waterfall of red from his eyes stared hatefully at the helping hand. Connor kept crying, "No!" at higher pitches until his voice seemed to shrink to nothing.

Ilene hid herself in the corner, hardly able to look upon the broken apparition that used to be a man. She laid her hands over her face. They felt stuck there. "Alpha, please..." she whispered.

The bell rang again. No one did anything. It rang again.

Now blubbering the word, "No," like a lost infant, Connor inaudibly whimpered for his mother with an apology.

Hearing another cannon go off, Ilene flung her hands from her eyes to see four ships lined in the distance from the broken wall. They were lined up like a firing squad before their intended target.

She expected the end to come. She curled herself up tightly-ready to have her virtues weighed by Alpha and to see Marlene again. She heard a splash instead of feeling a horrible impact. At least it was a miss. Yet it still shook the ship.

A wooden crackling flew into Ilene's ears as she turned to see the broken side of the ship, where Connor was, crumble away like grains of sand. Connor wailed as he fell into the sea with the rest of the ruined debris. Osiris fell too. He was too close to the edge of the damage. He was caught up in it.

Ilene found herself propelled to the other side while reaching for Osiris's hand from the jagged edge. It was only when she felt the full weight of Osiris jam her arm out of place that she suddenly regretted her sudden action.

Hanging on with both arms, and all of her strength upon his good arm, she felt herself sliding closer to the end. The back of her feet tried to latch around the table's legs behind her. Her ankles burned almost as badly as her arms. Her gritted teeth felt as though they were being stabbed through her skull. Ilene could not gauge Osiris's reaction as his head bowed to his fate below.

Ilene whispered, "Osiris, help me."

It felt strange to say, but she **did** need his help. Not his dead weight.

"Pull!" she said more loudly. "Come on!

Osiris's eyes looked up, revealing the despair lowering his wrinkles deeper than ever. "What's the point? I'll be dead like Connor. At least I won't suffer this way. At least, not as much. Besides, my arm's broken. I couldn't get myself up if I wanted to."

Ilene knew the answer to his dilemma before he finished his speech. "Swing your legs. Use them to get a hold on to the edge for leverage."

Osiris did not answer. His head was hanging down again.

"You're still thinking about it, aren't you? Whether you should let go? I know why you haven't done it yet. It's not because you're afraid. It's because you still want to protect Marius."

She didn't have to say any more. His head sprang back up. Even the furrows of his face seemed to wash away. Osiris's legs swung heftily, gaining momentum, until he finally locked his heels into the splintered edge. Ilene grabbed his legs with her other arm. With a solid grasp on his arm and legs, she finally hoisted him up.

They were lying on their backs afterwards- panting for life. The bell rang again. Ilene finished panting. "You're going to have to show me how to load that thing."

So he did. They spent the rest of the night fighting off the Ursians. Meanwhile, Crock and the rest of the crew managed to sail them out of the harbor. They were now in the open sea. The enemy still pursued after them, well into the morning and afternoon.

Ilene and Osiris grew pale from their sweat. Their eyes were fire-red and their muscles were numb pistons thanks to their ordeal of loading and firing non-stop with no break for almost half a day.

The only moments where they felt awake were when Ursian cannons slammed into or past their ship. Then they had to get down to brace in time to survive. Though, the single successful hit that the duo managed at one point also enlivened them as they hugged and jumped like gleeful school children while watching the Ursians sink.

Three ships were still after them.

CHAPTER 10 EYE OF THE STORM

After a while, the firing between both sides stopped. The bell stopped ringing. It was as if a peace treaty was signed that they were not told about. They almost hoped for more cannon fire. It was the only thing that kept them awake over the long hours.

Livened again, the two heard the upper doors crank open. They thought that it was cannon fire. They hoped that it was more cannon fire. They did not want to be nodded into sleep during this ceasefire only to have it end as abruptly as Connor's life.

But to their exhausted disappointment, it was not incoming fire. It was Mr. Hound. His usually crest-fallen eyes bulged out with concern.

"Up on the deck with you all. The captain has something to say."

On the deck, Crock peeled his blistered hands from the wheel.

Everyone gathered around in a circle.

"Here's what we're dealing with," he grumbled on his way down the stairs to stand level with his crew on the main deck.

"We're dead. All of us. I've never lied in my life. They didn't stop shooting at us because they got tired of chasing us. So, don't be singing no praises to the divine yet. They stopped chasing us because they've cornered us."

Once on deck, he pointed north. "That way may not look like nothing but another pretty ocean horizon, but beyond it lies the mountain continent of Vaalbara- Omega's arm. You may recall that in order to reach Ur, we had to sail through a narrow passage within Vaalbara's confines. For the island circumvents a large distance far greater than we can sail around."

"To your south," he continued, directing his hand shakily to the direction of the lined ships in the expanse, "is the enemy. And a clever enemy they are. They got ships coming from the south, southeast, and southwest. Whichever direction we go, you can bet your savings at home that they are ready and willing to charge us an empty-casket funeral for our families to weep over. We can't proceed north without eventually being driven into the rocks of the continent. These Ursian bastards must use this stratagem often on fugitives. Also... Osiris?"

Passing a red-eyed look to the captain, he listened to his leader's inquiry with intensity. "How is the status on our ammo?"

Osiris gave a monotone reply. "Nearly out, sir. And we lost Connor, by the way. Side of the ship is ruined too."

The captain sniffled and wiped his loosely curled hair. "Yes. Just as I calculated. We're nearly out. We're cornered. Nowhere to go. As I said: we're dead."

Marius chirped in. "And in further uplifting news, everyone: I've contracted an incurable illness."

Hound growled like his namesake. "Let the captain talk. He has a plan. Told me about it himself."

Marius couldn't avoid his joker's instinct to confront high stakes with mirth. "Ooh. Aren't we special?"

Crock disrupted the electric signal of hatred between the two mates with a glare. Once his eyes reeled in their attention, he looked up to the sky. All the other heads of the crew followed his gaze.

"Sky's beautiful for such a dismal occasion, wouldn't you say? As equal parts a naval man and trader, I know the seas. That is how I realized the misfortune of our current route. But we were too far into our getaway to steer back to Vaalbara's passage. Yet I also know the orbiting patterns of the isles above in the greater sea that we call the air. My compass-calendar assures this for me as well. I even know the routes of the less profitable isles, without populations. I know this because I was thinking of retiring from the naval life and setting my own post upon such an isle with my family."

A heavy pause. The captain still stared up. Ilene touched her hair. The blood was still there. But it was dry to the touch. She didn't want to examine its state at this moment.

The captain went on. He looked down at his crew again. "These forest isles are home to all kinds of wildlife and fauna. Tomorrow, one will be circling above our little stand-off. It will come in from the south. Right above our enemy. If we're as lucky as I want us to be, we can fire at the orb and the loosened stones could potentially weaken their ships or even end their lives. Maybe if we're even luckier than that," another pause as he sat wearily upon Ilene's throne still on the deck, "we could collapse the whole isle. Total assurance of wiping them out."

Osiris's arm instinctively grabbed Marius's shoulder. "But that could kill us too."

Hound replied, "Or give us a fine wave to ride out of this mess. Besides, the captain said that this assured their death. Don't you want out of this mess that our dear grace got us into?"

Ilene struck her aching voice out. "That's quite uncalled for!" It was what mother always said to her rude daughter making childish prattle at dinner. It sounded ridiculous in the company of seedy naval men. She kept yelling anyway. "I had nothing to do with this and... everything to lose. I-"

Crock verbally broke it up. "Enough. We're waiting for the orb in the morning. Everyone: stay at your posts in case of a sudden attack. For now, they're just waiting us out. But to their surprise, it is the opposite. Either way, someone is dying tomorrow."

Atlas approached the captain and drew him aside. "Sir, may I offer a request? Perhaps the crew on the cannons can get some rest? Mr. Hound and I can operate them in their absence."

The captain argued, "Then we'll have no one on the sails. How will we escape if this all goes south?"

Atlas reasoned, "We have nowhere to go, yes? Especially south."

Atlas spoke with a soft tone despite his great frame. The captain eyed the big man. Then he eyed Ilene. "Very well. Osiris, you two get some rest. But I want you ready to get up in case the boys need help on the cannons. I'll keep a vigil up here for the rest of the night. Dismissed until then."

The group dispersed. Osiris patted Atlas upon the shoulder and thanked him. Ilene rose on her tippy-toes and hugged him. "Thank you, Atlas."

The giant smiled and smoothed her hair out. "My lady, if you'll forgive me for being too personal: I wish to let you know that I admire your courage in these hard times. I had a daughter, Bethany, who died from a sickness. She was young. I like to think that she would have grown into a strong woman such as yourself. I'd hate to see anything happen to you."

Ilene had no words. She could only hug him again. Ilene tried to pretend that she was hugging Marlene again. But it somehow made her feel worse. She felt worse because the tears stopped. They were swallowed back into her eyes. Her face grew numb, and her heart felt empty.

Atlas left her as he jogged down into the cannon's room below. It was a total change that swept over her. Her body knew that this excess of tears for the fallen was affecting her mind's ability to handle a survivor's struggle.

So she let go of it all. She breathed it out until nothing was left as she soon found that she was the only one left on the main deck. She looked out to the sea and saw the ships that were after her royal blood. Ilene grew up with a concept of hate on a superficial level. She hated her bedtime. She hated chores. And she hated Marlene always correcting her. But those were only vague discomforts that she used the word for.

Looking at those ships, she felt actual hatred for the first time. It kindled in her like a forest slowly burning down. Stretching her hot malice from the reddened whites of her eyes, she eradicated each ship into utter desolation with each eye- blinking them into the black abyss. She repeated this vehement exercise for an extended period. She leaned against the rail with her staring resentment. It almost made her smile to think of the pain that such a travesty as their ships sinking would cause their loved ones. It would be a legion's mourning in Ur.

Yes. It **almost** made her smile to dream of such a potential vengeance. Almost. She realized the time she lost when her stern stare was broken by a sneeze. It whizzed from her mouth and shook her from the confines of her mind. Before she could catch her breath, she sneezed again. It continued until she seemed like a mentally convulsing lunatic making animal sounds. When her sneezing ended, she felt the ooze drifting down her chin past her dried lips like a fountain.

A handkerchief was pressed into her hand. It was the captain. "I came down to investigate the odd noise. Luckily, I both reloaded my gun and brought a handkerchief too."

Ilene swiped it and smudged away the snot as it flew down her face again only to be met by the same scratching process. "Never learned how to blow your nose?"

Memories of such lectures that came from Marlene bludgeoned upon her chest. Inwardly cursing the sudden return of feeling sorrow again, Ilene responded, "Some people can't whistle, captain. I'm simply no good at blowing my nose."

The captain agreed to this as he joined his elbows upon the rails. "Fair enough. This sea-air can get to you. I'm surprised that you're just now catching an ailment, let alone your maid who hit the water. I don't think she-"

The captain halted Marlene's mention upon seeing Ilene's descending brow. He tried to correct it. "She- she was a good woman. I'm sorry she-"

The brow fell lower. No words. The captain gave up. "Forget it. I'm no good at pep talks. Just get in your cabin and rest before that cold gets worse."

Ilene returned to her cabin. She saw the book from Lida on the bed. Someone must have brought it there. Ilene flung it upon the floor. She fell upon Marlene's bed- the last vestige of her friend. Her nose trembled a bit as she realized that she was sleeping while still wearing the blood-covered dress. Thankfully, Ilene drifted asleep before she could horrifically imagine what might have been done to Marlene's body.

Ilene dreamed of nothing. She never dreamed much in bed. Her dreaming was usually done while awake. Since life became a nightmare, this was her best solace. But the nightmarish life pulled her back when she heard a clatter on the floor. Kicked upright and blasting her eyes wide-open, she expected cannon blasts.

She saw Marius at her door instead. She quickly asked, "Shouldn't you be with everyone else?"

Marius shrugged and swung his eyes to the floor. "It's like Atlas said: we have plenty of people on cannons. We just got to be ready to jump back in. Besides, Uncle Osiris refused to rest. He's

114

still harping on keeping me safe. So, the old sea dog sentenced me to rest it out in his stead. But I can't sleep. Too much tension. I need someone to talk to and Crock is not too great at pep talks, so I decided on you. How are you holding up? I heard about-"

Ilene put her legs over her bed's edge and pulled a pillow into her chest. "I could sleep, thanks for asking. In fact, I could sleep for the rest of my days."

Marius joined her on the bed. "That may be sooner than you think."

Ilene struggled to not raise her voice as she said, "Please. Let's stop talking about death."

Marius raised his eyebrows in exasperation. "Hey. You started it."

Ilene looked out to the darkness rolling with the waves from the window. She looked to the serenity that the stark black portal offered. This sight helped her get to sleep many nights upon this ocean. "I didn't mean death when I said I wanted to sleep forever."

Marius looked out that same window along with her. "What **did** you mean?"

Ilene gripped the pillow tighter. "I've no desire to experience any of this. I don't want life to end. I just want it to stop."

Marius interjected, "You want a break."

"Yes. A break from misery. Isn't that what joy actually is, Marius? The absence of misery? I can plainly see that now. Can you see it?"

"Not a bad way to put it, I suppose. Myself, all I know is that I've been riding waves with Uncle O on one odd ship after another for a lot of odd years. And do you know why we did it?"

Ilene could only shake her head.

"Father ran us into debt. Took some bad gambles. We had to pay it off somehow. So… we took to work on the high seas. I was just a kid, expecting adventure with pirates and the like. All I got was back-breaking misery that turned me into the ape that you see before you today. We never did pay off his debts.

Those whom he owed came after him. He tried fighting them off, to no avail. Mother took herself soon after. So, we stick to the ocean life. We know no other way. We got nothing to look forward to on shore. I guess what I'm saying is that we shouldn't wish to switch out when we face death and misery. Otherwise, we might miss out on life and joy."

"But," her grip on the pillow was weakened, "it is so hard right now. And I don't see how things can get better any time soon. Marlene... she... she said she'd always be here for me, but now..."

Fresh out of tears, she groaned sorely. Marius wrapped his arms about her shoulders. "Listen now. I'm no Alphite priest when it comes to pep talks either. And I'm not going to promise to be by your side like Marlene did. Because, first: I'm not that kind of guy. Second: I may not be around to annoy her majesty much longer either. People die. You see it almost all the time on the ships. Just, I don't know, do this thing that my uncle once told me back when he was strong enough for sea life (before he got frail and one-armed). He said: 'When it gets tough. I want you to get tougher.'"

Marius almost sounded like Osiris when he said this. "Nice impression," said Ilene while finding reason to smile just a bit more.

"Eating, working, and sleeping with the old bird starts to tell on one. But do you get the advice? I know it sounds a bit like, 'suck it up,' but-"

Ilene intervened. "No. I get it. It's sort of like, 'what doesn't kill you makes you stronger,' right?"

Marius nodded. "Once we understand how alone we can be, it comes naturally to dig deep for strength and all that."

A pause blew into the room. Ilene divulged herself of the covers and pillow. Marius broke the pause by asking, "Are you hungry?"

"Yes. But let me change. I don't want to think of the smell while I eat."

Ilene changed into a bright sun dress with orange fringes. The given circumstances made her hesitant to pick such bright colors. Then she looked to her favorite blue dress ruined beyond reason. It was darkened black from blood dried and mingled upon it. It was a shadow of the cold pit that Ilene feared joining Marlene in. Surely, this was her mourning dress throughout the course of these unendurable events. The sweat and trauma that came with the dark dress clung to her as she took it off and changed into the yellow one.

It took some fighting to tie it around her waist. She no longer had anyone to help her. The thought of this was too horrible to repeat. It stabbed at her again. She no longer had anyone to help her. She tried to ignore this as she managed to get the dress on, although it became wrinkled through her wrestling with it. The dress also appeared lop-sided upon her form. Ilene almost walked out of the cabin when she noticed herself in the mirror.

Her hair had been blackened dry by the blood too. Each lock was no longer beautifully patterned. The strands were shriveled by the past brutalizing hours. No kind hands nor jibbing remarks stood behind her. She no longer had anyone to help her. Beating back each retreating eye-drop with her hand, she got a cloth and a cup of water to clean it out. Then, she got a band to adjust her hair into a simple ponytail.

She no longer looked like someone who had gained a miserable set of memories, but someone who had lost a lot of joy. The beauty that Ilene's maid brought to each day by virtue of her loving care was her life's greatest joy. She was crushed upon realizing that she took it for granted.

Ilene felt the disturbingly compelling words of Lida pass through her mind.

"Are you happy with following your maid's 'morals?' Or are you willing to cast them aside so that you'll **have** something in this life worth living for?"

Ilene took the book that was filled with the radical ideas that might well have shaped Lida's malicious ways. Ilene threw the book at the mirror with all of her hate behind it. The mirror cracked, dividing the image of Ilene into innumerable reflections. Some of its glass shattered.

A knock at her door. "Are you okay, Ilene?"

Ilene composed normal breathing out of her panting panic. "I'm fine, Marius. Be right out."

As Ilene looked at the shattered glass sprinkled over the book, she could only think of how both women (Lida and even Marlene) had cursed the princess of Pangea in their own special way.

CHAPTER 11 THE EMPRESS

How could Empress Lida make things worse for Ilene? The answer unfolded upon a balcony atop an old, unused observatory towering from Ur's royal palace. Though dwarfed by the old giant-prisons, the observatory still loomed over the populace. Upon the balcony was a woman in a white night dress, stepping out to take in the gentle air. A companion followed behind her. She looked down at her people.

"It is an ugly thing that I have done," sighed the empress supreme as she watched the candle-lit funeral procession taking place in the city square. The Ursian capital of Patricho was in sore lamentation for the loss of Emperor Hailus, Prince Jacques, and the other leaders. Everyone down there had their arms raised in the Alphite arch. They kept them raised, ever surrendering to the love of their lost leaders.

Their new leader, the first sole ruling empress in Ursian history, spoke on. "I don't think I could have killed them with my bare hands. I'm glad that I hired the soldiers to do it. I'm surprised at how quickly they got the job done. I hated to let go of my many friends, and my family... Even some of the corrupt politicians slithering in my husband's ear were good men deep down. But I'd hate to see my country fall more than anything. Family is family. But home is deeper than blood. Wouldn't you agree, Monote?"

The veiled stepson did not even look at the sad parade as he leaned on the wall. "I suppose I can't complain. I was the only one that you spared after all."

Lida spread her arms over the railing. "And why not?" She snickered through her teeth. "You're not **really** part of the family, after all."

Monote didn't flinch as he said, "If that fact excludes me from assassination coups, I suppose that works for me."

Lida smiled as she looked further into the weeping crowd below. A little girl being held by her parent was crying as the young prince's closed casket went past on its horse-driven cart. The child had both of her little arms hoisted high while her face was buried in tears upon her mother's shoulder. Even the mother spared her arm that was free from holding her daughter to raise it for an Alphite salute, albeit an incomplete one. Lida considered how much of a strain that must be. Such sweet piety for her leaders.

Lida's smiled widened. "Did you ever wonder why you were made to live as a subject of shame among our family in the first place?"

"You're talking about how I was allowed to live in the palace in exchange for my subservience as well as my exclusion from political affairs."

"Very perceptive. That is what I've always... respected about you, Monote. You're the lowest amongst the royals. People have assumed that you're a stupid bastard due to the circumstances of your birth. That, and the fact that you're usually silent, has made most think that you're a fool. But I've always known the truth. It is always the most intelligent who can keep their wisdom a secret."

Monote removed himself from the wall. "You know a lot about keeping secrets too, it would seem. You seized power through an arranged assassination and managed to convince the masses that it was the Pangeans that did it."

"You haven't answered why you think you were allowed to live with us instead of being thrown out in the street. By all rights, it was where you belonged. Or perhaps you should have been hung by the neck from a cliff before letting the Ursian Sea take your body away with your mother's. You never belonged with us. So why keep you around?"

Monote crossed his arms. "I always assumed that it was because father needed a scapegoat to publicly distract from Ur's poverty and over-population, not to mention the slight scandal of a divorce and second marriage."

Lida shook her head and grinned. "You're only half right, boy. I put the idea into the emperor's head. After the divorce from your mother, I married him almost immediately. But then word of your birth seeped into his ear. The country was massively divided on the issue. Should the benevolent emperor leave his child behind? Or should he contradict Alphite law with the presence of a bastard in the family? Should he even be allowed to live?"

Monote's veil covered his face's response.

She went on. "Hailus wished to merely leave you in an orphanage somewhere. But I saved you by suggesting that you be our subjugated ward."

Monote indignantly asked, "So **you** are the reason that I've lived my life in utter shame and loathing?"

Lida added, "I'm also the reason that you've lived in security. Would you really call **that** an ugly thing I've done?"

Monote stepped closer to her. Lida continued, gesturing to the sea of mourning candles flickering below. "It is just like what I have done to our country, our government, our family. We were going nowhere under Hailus. We had to progress."

Monote blurted out a dark chuckle. "So, you put those scapegoats to slaughter?"

"Oh, no. Now I've a new scapegoat: The princess."

Chuckling again, he mocked her original motives. "Aw. Are you upset that the girl didn't want to rule beside you? Perhaps this kindred spirit you seek in her is not so kindred after all."

"It is my wish to allow the lowly to rule. You, me, and even her. Can you honestly say that you didn't wish to lead in your father's stead? What kind of ruler would you have become? Do you not grow weary of hiding behind that veil in shame?"

Monote joined her in looking over the rail. "First law that I'd make is to have everyone wear veils like this."

"Why? To share your shame?"

"No. I've just grown accustomed to the privacy that this curtain about my face brings. I'd like to share such a power with the lowly as well. Hell, put a veil upon all the world. Why not? It's all ugly enough. Why must we reveal our faces- the intention behind them that people are all too poor at hiding? But, tell me more of what you'd like to do with the princess."

Lida looked down as if the plan was all laid out before her. "It will not be easy. But I think that I can work her rebellion to our advantage."

Monote interrupted. "**Our** advantage?

"I let you live. Twice. I want you by my side instead of Ilene."

"Would I still have been allowed by your side had she agreed to your generous offer?"

"I **still** let you live. Besides, I have two sides after all. Now you can have both."

"Lucky me."

"So you do know that we can't let the girl live?"

"Indeed. If she returns to Pangea, it will mean war. I hear that some of our best ships are seeing to that."

"But, what then? It will still get out that we've killed her."

"All that talk of taking the world on and you're afraid of war?"

"I fear nothing. War and desolation will come to the swine of Pangea by my word- just not yet. I must have time to convince other countries to join us in our conquest. In case she escapes our ships, we'll need to make sure she is hunted down before it is too late. For now: I will have to send my most trusted soldiers abroad to cast their nets. Perhaps I'll make a fund for a reward."

"And how can we afford that? We have little trade and alliance with other nations. The orbs barely come over our lands."

"As I said, change is coming from my rule. It all comes back to Ilene. First, I'll convince the Pangeans that I've kidnapped her for a ransom."

"Sounds like you want early war after all."

"No. Can't you see through that veil?"

Lida playfully pulled at Monote's veil before letting go. "Pangea will not attack us if we have their daughter."

"But what if they pay the ransom? We're talking about the wealthiest nation in the world."

"Exactly. If we continue to refuse the 'return' of Ilene, we can keep upping the amount. It could go on for centuries, really."

"Surely this cannot go on for that long. They may snap and attack anyway."

"I will not be idle in that time. I will use the wealth that they give us to strengthen our forces at home."

"And abroad? You mentioned some recruitment strategy of other nations too?"

"Again, Ilene will be our help in that."

"You seem ready to enlist her aid whether she wants to be of use or not."

"I will certainly make her unwilling. She will be a puppet. 'The vessel of **Her**.'"

Monote's veil nearly flew open as he gasped. "You don't mean the omen?"

"Yes, Monote. The Omen of the Ill-End. So, as it is written in *The Holy Volume*:"

"'And she shall come as an exiled killer. She'll gain the hearts of all men via her charming ways. But harken! For she shall wish to only deceive so as to gain the souls of this world. Her heart may follow human virtues, and she may yet believe them herself. But the great traitor dwells within her. The Goddess dwells within her. Omega shall rise again through and by her.'"

Monote carried on the verse with Lida. "'But fear not the vessel of disaster. Abase her. Keep her far from society. For if you don't, she shall divide all companies until the world itself is split into ruin- to her delight. Some weak hearts will take her in and help her influence grow. Verily, the hearts helping her shall join her in the arctic hole forever when the faithful woman shall arrive. In the name of Alpha, the faithful woman will gather an army of the holy few against the rest of the wicked world whom the Goddess hath manipulated. In Alpha's name, the faithful will smite the wicked. The happy-forever will come to all who join the faithful woman's side.'"

Finished with the scriptures that every educated Ursian citizen is indoctrinated with from birth, Monote smiled from below his veil. "So, Lida, you believe that Ilene is the possessed vessel for the spirit of the Goddess that betrayed Alpha eons ago?"

"All that matters is that it is what **they** will believe," said Lida stretching her hand over the still-saluting masses. "And that goes for the rest of the world."

"It will be easy given that she is heir to the most successful kingdom of the age. How the envious rulers below them will rush to our side to appease the superstitious and fearful multitudes."

Monote bowed graciously. "Very well, my empress. I shall stand at your side. I wish to rise over the crowds that once scorned my existence in the streets. Tell me how I may spread the news of the Goddess's rise."

"Come closer and hear."

CHAPTER 12 THE GLORY OF FOOD

Within the galley of the Pangean ship, two young souls shared a meal. In the room was a table surrounded by counter tops, and some food crates from the ship's most recent trade. The chef's death during the recent catastrophe left the two without a means to cook their own food.

So, they made do with the raw fruits and vegetables. Marius and Ilene each got a small crate and put them on the table to dig through. Marius chose a crate of apples. Ilene chose a crate of carrots. Ilene brought some of her water from her room. Marius took some of the ship's alcohol.

"It'll just be for washing the apples down," assured Marius to Ilene's concerned look upon his drink.

They began to eat, and their spirits became fattened as well as their bellies. They said nothing between each of their bites. Marius and Ilene began to grow two little, towering ziggurats of apple and carrot waste.

Mostly satisfied, Marius took some flavor craving bites of his final apple as he happily sighed, "Much better. I've always said that a good meal makes even the worst of days glad again."

Ilene winced shut one of her eyes, for the apple juice flew from the mate's mouth as he spoke. Ilene nibbled into another carrot and swallowed it. "Don't chew with your mouth open if you don't mind. But you're right. The food is indeed good. I mean, it's no royal banquet, but I too find that a good meal does help settle one's anxieties."

Marius swallowed his bit of apple and raised the remaining husk. "Hear, hear! To the glory of food!"

Ilene did likewise with her remaining bit of carrot, smiling some, daring to forget the past few hours. "To the glory of food! May it dwell happily in our bellies!"

"And beyond," saucily suggested Marius with an oral fart from his tongue to the snickering of both youngsters.

Marius further said, "I wonder if it is possible to become intoxicated with food as well as with drink. We're both certainly starting to sound like a pair of rowdy drunks."

Ilene shrugged shyly as she tossed the finished carrot stub into her pile. "We haven't eaten for so long. Being able to finally fill ourselves is, oh, what's the word...?"

Before taking another series of chomps into his apple, Marius suggested, "Euphoric?"

Ilene's eyes squinted merrily as she agreed. "That's it! I'm in euphoria over food!"

"The glory of food!" Marius shouted through his filled mouth again as he raised his apple and slammed his fist triumphantly on to the table.

Ilene slapped his dense shoulder like a whip. "Stop that, you! You're getting apple sauce all over my sundress. I'll have your disgusting arse thrown out of this restaurant if you don't behave properly. Now chew your food."

"Yes, ma'am. Sorry, ma'am," he joked.

Ilene got another carrot from the crate on the table and raised it as well before devouring it. Ilene exerted her happiness a bit too far as she considered what awaited them back on deck. Her smile and squinting eyes faded into the floor.

"Too bad a meal, no matter how good, can't allow us to forget those ships waiting for us up there."

Marius swallowed his apple bits and looked to Ilene's sad face. He missed her smile. "Don't worry, princess. Maybe they got bored and left us."

Both managed to snicker at this superfluous theory as they faded into a thick mist of silent brooding once again.

"Fat chance, right?"

"Grossly overweight."

"Speaking of which," wondered Marius, "how many carrots have you had exactly, little lady?"

"Too many," admitted Ilene. "I've always loved carrots. I once tried to eat a whole basket of them before a dinner when I was just a little princess."

"How did that work out?"

"Marlene found me stuffed into the cabinet with nearly half of the carrots in my mouth. She lectured me as she whipped me all the way to my room. Went something like this-"

Ilene began to resurrect her maid's voice: "'You ought to be ashamed of yourself, little Ilene! The grand Duke from the colony of Rodinia came all this way for a finely roasted pork and now you can't eat dinner with him because you've spoiled your stomach!'"

"'Oh dear,'" mocked Marius using an impression based on an uppity accent found amongst the aristocracy in Rodinia, "'how dare that impudent child not dine in my majestic presence? Oh, well. More roasted pork for my fat self.'"

Marius slobbered loudly into his next apple with exaggerated ravenousness.

"And it came at a higher price than that," continued Ilene using a faux ominous tone in her voice. "For you see, I was never to eat carrots again after that night. I got a severe stomachache from all those carrots, and I puked all over the sheets in my bed."

"Don't be embarrassed," said Marius as he patted Ilene's hand during her red blushing, "I puked during most of my first few days out at sea. The mates still joke that the ocean looks slightly greener these days."

"I thought that I noticed that the sea was a little contaminated."

"Ah, so you **did** notice." He laid his hand over his face like a dramatic actor. "Will my shame ever end?"

Munching on her carrot again, Ilene said, "So, anyway, I got my spankings for that re-coloring of the sheets out of it. But I got some fine new indigo sheets out of it too. I still sleep in them at home. Only, I couldn't eat carrots after that. They made me think of how sick I got."

Marius tossed away the last of his apple. "They don't seem to be making you sick now."

"I think I needed to eat them again, though. I needed a sweet treat from childhood to lighten the darkness of these days."

Heavy silence fell upon the room again as the two stopped eating. The ship creaked with a yawn.

"So," began Marius, "what are your plans when you return?"

Ilene leaned back in her chair, trying to consider the slim chance of their surviving. Her eyes tried to stretch out into the unimaginable future that lay before her as she let a gasp of air out.

"A funeral. I'm going to have a funeral for Marlene. And I'm making sure it is an event. I know that only royalty has great gatherings upon their deaths. But I'll make sure that she gets her proper respects. She was more than any queen or king-more than any mother, she was my friend, my..."

"Guardian angel?"

Ilene was trapped between smile and frown. The smile grew

from realizing that Marlene was always there for her, just like a guardian angel. Marlene was there for Ilene's first step to help her if she fell. She was there to teach Ilene how to read, and even corrected her when she was wrong. Marlene was even going to be there for Ilene's wedding day. That's when the frown interfered. To realize that no more of these memories could be made left Ilene feeling detached from the world in a way that she could never redeem. For Marlene seemed to center Ilene's world. And when Ilene's angel died, Ilene herself felt like a fallen angel.

Marius further inquired. "Well, funerals are funerals and all. The real question is: what are you planning on doing after it's over?"

The thought of this came to Ilene like a bullet through her head. The princess closed her eyes while imagining the sneering lips of an empress that told her what one must do to get what one wants in this world. Those same lips ordered the death of Ilene's angel. Ilene started to think that maybe Lida was right. Ilene's eyes blazed open.

"War. I want my parents to wage war on Ur for what they did. I want them to bring those old giant-prisons down upon their miserable heads!"

Ilene struck her fist upon the table. It had the fierce finality of a judge passing a death sentence with a gavel. Ilene's cup of water fell, but she didn't care. Her eyes remained fixated on her plan for vengeance. Marius put his hand upon her clenched fist. Ilene went red again, but not with shyness. She was red with fury this time.

"Ilene, calm down. You're upset. You don't mean that."

Ilene yanked her hand away from his. "Keep your hands off me! Do you think that I'm just some frail, pampered little princess? Well, I'm not! And I'm going to make sure no one oppresses me again. I'm starting by helping the captain flatten that Ursian scum outside."

Marius argued, "Look, there's no doubt that we need to kill to survive in this situation, but you're talking about killing an entire nation filled with innocent people for a personal vendetta."

Ilene squinted with contempt. "So, you're on Lida's side now?"

"No! I just don't want to see a lovely girl like you turn into a cruel woman like Lida. Besides, you can't declare war on a country. Only your parents have that authority."

The mention of her first oppressors made her turn away with disdain. "I know that my parents have all the authority on this matter. Some things never change. I simply draw satisfaction from knowing that even **they** will not ignore how brutally I've been treated."

"I just know that you couldn't live with yourself if you felt responsible for so much death."

"Let's get one thing perfectly clear: you **don't** know me. You didn't even talk to me until the last day on this boat. So, you don't have any cause to judge what I think is righteous recompense."

Marius grabbed another apple in frustration. He got up from the table and stood by the door, away from Ilene. He did not eat the apple. He only stared into it as if he were Alpha judging the world in his hands.

Ilene couldn't help but break a bit from her anger to ask, "Did you really just refer to me as 'lovely' as part of your argument?"

She wiped her out-of-place bangs back. They were tussled by her yelling.

Marius smirked a little before putting the apple back on the table. He stood over Ilene, staring into her lost eyes and desperate grin. He frowned again. "I've seen a lot of killing in my short time at sea. Some of it justified, most of it... not so just. Sometimes I only looked on. While other times, I participated. I'm not proud of it, but I know what had to be done. I won't say that the situation we're in now is a typical day, but the crew and I know the moral stakes even if we don't talk about them. There is a kind of... respect that we give our enemy. Because we've seen how horribly vile people can be to each other. You're still young. Despite what you've seen, who you've lost, you're still innocent. You've no blood on your hands. I know you want back at Lida. But, leave the retribution to people like me who are used to it."

He put his hands on her shoulders as he begged, "Please don't look for revenge. You'll find it. And instead of satisfaction, you'll feel a ton of hurt instead. Because I went after the man who killed my father for his debt. After searching for days on the docks of Pangea, I found him standing over the pier one night. It was just the description that Osiris gave of the man that he chased off. I pushed him right in. No one saw. His limbs began to kick out to the surface. He began crying for help. I then jumped in to hold him down… to the very last bubble. I don't want you to feel the way that it has made me feel since then- not a nice girl like you. Stay safe. Stay pampered. Maybe that's how we should all live. But we don't. We can't. You can't help who lives well or vile in this world and neither can I. Just keep your hands clean. You'll never get rid of the shakes that come in the night when you think of all the faces that you've wiped away."

Marius pulled himself away from Ilene. He put his hands to the wall. His face was hidden from her, ashamed. Ilene exerted out the next question, slowly with care. "What… what are **you** doing when… if… we return?

Marius raised his open palm, his answer on an invisible platter. "This. This job is all that there is for me. Going to place after place that the high powers say that I need to help provide the grunt work for: trade, naval support, royal transports- all while never knowing who I'll meet or who I might kill."

Ilene walked up to comfort him in the same way that Marlene comforted her. She stopped before putting her hand on his shoulder. She felt that it was too much sorrow for someone in her state to bear. She tried to talk the poor man up, though.

"You don't have to do this for the rest of your life if you don't enjoy it."

He bitterly snorted. "Welcome to the real world, your grace. There isn't much room for a layman to move up."

Ilene zoomed her eyes into his until they were locked. "Perhaps you can marry up."

He stammered. "Ilene... I... I can't."

"We can try. There are many young bachelorettes in Pangea's aristocracy. I know some of them. Perhaps I can get my parents to convince their parents. Then you and Osiris don't have to trek the terrible seas anymore."

"Perhaps. That is very generous of you."

"Marlene always said that the best revenge was living well."

The well-said statement was followed by a rumbling outside the ship. A well-aimed shot was fired.

"Down!" Ilene felt a great weight claw upon her and wrestle her to the floor as the walls splashed open with crackling thunder.

A ball zoomed through each end of the galley, just above the floor-bound couple's heads. They could see that it was morning outside the newly windowed walls. The Ursian ships had their sails up, in-bound for the Pangeans. The orb that Crock predicted hovered over them as a giant spectator.

"They must have figured out what we were planning when they saw the orb come in. They're primed to kill us!"

CHAPTER 13 FIRE

They jumped from the room as it was ripped apart by a volley of relentless cannon fire. They sprinted up each staircase on their way to the deck. As they reached the top of each step, more cannon balls made the staircase disintegrate in a hailstorm of splintered wood.

Marius pushed Ilene along to keep her out of the line of fire. He slowed his own progress in doing this. A shot flew between them. The shock of its feedback left them separated by a gaping hole in the staircase's structure.

"You've got to jump!" she shouted.

"Just go!" he retorted.

The sudden flux in the broken ship's balance left its body on the verge of bursting at the wooden seams. It moaned horribly. Ilene could hear the captain's bell, madly ringing in answer to the ship's gurgling swansong. Ilene then felt a strong sea wind that trembled her and Marius's clothes as they were ruffled into a thousand different shapes a second.

Ilene could also see the wide blue sea and sky shadowed by the on-coming ships with the hovering isle floating intow overhead. This wind did not help with the ship's sudden imbalance as it rocked the vessel severely. This crisis nearly caused Marius to fall out of one of the holes in the wall as the ship's tilting pushed him.

But the force of the Pangean's return fire swayed the ship back into the opposite tilt- enough to wobble Marius away from the hole. This shift in inertia caused him to fall hard with a bone smacking sound that made Ilene gag a little. Ilene held on to the edge of the wall during this swaying, and she stiffened her legs with all her might.

"Jump, jump!" repeated Ilene- ready to beg for as long as she had to. "I'll catch you! I will!"

Bruised and groaning from the pain of being slammed about, Marius had no will for arguing. He could see in her eyes that she was not going to leave him in the same way that she had to leave Marlene.

He jumped over the rift. Ilene launched both of her arms out to grab him. She locked her fingers into his sweaty elbows and struggled against their slipping. He swung into the staircase's jagged edge. His knees were stabbed into the splintered wood. Small, but unbearable spurts of blood spotted his legs.

"That hurt...!" he mumbled with a small yell.

Ilene's ankles were giving. Her sweat was a waterfall ready to pull her down. A new shot was barreling towards them. Ilene didn't know what to do. Ilene was grabbed by strong, familiar arms that whisked both her and Marius from the edge.

"I got you both!" said Atlas.

"Hey, I helped too," protested Osiris, whose arm was still in a tightened grip about Atlas's bicep. Osiris then asked Marius, "You didn't think that I'd let you go for a dip with a pretty girl without my permission, did you?"

The good cheer aroused by the party's safe passage past death could not continue as they heard Crock from atop the deck. "Get up here now, fools! Only Mr. Hound and I are on cannons! We need all of you up here!"

The group ascended to the deck. The deck was in ruin. The mast's sails were in tatters. Holes were lined upon almost every step. A fire bubbled over the stern where a game of catch was once played on a lazy afternoon at sea. Ash snowed in the air, with the isle creating intense shade from above. The isle was nearly straight above the enemy ships. These ships were so close that everyone could see the faces jeering and rioting with their swords for a chance to see the proud Pangean nation fall as surely as this dying craft.

Trotting over what little deck was left, they made their way across. The ship wailed upon each stamp, threatening to snap the floor. A descending cannon ball was spotted by Atlas, and he gathered the whole of the group in his arms and rushed them into the door of the lower decks. They all fell down the stairs before the ball crashed through the main deck.

As they scrambled to their feet, Ilene caught Hound in the midst of pulling the rope for a cannon. The resounding cry of the blast nearly splashed her back upon the floor. Crock was rushing to load another round. Both men were drenched with sweat and sea water. Both had their sleeves rolled up and their shirts unbuttoned. Crock's hat was gone. The man seemed shortened and demeaned without it, revealing a balding head with his grayish beard slithering down his war-wrinkled face. Hound kept his hat on, veiling his eyes still.

"Don't just stand there!" yelled the captain with the same authority, but with a touch of nerves. "Atlas, Osiris: I need you on firing! Marius, Ilene: I need you on the ammo! Target the orb! Bring it down and we can still win this!"

Marius began to reason, "Captain Crock, that orb has gotten too close to us. Bringing it down into the water now could kill us too."

Crock took the ball that he had picked up and shoved it into the chest of Marius. The younger mate barely wrapped a hold on to the ammo before its impact drew out a lot of breath. "Go back to the deck and take another look at what's left of this battered carcass of a ship if you disagree, boy. I told you: we're going down anyway. We might as well take them with us."

With unnerved sweat jumping from Marius's brow, he brought the ballistic burden to the nearest cannon. He spouted, "Sir-" attempting to salute. But Crock carried on with his work before Marius could finish with, "-yes, sir."

Ilene began handing ammo to Atlas, though this raked every fiber of her pampered arms with soreness. Atlas fired them as quickly as Ilene could hand them. As the firing went on, Atlas began to out-pace Ilene and take ammo to load ahead of her. Ilene could not tell if Crock disputed this practice as the sequence of blasts drowned all words out. Ilene pushed on with her task anyway. She could tell that Atlas didn't want her to get hurt, by the looks that he gave her. But during this hard battle, Ilene understood that it was either her life or theirs.

Enemy ballistics began to rain through the chamber's wall. They made Ilene stop her routine with paralyzed fear, only to start it again. She saw everyone else fighting just as hard. They were growing as red and sweaty as her.

Ilene saw Marius handing his ammo to Osiris in droves. The uncle and nephew were a good team in keeping pace with one another. Their synchronicity in timing their hand-offs showed a strong bond in how they looked to each other between every shot. They knew that they could be looking at each other for the last time. They were brief glances of respectful farewells linking each eye.

The Pangean's shots began to chip away at the above orb. The stone isle's side began to fall in mounds upon all of the enemy ships. Most of the debris hit the water. This started to make waves that shook the ship's floor into a frenzy that made everyone lose their footing. The cannons remained in their place as they were bolted down to prevent them from falling about during such circumstances. The same could not be said of the cannon balls that rolled about the place during

146

this wavering of the ship from the wave's weight. One ball crunched into the shoulder of Osiris's broken arm. He yelled out in misery. The floor lurched up into an inverted incline, ramming everyone into the chamber's opposite side.

Atlas managed to hold on to one of the cannons during this inversion. When the wave subsided, the ship re-leveled itself and dragged everyone back to their original footing. Hound got his head clanged against a cannon during this chaos. His hat was knocked off as he was laid out into a corner-dead or unconscious. This wasn't the only blow to the crew. A mountainous noise, sounding like an endless horn's call, blared as a mound of falling rocks began rapidly trickling on the above decks. The mast's base was demolished by one of them. Osiris could hear the spire toppling. From its high-pitched scraping, he could tell that it was falling into the cannon's chamber.

Marius tried to help his fallen uncle up. "Are you alright?"

"Marius," whispered Osiris. Then he turned the whisper into a raw cry. "Get down!"

The last thing that Osiris felt before the mast broke through the ceiling, as well as into his back, was his hands safely forcing Marius out of the way. Marius got up to see a room with the floor cracked by the sudden weight. Dust fogged every direction. As the dust cleared some, he could see the mast's tip piled atop a splatter of human organs and a weakened hand twitching under this mass.

Noise barely chirped from Marius's heavy throat. Marius crawled sloppily to the hand. Osiris was already dead. Only the muscle spasms in his good arm remained. The hand grasped about thoughtlessly reaching for anything. Marius caught the hand and felt its falling heat before it lost all residual energy. Marius put his other hand on top. He wouldn't let go. He wouldn't stop crying. He couldn't make a noise from his burdened throat. He bowed his head deeply into his uncle's hand.

The mast's descent was almost perfectly placed within the center of the room. The impact scattered the ammunition about the floor. The rest of the crew steered clear from the wreckage just in time thanks to Osiris's warning. They were all spread away from each other. They scrambled into some corners of the room for their respective escape routes from the cataclysm. Ilene nearly tripped into the corner wall as she wobbled over the still dormant body of Mr. Hound.

Atlas and Crock tried to recover their bearings as they returned to the cannons. But when the dust finally cleared, Atlas's eyes were shocked to see the desperate loss that Marius was enduring. Crock jabbed at the shoulder of the man to reignite his actions.

"Come on, Atlas. There's nothing you can do. We've enough problems on our shoulders. That isle could fully break down with just one more shot."

Atlas was about to fire again after Crock loaded a ball when he saw the largest of the day's shocks that made the big man feel very small. Something mountainous was seen in the distance. A giant's legs were falling into the water. They fell into the water far behind the floating isle's edge. The rest of the great body descended into the water like the eruption of a volcano-slow and awe-inspiring. A low and mighty hum drowned out even the cannon fire.

The giant was bare naked except for a waist-skirt made from what looked like the scales of a leviathan sea monster. Though smaller than the isle, the bare giant towered over the ships. Thus, an intense myriad of waves grew from his landing into the sea. Ilene was just getting up when the tremendous arrival of the giant shook the very ocean floor. She trembled at the sight of the arms that could swat away all the ships with one blow.

Atlas scowled at the sight of the large fugitive that came from the supposedly deserted orb.

Then Atlas stared more intently at Crock. Crock met Atlas's gaze and was grabbed about the neck before the captain could explain himself.

"You said that this isle was deserted," Atlas growled to his commanding officer with a tightening vise. "Let me guess, you came across this in your travels. You thought it'd make a good place to start your own port. Then you discovered that the last of the giant race lived there. So, you let it slide until your opportunity came. And what better way to get what you want than land it on our enemies? Then what? Kill the survivors? Drive them out? You wanted to finish the job that the Ursians started years ago. They did it for power. You're doing it for profit! You're worse than them!"

"Please," hacked Crock, "I wanted to leave something for... my family."

With the weakest breath left in his voice, Crock whispered, "Live or... die... I wanted to leave this isle to them. My son... needed land for... business."

Atlas was partially touched by this confession. So, Atlas released Crock to his relieved gasping. The large man was made much larger as Crock dropped to his knees in a panic for air. Atlas spied out the window as he noticed that no new shots were fired by the Ursians.

"The waves seem to have sunken all the enemy ships. Looks like your plan worked, at least the part that we agreed upon."

Crock raised his worn eyes as he wanted to cry out for celebration but could barely muster up a cough that cast his visage down again. Atlas was not so touched as to morally release the captain as he did his throat.

Atlas stared out at each ship as they were torn to pieces by the raging sea. "Growing up in the slums, the other kids always accused me of being akin to one of those giants."

Atlas began an impression of one of those children so

accurately that he surprised himself. "'Stone the giant! Cut the fat giant down to size! HAW! HAW!' Those stones that they threw caused the first pain that I ever remember feeling."

Atlas rubbed his arm where an old scar lived. "I was too big to fit in. Dad said that it wasn't because of that. It was because someone my size should not be so gentle. He said that I was too much like my mother- Alpha, rest her soul. He constantly suggested that I take to sea life, become strong like him. I did not become a sea mate for his approval. I did it to get away. I wanted to live away from the taunts as well as the other miseries of slum life. Part of me also wanted to venture the seas to, perhaps, behold one of these endangered behemoths said to still wander the ocean. Most believed them extinct. Others could only dream of proving the myth true. I think that's why we have myths. They give us something to think of other than our own poor lives."

Crock put his hand on the cannon, brushing against one of its firing ropes. Atlas looked out at the only person that far exceeded his size. "You managed to find one, sir. Out of everyone, it was you. You discovered one of the greatest mysteries of the world. While some of us only could look forward to work, marriage, and death- you had the opportunity to change the world."

A sad pause. Atlas spoke on since no one else would. "My wife was the only one who was kind to me, from childhood onwards. We had a daughter. She got the same disease of my ill-breeding that I have. She was big, too big. The kind of big that one cannot craft into a frame like mine. She could not move. Eventually the strength that she needed to move made her young heart give out. She never stopped trying to move and be strong. If I could only describe the kind of conviction that it took for her to get out of bed each day-!"

Atlas began to lose control. Leaning over Crock again he said, "I've seen what I've had to do for my family, Crock. The horrors that you've done to that giant are all on you. What if the rest of his family was left on that isle?"

Crock croaked. "My boy, Pratt, he was in debt. We needed to help his trading company, or his family was going to lose their home."

"So you decided to do this at the cost of that giant's home?"

Crock and Atlas were both silent. The ship was silent. The cannon chamber was practically the only part of the ship that was still able to float. Ilene crawled to Osiris's hand and linked her arms over the bowed head of Marius. She watched the two men begin to stare at each other for a long period.

Finally, Crock spoke up with his full breath back. A conviction rose steadily from his voice. "I was... **am** willing to pay anything to help those I love."

Crock then jerked the cannon's firing string. With perfect timing on Crock's part, the ball managed to strike the knee of the giant. Sprawling back in agony, the behemoth crumbled his head into the side of the isle's soil. The force of this impact was so great that it shattered the ends of the isle's lower ground. This created a stream of mountainous boulders and rocks galloping into the water. What followed was the billowing of an army of waves from this avalanche. Most of the ripple effects from the upset ocean were cut off by the towering legs that managed to regain their footing in the leagues at the bottom of the sea.

Enough surfs slammed past the crew's legs to feel these ripples shake the ship in every sickening direction that their beaten bodies could barely endure. Ilene yelped as she was hurled to the other end of the chamber, away from Marius who held on to the busted mast.

That was not even the worst of it.

With the gravity of the isle's orbit upset by this large portion broken off, the orb faltered and quaked like a teeter-totter during a storm. Then it fell. It speared its way into the sea. It created the god of all waves. It even over-took the hapless giant, made a drowned ant before its might. The wave was encroaching quickly to the crew's cabin.

"Even my soul, Atlas! I'm even willing to pay my soul to help my son!" He cackled madly and shook his fists before the horrified face of Atlas. "Now Pratt will always succeed. He can make his own port, even a nation!"

Crock stopped laughing as he voiced a sudden concern. "Oh, but how to tell him? He will! He must!"

Crock kept cackling on anyway, grasping Atlas's shoulder to

hold himself up as if he were overpowered by the funniest joke of all.

"You old fool...!" cried Atlas looking helplessly out the window. "You killed us all..." he mumbled listlessly. Atlas rubbed his head with his hand. Unable to bear all that lay outside the window, Atlas slumped down. He closed his eyes and breathed softly. He opened his eyes as he pulled a picture out of his pocket. Atlas stared coldly at the picture as the wave closed in.

Crock broke from his revelry. "Is that your family?"

Atlas did not answer as he kept looking at the picture. Crock slumped down next to him.

"Maybe I'll see them again," Atlas finally said. Another pause lay under the water's steady rumble. Then in bitter after-thought Atlas said, "But these people: Ilene, Marius... and poor Osiris... they won't get a chance at anything. Were they part of what you were willing to sacrifice for your prosperity?"

Crock balled himself up as the wave rumbled closer. "Let's let each other die in peace," he whimpered. "That's an order."

Ilene closed her eyes too as she took in the calm before the disastrous end. Her last sight of the crew saw Atlas and Crock balled up like sleeping babes, Mr. Hound still spilled upon the floor, the mast still planted over Osiris's ruined body, and Marius staring with haunting serenity into her as he held on to Osiris. This calm did not last very long.

The walls split with the fury of a thousand cannons. Ilene felt the effects of the bursting onslaught. Like hounds on a hunt, the gushes of liquid swept her body into a jerking whirlwind of chaos. Ilene's eyes were clamped shut throughout the ordeal.

She felt everything spill over her as the world became cold and quiet. She heard air-bubbles break from her nose. Ilene felt herself floating in the loose underwater gravity. She felt lost within a womb of timeless infinity. Infinity hurt for a finite moment as she bumped into the edge of the ship's hole before getting sucked out. She had to reach the surface. Air dwindled with each sting in her neck.

CHAPTER 14
DROWNING

Ilene wavered her hands toward the direction that she vaguely understood to be up. She dared not open her eyes. As a child, she once opened them inside the bath water. She just wanted to see what it looked like in the underwater world even if it was the few feet found in the tub. Expecting to feel a cool bliss come over the eyes, little Ilene only felt the flaming darts that stung from within her lids. It was the soap that suddenly infected them.

Though the soothing comfort that the maid brought to little Ilene was a blessing, the pain that she felt in her eyes that day felt stronger than any healing kindness. Rowing her arms higher was a battle to beat her fading air. Ilene felt something sliding from her head. It stung. She had to hold on. She had to keep rowing.

She felt the air of the above world finally wrap around her hand. She craned her head free and sucked in all the air that her selfish throat could take. She could barely hold herself up. The dress encircled about her. It held her up like a flimsy raft. Yet it blocked off her arms from paddling. So, she bunched a handful of it into one hand while paddling with the other. She kept shooting her paddling hand out for something to support her above the water. She kept getting sucked back into the deep by small waves only to kick her way back up. Wreckage swam about her.

She tried to grab whatever piece of wood she could find, yet none could support her weight. Punching furiously, she refused to be pulled back down. Her limbs were beginning to give out. A fire began to develop in her very bones. When Ilene resurfaced upon her fortieth odd attempt at floating on a piece of wreckage, Atlas's body rose in front of her sight.

She breathed out relief as she said, "Thank Alpha, Atlas. Perhaps we can-" He did not rise further. His large form bobbed above the surface. His face did not rise from the water.

"Dead..." Ilene said with a chill scratching her chapped lips. Atlas's body was big enough to support Ilene. But from the moment that she laid her hand on his slumped back, she felt so wrong. So, Ilene let go of the stiffened back and resolved to find a different support.

Before treading off, Ilene patted his head. The water made a strange smacking sound between their skins. "Thank you. You deserved better than this. I hope you see your daughter again in Alpha's happy forever."

Ilene swam away and could not help but look back as she saw the world printed on the mighty man's back drift off into the distance. *Perhaps he'll float all the way to paradise*, Ilene half-hopefully considered.

She was suddenly further washed about by the remnants of

the great wave, creating hills that flung her waywardly while forcing her underwater deeper than ever. She rose once more with winded breath and weary bones. She gasped for relief as she hugged upon the largest piece of wood yet. It was only after hanging on for a moment that she realized that it was the bookcase from her cabin.

Those nostalgic stories were now Ilene's only safety net. She placed her knees into an open space in the shelf's cubby hole. Feeling the case's masonry buckle slightly, she wrapped her arms around the edges in case the bottom gave out. Ilene paddled the makeshift boat awkwardly with her hand until a thin piece of driftwood came by. She grabbed it and used it as a makeshift oar.

With some stability finally achieved, Ilene looked back to the isle. It had settled into the water. It looked like a regular island at this point. Remaining tuffs of waves sprouted about the open sea. They waved up and down like gentle cradles. They were an acceptable distance away from Ilene. She still had to escape them. She looked for the giant as well, but she did not see him. He must have escaped... or drowned as well. Her survey of the water also presented some of the ship's ruined corpses that seemed half filled with sea.

Ilene's survey was interrupted by a chunk of such wreckage that bumped into her vessel. Ilene had to row around a maze of debris. Sometimes she would have to poke at a chunk of wood with her oar to angle herself from drifting into it. While difficult to navigate, her time on this shelf offered her a gentle calm.

The drifts of the water sounded like rain that would drip upon her window at home. Ilene would sit by that sill and listen intently to each drop when Marlene got to a boring part in one of the very books that she was crouched next to. Remembering the similarity of the sound, she smiled sadly and rubbed one of those books.

Speaking to her maid that she knew couldn't hear her, she sighed, "'Why didn't you skip to the exciting parts?' I'd always ask. Seems to be the opposite in real life. I'd give anything to jump past the pages of this horrible day."

Upon speaking aloud this melancholy thought, Ilene passed her countenance into a numb mourning for all those lost during the ship's sinking. She nodded respectfully upon thinking of Crock's stoic leadership, even if it had dark motives. She shook her head upon thinking of the noble Atlas and the woes leading to his ruin. She covered her face upon thinking of Osiris's horrific death. No one should go through that. She let fall her arms to the side of the shelf upon thinking of Marius. He was someone that... could have been more.

But he wasn't. Now Ilene must live with thinking of what could have been with him- with all of them. Ilene continued to try rowing through her misery. She figured that she might as well. She couldn't go back to those happy memories without feeling sad. She feared and believed that she would be dead soon anyway. It bothered her how much this fact didn't even scare her anymore. Her faith in Alpha's happy forever seemed to be a hallow comfort after all the trauma implanted in her soul.

Ilene kept shoving through the fragmented maze of lost crafts for over an hour. In that time, the tuffs of waves came together. They eventually conglomerated into a much larger wave. As they moved closer while simultaneously joining as one, the greatest wave got bigger and closer. It preyed upon her as a beast preys upon a victim in the wild. Ilene felt the tremors of the wave as it gained proximity. Hanging over her by the time she turned around, fear seized her before the wave could. Ilene tried rowing faster. The wave's shadow still outpaced her.

Within the wave overhead, Ilene saw an even more terrifying sight than impending drowning. Near the top of the beast's wet jaws was an Ursian soldier caught in the maelstrom. He must have survived his ship sinking too. Seeing the girl that his crew was ordered to kill aroused in him a last-ditch passion to finish the mission. The soldier didn't want to chance the possibility of the girl surviving the wave. So, he jumped out.

Sword drawn, he nose-dived for his trembling target. The target moved as Ilene hopped out of the cabinet and swam under it to use as a shield against the killer and the wave. She over-turned the case to create an air-pocket within the cubby hole. Ilene watched as the tales of her days-gone-by fell into the water. The killer landed atop the case. His knees quaked the shelf as he pierced it with a pulsating violence that made Ilene believe that she was stabbed. She was rather scratched within the side of her arm by the sword punctures from above. She cried out. Now sprawled on the case, the killer could see the hole that he made. He heard that he was right on target for his kill. He knew just where to hit next. The wave was so close. With a rough vow, "For the empress," he raised his sword for the second strike.

But the second strike came from the wave instead of the killer. The weight crashed upon the killer and the cabinet. The wood pounded upon Ilene's skull. The impact left her reeling back into the depths. Ilene tried to shake it off and swim to the surface. She ripped a sleeve from her ragged dress and pressed it to her bleeding arm. If her eyes were opened, she would have seen the killer coming right for her. He lost his sword in the chaos of the downpour, but that didn't matter. His eyes were fixed wide open to close in on his target. The two were reunited with his hands clawed about her throat.

Ilene let out a shrill gasp- a fatal mistake underwater. She knew what was enclosed on her even without sight. She tried to kick him off. Her dress held her down in the watery gravity. Her body writhed with her heartbeat. Each of her nerves blipped with an inner chirp of fleeting agony. The killer held his grip, stare, and breath firmly. They floated in the current, spiraling weightlessly past the bulk of the sinking ships. The broken crafts were like wafting leaves in the autumn.

Ilene was doomed, but she was not giving up.

She pressed her nails straight into the man's eyes. The blood oozing out moistly ran down her fingers before fluttering into the ocean's mix. She was glad that she kept her eyes shut so that she could spare herself from the sight of the man's horrid face in this ugly torture. Ilene did not want any more nightmares in bed than she had already gained. Ilene pressed further as her eyes gritted tighter shut. She could feel the blood vapors from the man slithering into her nose. Or, perhaps it was her blood, or a combination of both.

His grip loosened. Ilene pushed her way out of it. She suddenly felt something floating in the water touch her hand. It felt like the wood of her makeshift oar. It was. So, she held it with both hands and jammed it into the man's throat that she figured was still close to her. It was. The splinter of the wood tore his neck up, polluting the ocean with more blood gassing about. She hoped to have finally stopped him.

She apparently hadn't as the man pushed her off. Knowing that he'd swim after her, Ilene had no choice but to open her eyes. It was an unwelcome sight as her vision jutted awake. The water was not a vastly blue dimension. It was red. The blood smogged the water's very atmosphere as it stung her eyes almost back into shutting again. She saw that the killer was enveloped in this blood's fog like a soul's spirit crimsoned with its sins. She could see that they were not as far from the surface as she believed. She also saw the soldier's lost sword floating up top too. She rushed her way to the surface.

Ilene popped out breathing in more deeply than ever. Ilene soaked in air like she was a dying elder. A brief gasp from her joyfully freed lungs sounded before the killer erupted forth in red fury from the water. He screamed with a hoarse howl for revenge. He punched her, blackening her eye. With the harsh turn of her head caused by this blow, she saw the sword he lost. She grabbed the heavy weapon with both hands. The killer moved in for another strike. Swinging with strength that she didn't know that she had, the sword rent in twain the rest of his neck. His remaining body slipped downward. His head remained resting above the shaking waters.

Ilene grew cold. She looked upon the sword decorated with the smear of gore. Ilene dropped it from her hand as if it were hot. She watched it float away. She hoped that she'd never see it again. As the sword drifted past the dismembered head, Ilene's eye got caught upon it. Its eyes stared dully facing the sky. Its chapped lips hung open, filled with an excess of blood flowing like a small fountain. Ilene was transfixed to this macabre sight that she had crafted. She held her arms around herself while trying to keep herself afloat by whipping her legs about.

Ilene could not say how long she stared at what was left of her would-be-killer. It was long enough for a storm to develop about her. Her blackened eye, grown swollen, stung when something tapped it- a rain drop. A downpour began to cover this ghastly tragedy. The head was shrouded in the torrent. Clumsy gallons of rain clapped about Ilene like applause. Ilene felt weighed down by its power. Ilene was also overcome with shivers and shakes- just like Marius said. Ilene reasoned in her scrambled heart that perhaps it would be best to let the rain have its way and sink her into the deep.

The princess lost everything. She lost her best friend. All hope of surviving was gone. Even if she did make it, she had nothing to look forward to in going home. Her parents wouldn't even let her leave the palace if she did survive. Now she has become a killer. What hope in a peaceful after-life could she even dare to consider? The world before her seemed to be nothing more than a meaningless splatter of grayish scribbles with dancing dots. There seemed to be no point in continuing only to get lost again.

Yet as she felt the blood from the killer wash away from her skin and clothes, she understood that time washes away all of life's messes. Marlene had once told little Ilene that when she accidentally spilled some milk on a patio at home. Despite this, mother began to deride her carelessness. She called what she did evil. Ilene was sore afraid. 'Evil' was only a word used for doomed and hated monsters or sorcerers in Marlene's stories.

Marlene asked the queen to let her discipline the girl for her. The queen agreed. But Marlene did not discipline her. They simply wiped away the milk with some rags moistened by water. The milk's stain remained. Marlene told Ilene that the milk wouldn't be stained there forever. All the bad things that happen will go away eventually. Sure enough, the milk's stain evaporated next week. Time washes away all messes.

Ilene flapped her arms awake with resolve to go on. She defied the apparent bleakness of the world. She wanted to fight beyond the misery. But before she could get beyond it, she had to face more as she bumped into the dismembered head out of the darkness. It was still afloat, but its mouth was bogged with rainwater rather than blood.

Ilene picked it up. "I'm sorry I killed you," she told the head. "Your life was worth more than this. I know it. You probably had a family and friends."

Ilene bowed to give a respectful silence for the dead man's spirit. "But I have those things in my life too. Given how gleefully you went after me in the name of your empress you must not have thought much of your loved ones. But I do think much of my loved ones. But your life was still worth something, no matter how badly you abused it. That's why your passing was unfortunate. But your life simply wasn't worth ending mine. I'm sorry. May your virtues weigh more than your sins on Alpha's eternal scales."

She laid back in the water while putting the head aside. The head's face flipped over into the ocean. Before swimming on, Ilene heard a crunching sound blast out. She assumed that it was thunder. But Ilene knew a crunch when she heard one. She turned to see that the head was gone. It couldn't have floated away so quickly. And it was obviously too buoyant to sink.

The answer rose from the water. It was a leviathan sea beast that loomed over little Ilene- casting out what little light was in the storm. It cast her whole world into an empty black.

CHAPTER 15
PREDATORS
AND PREY

The leviathan was the most feared species of fish. It had a bio-illuminated antenna stock that shined like a spotlight over its food. It flashed upon Ilene with a blinding intensity. Its vast size allowed its species to actually eat the whale into extinction. It ate any creature that it was bigger than- almost all of them.

Ilene was its next morsel. Its jaws cranked open. The water flowed into its maw, sucking Ilene in. Ilene tried to swim from its damply darkened cave of a mouth. It was no use. The leviathan was about to clamp its teeth down.

Before a bite could be taken of Ilene, a bite was taken of the leviathan by the one creature that it was dwarfed by. The giant burst from the rain's veil to pick up the shrieking sea serpent and gnaw into it. Colorful intestines rained along with the storm. The smell was awful and boiled Ilene's stomach. Yet Ilene was alive. This feeling of salvation sank away when the giant threw the leftovers miles away and he craned his head down to the frightened girl.

The giant's voice deafened Ilene's ears with its thunderous

blast. "You are one of them! Those who destroyed my home. My family was there. Now they are gone."

Ilene tried to explain herself. "Please don't kill me. I-I-"

She hated stuttering. She composed herself. "I had no part in it. I didn't know that any one was on there, that is, it was the captain who-"

The giant lifted his hand. Ilene shuddered to think that he was getting ready to swat her out of existence. It appeared that he was rather lifting the hand to his ear to hear her. "I can't hear you, girl. You're like a buzzing insect."

Ilene repeated herself without stammering this time. She raised her voice.

"I still cannot hear you."

Ilene screamed her words at the top of her lungs. She coughed. Her throat felt sore.

The behemoth scratched his beard with the grading sound of earthen crust crumbling together. "You say that you didn't know, but this leader of yours did? That's an awfully convenient excuse."

The fringes of Ilene's dress were picked up by two of his fingers as if they were giant tweezers. She was hoisted from the water. This left her suspended aloft like a decoration hanging over a cradle. Being brought so high all at once was a thrilling horror that made Ilene feel as though parts of her heart were leaping from her mouth in between shouts of surprise.

"What's to stop me," the giant asked, "from killing you for justice? How would you like it if I came to your home and destroyed it?"

Ilene's mouth was clapped shut for an answer. She was transfixed by the orb-sized eyes narrowing over her. His skin was like a mountain slope with his rigid wrinkles and elder hair seeming like snow. The giant ripped his gaze from Ilene to lay his heavy head into his arm to hide his weeping.

"I mean," he sniffled with a deafening trumpet, "our people have been hidden away for generations. We were never violent. Then your kind drove us away. We only wanted to be left alone. Now Marl is gone. Your people killed him. Cannon fire struck him down. It was just me and him after my beloved Venita passed. Oh, Marl, my son..."

He lamented and dropped tears that mingled with the rain. He hardened his voice again. "And it is all because of your kind. I vowed to never strike back at humanity as did my father and his father before him. But now I've no longer a son to pass that philosophy down to."

"Please," begged Ilene. She implored her hands out in supplication.

He placed her on his open palmed hand. Ilene landed on it roughly, tumbling a few extra feet. Getting back up, Ilene saw his other hand rearing up for its dark execution. Ilene was to be pressed down until dead. But a voice stopped that fist. It wasn't the giant. It was Mr. Hound.

"Do you like bleeding out slowly until dead, monster? No? Then desist your actions."

The morose man was seen standing in the hollow of the giant's collar bone. He held a musket over the softest part under his Adam's apple.

"What is this? How- **what** is poking me?" The giant's raised fist turned to investigate with a series of grasps about his body. He looked like one searching for an itch to scratch.

"That would be my musket. Found her in a chest full of ammo that whisked me to safety after I awoke to find that I was minus one ship. And what do I happen to drift to? The deserted isle that our captain added to the sea? No. I bump into a big, hairy leg. Charmed, I'm sure. Despite the stench, I climbed the heights of your anatomy with your hairs as my grappling holds. I don't wish to go into further grisly detail regarding the unsightly sights encountered during my journey. Suffice to say that, in the end, it was preferable to drowning. And unless you want to gargle a splash of gun fire, you'll put the girl on the other side of your collar bone and bring us to the nearest orb trading center. Does my insect-like buzzing come through clearly to you?"

The giant paused indignantly. Ilene breathed hurriedly, not knowing if she was on the brink of rescue or more danger. As the titan moved Ilene to the edge of his collar's hallow, Hound mocked him.

"There you go, boy. That's the proper way to treat royalty. She's royalty, you know. While we're talking labels, tell me what your name is. I'm no good at naming new pets."

As Ilene settled into the fleshy seating, her back upon the side of the bony collar, the giant groaned formally. "My name is Marl. I too am no good at coming up with names, human. That's why I named my son after me. Marl."

Ilene looked to see Hound across from her. He held the musket dead in the center of the large throat's tingling flesh. Hound's fingers were twisted upon the weapon, itching to thrust and fire. Hound's clothes were darkened and ripped up just as fiercely as Ilene's. Somehow, the man kept his hat. The hat made a cowl over his eyes, as always. There was something different about Hound, outside of his neck mussed up with sweat down to his own collar. For the first time, Ilene saw Mr. Hound smile. His teeth were hanging sharply out of his mouth like unsheathed daggers.

Hound made somewhat of a greeting to Ilene by making a mock bow, musket still in hand. "Nice to see that pretty face again, princess. Finest sight I've seen in this past hour."

Looking over Marl's hill-sized shoulder, the mate grumbled, "Not that it was much of a contest."

Ilene widened her eyes with surprise. "Has it only been an hour since we sank?"

Hound nodded. "Just about. My dad's watch survived. See?"

With Hound's trigger hand weighed clumsily over its mark, his other hand fumbled a watch from his pocket. The watch was brass with splotches of gold painted about it. "He carried it with him while he was in the navy. Good times. He always taught me to stand by my country and all that father/ son stuff to keep me disciplined until I left that shack."

To mock Marl, Hound added, "Isn't that right, Marl **Junior**? Oh, I'm sorry. I meant Marl **Senior**."

Marl shook his two passengers with his failed attempt at holding back his sobs. Hound giggled childishly and smiled through his teeth again.

"What-" She hesitated. "What about the other survivors?"

Hound pocketed the watch and frowned grimly once more. "I wasn't the only one on that ammo box when I woke up from my headache. Crock got the bright idea to hold on to it too. The two of us were weighing it down, though. He said that his old years were wasted on surviving, or something like that. So, he let me stay on it. He swam away in search of something else to float on. Then a big wave got him."

Hound kicked the side of Marl's throat cruelly. "No thanks to your over-sized wading about, Mr. Marl Senior."

"All in one hour," Ilene whispered sorrowfully. A heavy moment passed quietly.

"Enough moping. Let's liven our feet to the future. Still with us, Marl? You haven't drowned from this rain, or your tears, yeah?"

The giant stiffened to attention. "Very good. Now then, I'll guide you to the nearest orb. First, we'll need to get past the Vaalbara mountains northward. Mush!"

Ilene felt pushed to the soft of Marl's neck. She saw the world turn clockwise and thrust forward. Ilene bobbed up and down with each of Marl's tremendous steps. Hound kept his balance by stretching his legs out and digging his heels into Marl's flesh.

"Mush!" he repeated louder with a bigger smile.

CHAPTER 16
STAND-OFF

The rain died away eventually as the large conveyance named Marl carried his passengers along. During these long miles of strides, Ilene began to settle herself comfortably into her unconventional quarters. She worriedly flashed a few looks to Hound as the mate kept his musket pinned above Marl's throat. The throat was constantly swallowing deeply in fear.

While Marl stepped over the Vaalbara mountains, Ilene fancied a look at their vast landscapes. It was just as the late Crock said. The mountains stretch beyond each end of the horizon. Yet from this vantage point atop Marl's collar bone, the sight seemed greatly diminished. A steady wind tickled Ilene's skin. This gave her goosebumps and made her wish to sit back for fear of falling.

The mountains crumbled under Marl's feet as he made his way through. He flinched slightly as one may do while trying to walk through thorns. Finally returning to the sea was a relief to the blistered sores throbbing on Marl's feet. This comfort for Marl was a discomfort for the two passengers. The rocks being dragged under Marl's heels created a rumbling noise that covered up the dead air between Ilene and Hound. The quiet of the sea made this more evident. The awkward quiet soon snapped to a stop. It was Hound's turn to glance at his companion.

"I never did receive a cordial thank you for my rescuing her grace."

Ilene shot a look back at the sternly faced Hound. He let his eyes beam out of his hat. Ilene's first look into those eyes transfixed her. They were of a cold, unblinking blue. He had wrinkles curtained under his eyes as well, snitching that he was middle aged.

Staring at this cruel face, Ilene was reminded that she did not much approve of Hound's treatment of Marl. Despite trying to kill her, she still sympathized with the old and weary giant. Hound should not have pressed his will so rudely upon poor Marl. If anyone used Marlene's death to get under Ilene's skin, the young princess was not sure how she would react.

Nonetheless, this was not the time nor place for the girl's personal judgments. So, she promptly jabbed out a thank you.

"So..." began Ilene with an elongated tone, "what is the plan for when we get to the orb? Will you arrange for a ship to take me home?"

Hound rubbed his chin. He pulled his hat over his eyes again. "Of course. I'll need to figure out how we'll arrange that. We got to be discrete. I can't parade you about and tell everyone that you're the princess of Pangea. Too many cutthroats in Princeberg. It's one of the most crime ridden of the orb-trading posts. Just stick close to me and keep your mouth shut. I'll handle things."

Ilene nodded dumbly. She tried to keep the conversation alive as she felt it slipping into the coffin again. She stumbled for an idea until she came across a conversation piece. She didn't realize how foolish it was until it passed out of her.

"I must say, you certainly talk more atop this giant than you did on the ship. I took you for the quiet type."

Mr. Hound put his free hand upon his back and stretched it from behind. "You are correct. That's because back during our ship's pre-sunken days, I'd chat up everyone onboard. Nothing wrong with that, except I tend to ramble. So, Crock chewed me out one day and told me to keep it shut. So, I did... when necessary. Now there's no captain to chew me out. Besides, taking charge like I am now calls for me to speak up more than I usually do. It's quite liberating, actually."

Ilene asked, "Do you have any personal plans after you return me home?"

"That's a personal question," quipped Hound. "I suppose that I'll end up getting knighted for my heroic feat. 'Sir Hound' has a nice ring, don't you think? Maybe our good king will even offer me your dainty hand in marriage. That wouldn't be a bad day's pay."

Ilene started up and kicked back at the idea of being with this slimy man. He had to notice of course.

"Kidding, of course. Keep it together now. I like riding solo just fine, thanks anyway. There's a plenty wide market of women to keep me in good spirits, if you take my meaning. Besides which, I may take up a more grounded trade. Anything to keep me out of wild countries like Ur. Not to mention the even wilder seas."

Ilene accidentally blurted out an unexpected yawn.

After a definite pause in reaction, Hound said, "Why don't you get some sleep, my grace? I'll wake you if something exciting happens."

So Ilene let herself be rocked asleep by the rhythmic swaying of Marl's steps.

"Ilene. Wake up."

Ilene did not stir.

"Marl, be a dear, and make a loud cough. That should start her up."

Marlene used to say that even an avalanche falling through broken glass could not wake that girl from her over-sleeping. The giant's cough was very much like such an unlikely sound even if it did do a good job of jolting Ilene's sloppy eyes wide open. Her hair was sloshed into a scribbled mess. Even her hair braid made it worse by holding the ponytail back in its wrinkled slouch.

"What is it...?" demanded the cranky princess. She was not a morning person.

"We're almost upon Princeberg," answered Mr. Hound.

Miles off, Ilene spotted the floating rock that held a series of jaded, nearly colorless, buildings. One of the orb's pulley platforms was on its way up. Ilene saw a ship sailing away. Most of the crew's mates were ignorant of the giant behind the route. Some of the lazier ship members relaxing on the stern saw the colossal sight. Except, they resolved that it was best to keep their vision a secret. It's bad enough that the captain accuses them of being lazy- let alone mad.

"The idea," explained Hound, "is to get to that pulley's platform bringing in traded goods. You can see that the orb is too high for even our slim friend to reach."

Hound began addressing his slim friend. "So, Mr. Marl, I'll need you to pick up the pace before the pulley flies out of your hands. Ilene, I need you to be ready to jump on to it when we are close enough."

The giant's strides sped up and were like the galloping of Ilene's favorite horse back home. But the beloved beast, 'Sweetie Bird,' as Ilene called it, never galloped so hard as to jumble the foundations of the world. It was during this vibration of Ilene's footing that a terrible thought filled her to the brim with worry- ready to spill over.

"Mr. Hound, what if Marl tries to kill us once we're off his body?"

Marl's progress came to a full stop. Ilene nearly wobbled off, but she managed to cushion a bump of her head on to the collar bone that acted as a kind of safety railing. Somehow, Hound still did not waver an inch.

Hound disapprovingly rolled his eyes. "I doubt that the old brute could have devised such a thought. But thank you for putting it into his little brain. Since this factor has put a halt to my schedule, let me tell you both how I intended to deal with it. You reading me, Marl? You've been a good boy during this whole trip. Don't you misbehave now that we're almost finished. I'm keeping this musket trained on your throat. I can tear it up just as well from a distance as I can up close."

Marl snorted. "Don't tell me, Hound. You just so happen to be the best marksman in the Pangean army."

Hound returned, "Care to gamble on that not being true?" Hound turned his head to Marl's large eye cast down on him with resentment. Ilene did not see what kind of soul-piercing stare the mate held on the giant. But it seemed to work as Marl's resolve melted from his eyes before giving in.

"Very well. I'd sooner be rid of you marauders, anyway."

He went on. As Marl sprinted closer, Hound said, "Almost there! Get ready, Ilene!"

Ilene fought her way into standing upright. But each mountainous tumble caused by Marl's epic strides kept kicking her to her knees every time she got up. The vibrating sensation abruptly stopped as Ilene found that she was staring down at the rising platform.

"You've got only one shot! Jump before it goes past." She saw some merchants upon this platform. They were surrounded by their latest spoils from a recent trade. Marl's appearance caused a great commotion among their company. With the giant standing before them they could only stand back in awe. Seeing Ilene peering from the collar bone's alcove, the merchants pointed and made indistinct chatter. Ilene looked past this and took in how high up they really were. She gulped.

Betraying her instinct to hold back was an instant regret. She aimed with her eyes and leaped out before any hesitant thoughts could stop her. Suspended in mid-air, she saw the swirled clouds and deep sea below, and became conscious of her body's heavy obligation to gravity weighing down into the pits of her stomach.

She reached her hands out to the platform. Its safety was mere feet away. She thought that she was going to miss it as she shot through the air for what seemed like hours. Her heart jumped directly upon the line between fear and joy when she felt her fingers tap on to the wooden platform. Her dress fluttered like a surrendering flag in the heights of the wind.

Unfortunately, she also felt the splinter on the wood's floor sting into her tender flesh. Ilene was nearly rebuked back to her fall when a pair of hands grabbed her arms. It was one of the merchants. This man wasn't in the best of shape. His heavy breathing upon bending down alone made that obvious. So, he was nearly pulled down along with Ilene.

"Would anyone mind offering a helping hand?"

In response to the curt demand, the rest of the men grabbed his struggling body. They heaved with a far greater strength than they needed as the whole of the party that Ilene joined nearly flung itself over the other end of the deck. The only obstacles that kept them from falling over were several valuable boxes getting pushed into the ocean's cruel waters.

"No!" complained the man. "Not my goods! This is not good. That merchandise was hard haggled."

There was no time for materialism as it was Hound's turn to jump. The platform was practically on level with Marl's collar bone. Hound kept the musket trained on Marl with keener intent than ever. "Moment of truth, Marl. Don't disappoint me."

So intent on keeping track of his mark, the mate looked at the deck's elevation to time it so that he could jump backwards without losing a bead on the target. He fell back perfectly into the floor. Before the merchants could surround him, he jerked his head up to prepare for the possibility of having to fire. Hound nearly pulled the trigger before he realized that he did not have to fire.

Marl only stood there and watched the human aim for him. The giant's boulder-rivaling eyes gleamed upon Hound with a generation's worth of resentment. When the platform became raised out of Marl's reach, Hound unwound his stiff vigil and smoothed his head back to the floor. The former sea-mate cooed out a serene breath of satisfaction.

"Do you know what the stupidest part of our escape was?" whispered Hound to Ilene, looking down upon her protector with concern.

Before she could attempt an answer Hound, blurted out, "This musket wasn't even loaded!" He sobbed out mad cackles.

The merchant, still staring down at the sea, spoke up. "I hate to interrupt your revelries, my mysterious guest."

The trader spoke with a cautious foreboding bubbling in his voice. "But it seems like your tall companion isn't quite done with you."

Everyone gathered at the edge to discover his meaning. Marl arrested the nearby ship from the sea and held it above his head. The excess water showered from the ship's bottom crevices, creating a liquid curtain over the strained muscles of the titan. With a bellow of rage, Marl launched the great ship at the platform.

As the ship hurtled closer, Hound shouted, "Hang on to something!"

Ilene grabbed the nearest chain holding up the deck by the corners. She squeezed it with both hands and all of her might. She was too scared to even shut her eyes.

CHAPTER 17
PRINCEBERG

Ilene was simply too scared to even keep her eyes closed for a second. Marl's throw fell short of hitting the rising platform full on. But the top of the mast crashed through its edge. It was the crow's nest that got sliced into the flat surface like a knife through butter. Ilene's mouth raised open widely as this impact rattled the platform.

Every sight turned into a scribbled mesh. The crow's nest even had a passenger. This man, seeing the sudden ascent into the deck, jumped out to avoid being sliced. But the inertia threw him down to his death.

All this chaos knocked even more boxes from the deck. "Aw, come on!" whined the pudgy merchant. "I really should have tied those down!"

But Ilene's thoughts were not on profit. She beheld the men falling off the ship or hanging on for dear life as it sailed into the death grip of the sea. She could hear the weeping and wailing in an unharmonious chorus.

It was the most horrible sound that Ilene ever heard.

"All those deaths," murmured Ilene.

Seeing that the crisis was passed, Hound mocked his failed killer. "You couldn't hit me even if you had a whole fleet to throw."

Hound kicked the last box in Marl's direction. The fat merchant gave out a shrill cry of dismay. "Was that really necessary?"

The platform nearly reached the opening to Princeberg's orb when Marl yelled a vow. "One day justice will come to all! To the large and the small!"

With that, the giant and the sea were swept out of sight by rock formations passing their ascent. It was dark in this vertical cave. Yet it passed a calm over Ilene that she savored.

Hound whooped and sighed graciously. "I can't believe that I just faced off with a giant. I say, my dear," to Ilene, "care to buy your knight in shining armor a drink? I know a wonderful pub around here. I'd dare even call it the best. It's been years since I last saw it. If I could only remember which part of town-"

The pudgy merchant violently poked Hound's chest in anger. "You're not dealing with a giant anymore, boy. Now you're dealing with me!"

Bemused, Hound asked, "Do **you** know which pub I'm trying to remember? I think it's called the 'Snake's Foot' or 'Gorgon's Ankle' or something like that."

The merchant grumbled aloud. "No. But you're working off the money that you and your lady friend owe me for all of our lost goods because of your wild scene. So instead of going to a pub to drink, you're off to my pub for work."

"Sorry to disappoint you, friend," scoffed Hound as he flicked the man's hand off him. "I'm in between jobs and I don't wish to work under someone lesser than myself."

The platform reached its destination. Past the hole stood the upper crest of the orb where its populace dwelt. This part of it contained the backyard of a two-story brick building, surrounded by fences. An automatic steam powered pulley winch stopped its coiling and locked itself in place.

In the spotlight of the sun again, the merchant clashed into Hound. Before the next cock could crow, the two were wrestling on the ground. Hound grappled the man into a chokehold.

Ilene hurried to break it up. "Please let the poor man go, Mr. Hound!"

He wouldn't stop. The merchant squawked in pain.

Ilene played her only card. "That's a royal order, Hound!"

Hound dropped his jaw as well as his hold.

One of the other merchants jumped back, jingling the bells on his jester costume.

"Hold on, I know you."

He looked Ilene over to make sure. "You're Princess Ilene! From the ship where Isaac got beat up."

"Which one?" asked a slender man in a moustache and overalls.

"The one where he lost those boxes, Craigson."

Coughing back to life, the pudgy Isaac flourished his cape up and adjusted his hat. "It wasn't my fault! Indeedly so, if you see your captain tell him that he owes me for the lost materials."

"We can't," Ilene solemnly said. "He's dead. They're all dead. At my wedding party, the Ursian royal family was killed by the empress seizing power. Then she proceeded to kill the crew when I refused to join her. We are all that's left."

The merchants stared sadly. Jake bumped Isaac's shoulder. "Remove your hat in respect."

Isaac fumbled it off. A moment of silence withered past. Isaac put his cap back on as he clumsily tried to reignite conversation.

"Well, er, be that as it may, outside of this incident, I find that this revelation gives you two all the more reason to stay with us."

"Why?" barked Hound.

"Well obviously," scorned Isaac, leering at his newest rival of many, "you two are trying to get back to Pangea, aye?"

Ilene wiped her eyes. It hurt to touch the still blackened one. "Aye."

"Then," announced Isaac with business-like formality trumpeting, "you'll both need to work up the money to get safe passage to Pangea. Besides, no one can know you're here. There are beasts dressed as men here in Princeberg that should never be put near royalty."

Jake slapped Isaac's shoulder with more playfulness. "That includes you, ya brute."

Isaac stared at Jake. "Know your place, boy. I'm your employer. And do you not recall that you and I both performed for young Ilene's amusement back in the day?"

Jake placed his hands together in wistful nostalgia. "How I long for those days."

Isaac bitterly told Jake, "We wouldn't have lost our jobs as royal entertainers in the first place if you weren't fooling around with that servant girl."

"Mark you, Isaac," Jake growled, "it was true love. Something your hard heart can't fathom."

Ignoring Jake, Isaac returned to his formality. "That brings me to the reward for our services. When we return you, we wish not for money (though it wouldn't hurt). We only wish to have our positions as performers returned."

Extending his hand out, Isaac asked, "Do we have a deal?"

Ilene shook his hand and bowed. "Good," he smiled. "Now let's get us something to eat."

It wasn't a table set by an emperor. But the meal did Ilene much good.

She sat on the stool at the concession bar. The place had over a dozen tables with chairs scattered about. As Craigson got some bread and cheese that they had in storage for their guests, Isaac apologized that there wasn't much more food.

"It was recently lost from us you know."

Hound ignored the obvious jab pointedly directed at him. He instead scarfed the food down before Jake could even return from the backyard's pump with the glass of water.

Ilene did not finish her meal as quickly, but she savored it along with the cup of water to wash it down.

Craigson worriedly spoke to Isaac on the side. "You make a good point, boss. What are we going to do about business without our order of food? Wasn't our latest supply of booze in that order too? Better yet, since the ship's been destroyed, how can we count on future deliveries?"

Isaac removed his hat to stroke his curly locks. "We'll have to borrow some from a local supplier. We could fall back on more of the entertainment aspect of our business. I've still got that new play I wrote."

Craigson refuted. "No. We are not performing another one of your melodramatic travesties."

"This one is a classic. I'm sure of it."

"What's it about?"

Isaac smiled and said, "The fall of the Goddess."

Craigson shook his head. "That old story?"

Isaac said, "Listen. I rewrote it to make the Goddess more sympathetic than legend dictates. It will have them weeping in the aisles."

Craigson snorted. "Yeah. Weeping for their money back."

Isaac tried to assure his brother. "Just trust me. This, and deliveries, is all we've got. We need to keep the place going somehow. You know mortgage is due this month."

Craigson angrily added, "We still owe some from last month too."

Flustered, Isaac sat down- putting his feet on one of the tables. He turned to Ilene. "Don't fret. It's bad for sleep. We got our new employees to help us. One of whom will not only manage to fill the role of the Goddess that we need, but will also guarantee us a ticket back to our old jobs."

Craigson sat down across from Isaac. He gave in after looking at Ilene as well.

"It's a long shot. But it's better than no shot."

Bringing his proposal home, Isaac laid this out. "If we win, we gain a happy go-lucky life again. If not, well, we didn't have much to lose to begin with, did we?"

Craigson nodded happily. "I'd drink to that if we had drinks left."

"Spoken like a true optimistic opportunist!"

They touched imaginary cups together while making a fake 'clink' sound.

Ilene approached them with her dirty dishes. "I'd be happy to clean these for you."

Isaac looked in shock at Craigson. Turning back to Ilene, he said, "No you wouldn't. You're a princess. Jake does the dishes around here."

Jake wiped the table of crumbs with a rag as he mouthed off. "That's only because I tend to poison the food for customers that I don't like."

Ignoring this scoundrel joke, Isaac told her, "True, you've much work to do for us. But we've no need to bring you to such lowly service all at once. Perhaps your knight Mr. Hound would...?"

But Isaac couldn't find the surly sea mate.

Jake explained. "He already went upstairs. Decided to make himself at home."

"Did you tell him which were the guest rooms?"

Jake pondered. "I think I forgot."

Depressing a jumbled mutter of curses, Isaac assured Ilene again that they'd get the dishes. But Ilene told him that she used to do them with her maid in the palace.

"Taught me responsibility."

"Well, that won't be your responsibility here. At least for tonight. You've had it very hard. Go upstairs. Sleep. Unwind. Jake will show you to the room."

"Are you sure?"

"Absolutely."

She bid them good night. She laid her hands on their shoulders. "I thank you. You're wonderful men."

"We try," said Craigson, grinning.

As Ilene exited the room with Jake, Isaac called to him. "Make sure that Mr. Hound rogue isn't in my room."

"What if he's in **my** room?"

"Well let's hope that he brought a girl in with him. Then you'll see how we felt when you brought one into ours. So there!"

Jake led Ilene away, lost for a reply.

Craigson asked Isaac, "Do you think she'll get on our nerves?"

Isaac sighed. "I've lived and worked for years with you two. I think I can handle a princess."

Ilene was up half the night thinking of the man she killed. The shakes were beginning to take her- just like Marius said. The Ursian's grimacing face was floating over her from the waves of blood. The wave's darkness overtook her so much that she was eventually taken by sleep as swiftly as death.

CHAPTER 18 ROYAL SERVICES

The strangely white sun light came into Ilene's window and awoke her. Ilene woke up feeling cleaned within her eyes, especially the healing black one. Yet she felt dirty for sleeping in her soaked dress. This did not concern her as much when she looked about her cramped quarters. It was practically a closet that was barely fitted with a window, bed, and dresser. The dresser had a mirror that she looked at to view a new problem: the state of her hair.

It was like discolored seaweed washed about the shore. She removed her head band to see her locks bulge out into rags more than ever. Her heart fainted sadly knowing that she'd never know the motherly touch of her maid upon her hair for comfort and cleanliness. She pouted to think that even fixing it herself may never make her feel spiritually clean either.

Growing annoyed with the needy longing, she mentally forged a bullet to blast away those quivering eyes helplessly vying for tears that would not come. Trying to brush off her sorrows, she found a comb in the dresser's drawer. Missing Marlene wasn't going to fix her hair. So, she got to brushing.

She looked out the window to see that it was fairly early. She wasn't usually one to get up early. But the spare sleep from yesterday must have caused her to rise before the sun. The dim clouds signaled that this was probably meant to be a foggy day. Then Ilene's brushing halted as she noticed something strange: snow. She could not believe the sight of it filled upon the streets. She continued brushing only to keep making double-takes at the window to validate her doubting eyes.

"Why is there snow outside?" asked the shivering Ilene after she later went downstairs to see Jake sleeping on the bar counter. The jester's body blared out in waking surprise as he fell over behind the other side, loudly crashing into the floor while breaking the mug of beer that was dripping from his hand.

"My goodness!" cried Ilene with her hands over her mouth. "Are you okay? I didn't mean to scare you." She rushed to see over the counter. She was afraid that he was terribly injured given his silence.

Jake popped up from the counter while waving his hands out and molding his face into a devilish snarl. "Boo!" he exclaimed.

This paralyzed Ilene's concern. "There now," the jester said calmly. "You scared me. Now I've scared you. Now we're even."

Ilene patted back one of her newly straightened bangs near the confines of her pony-tail's band. Her hair was still unkempt given the amateurish structuring. But it looked better than it did before.

With this swiftly done, she said, "Seeing you fall scared me more than the relief of seeing you back on your feet again. I mean, who says 'boo' to seriously scare people? I'm not a child. In fact, I'll be 17 next month."

Jake burped and picked one of his ears. She found it most unbecoming. So, Ilene turned from his loathsome manners for a beat. "So," Jake asked between a few yawns, "why did you awaken me? Something about snow?"

Ilene sat at her bar stool from last night. "That's right. Why is their snow outside? Isn't it summer?"

Jake wiped the broken glass from his chest. He had a thankfully small cut that he wished to hide from the sensitive princess. Isaac told him to leave a good impression on the girl last night. Jake wanted to return to the palace most of all, even more than Ilene herself. Holding to this hope, Jake turned from Ilene while reaching down in the lower cabinet to grab bandages as well as a new drinking glass.

"Right. I sometimes forget that the weather is different down there. What you've asked is the chiefest of questions by tourists who first arrive upon orbs like Princeberg."

Jake secretly set the bandage and then got the last vestige of a bottle to pour into his glass. "I'd put it in layman's terms, but you're not exactly a layman. Then again, **I'm** a layman and I don't know any other terms. So, I'll use layman's terms."

He turned and hid the wrapped-up injury under the cleft of his arm pit while sipping the glass with his other hand rather loudly. Misdirection: the key to a great jester as well as magician, a favored motto of his life's profession.

"You understand how the sun goes around the earth?"

Ilene laid her chin on her hand. "Actually, the earth is the one that goes around the sun."

Gulping down the drink, he rasped a reply, "It's too early for the likes of me to keep track of my sciences. I don't even want to **know** what time it is. Anyway, that same orbiting deal is double fold for the orbs. Since they're rotating so near our world, they pass into new seasons every few weeks because the orbit encompasses all the world in that time."

Ilene took her chin from her hand, approving that she understood. "I get it. Since it moves around the earth so fast, it gets to experience all the seasonal shifts more quickly."

She shivered as a stiff wind whipped through some cracks in the building.

Unshaken by the breeze, Jake slurped in the last of his drink. He looked forlornly at its dry bottom. "Aye. What you said." He looked up at her. "Can I make you some breakfast? I think we got some of that cheese left. You look like you could use a blanket too."

Ilene fasted from breakfast. The cheese from the night before made her a little queasy. Before long, everyone else made their way downstairs in sequential order. Mr. Hound was the last to wake up. He found Ilene and the three merchants gathered about a fireplace by the dining area. They heeded to the words of the girl now wrapped in blankets. She seemed to be upon the tail-end of a funny story.

"And that, friends, is why you never bring two pigs near the royal throne room. Mother and father could not sit upon their seats for weeks."

Her new trader friends burst out into jovial cackling. Jester Jake could appreciate the humor most of all and laughed the hardest. It had been a long time since he could stand back and enjoy laughter during his sorry course.

"Ah. Hello, Mr. Hound. Princess Ilene was just telling us of her wild youth. They never publish such fascinating stories in the *Daily Pamphlet.*"

Hound grumbled gibberish rudely. Cleary not a morning person.

Craigson said, "Speaking of the local paper, could you pass me that copy of the *Pamphlet* on the counter over there?"

Hound stared harshly at Craigson. "Consider it your first duty in our employ," encouraged Craigson sharply.

Hound snatched the paper and unceremoniously handed it to the waiting palm of Craigson.

"There's a good lad," the trader sneered as he opened the news document.

Hound ignored him and sat upon a rug before the fire. Hound was at the foot of both the surrounding couch and two rocking chairs. Ilene rose from her centered rocking chair. "I say, Hound. I wish to show you my new clothes. The lads picked them out to replace my ruined dress."

Hound peered over to see Ilene remove the blankets as she presented her new tunic. Her clothing acted as a combination of all three merchants' wardrobes. She had a poofy, blouse-like shirt with overalls padded over them. She had a worn-out old jester's collar with bells over her chest and even more bells at the ends of her sleeves. She also had a pair of pointy shoes and a velvet cape to match Isaac's own.

"We each gave her one simple set of duds and she still insisted that she was too cold. So, one thing led to another and..."

Isaac sighed with further cackles vaporizing out of his icy mouth.

"How long must I stay bundled up like this?" asked Ilene.

"Only for a few weeks, my dear," assured Isaac. "Then it will be spring."

"Then you can strip for us," darkly inferred Hound to everyone's sudden discomfort. The look upon his face over Ilene did not help either as it was unblinking, grinning with no sign of feigning. She was cold. So, she put her blankets back on.

The discomfort was ended by Craigson, too absorbed by the paper to listen to the conversation, screaming with joy. "We've got it, lads! Our ticket to success! Look here and be merry!"

Craigson spread the paper out for all to read. He pointed to a notice:

Local warehouse on the corner of Inkle Lane and Bash Street open for cheap sale. Renovations required upon buyer's purchase. Details disclosed at neighboring home of owner on Inkle Lane. Ask for Barnaul Ladson.

Craigson declared, "We're cheap. We can surely fix up that building too."

Isaac exclaimed, "And we can surely put on my play there."

Craigson frowned, "No. I meant that we could use it as a supply house for the local trading plan we had."

Isaac reasoned, "Why can't we do both?"

Craigson slapped the paper on the floor. "Isaac. We're a pub that acts as a delivery and trading service too. We can't go off pretending that you're still in your lofty world of the arts."

Ilene intervened with curiosity. "What's this about a play?"

Isaac ignored Ilene as he replied to Craigson. "We could potentially bring in more buyers with the publicity that could be involved with the show. And you want to throw that all away?"

Craigson hotly stomped in front of Isaac. "I'm not getting on that stage to be laughed at."

Isaac retorted, "So what do you think is going to happen to you when you go back to the palace to perform?"

Craigson stomped away and adjusted the wood in the fireplace with a poker. "That was different. It was royalty that we performed for. I got to sleep in a comfortable bed after eating a fattening meal every night. Here-" he flung out a sloppy hand wave meant to represent the whole of Princeberg. "-I'm just another pauper to be mocked. I want to stick with what practically yields a profit and keep our heads down."

Craigson poked the wood with growing frustration. "Besides, what if Ilene is recognized during the show? We can't have that."

Ilene's face glowed with delight. "Am I in the show? What's it-"

Isaac cut Ilene off to grab Craigson's shoulder. "Some make-up will fix that for her. Don't mix up what this is about. If the stage bothers you that much, how about I have you work the curtain backstage?"

Craigson thought on this. "Well... I guess that this public event **could** bring in some more buyers."

But Isaac snapped into worry again as he realized, "Egads! If you're not in the play, we need musical accompaniment. And Jake can't play to save his soul."

Jake said nothing and only snorted.

"Who can I get to play a violin on such short notice? We're already going to put a lot of money into this deal."

Craigson's poking of the wood grew limp and careless as one of the blazing logs rolled out of the fireplace as a result. Everyone scattered and yowled wildly. Before the log set fire to the rug, Hound rose and promptly kicked it out the window by the entrance's door. The broken glass welcomed in a freezing breeze that bit into Ilene from across the room.

"I'll help you fix the window," Hound said after a pause. "Also, I was going to say that I can play the violin for you."

Ilene perked up despite the minor crisis shocking her. "Excellent. What character am I to play?"

Isaac said, "Only the Goddess of all creation."

Ilene paused, transfixed by the idea. Then with over-dramatic flair, she announced, "Tis the role that I was born to play!"

They cried hurrah before proceeding to work on hammering a board over the busted window. As they finished nailing up the window's board, a new burst of frigid air blasted into the pub. The front door was open. Customers. They didn't look friendly. They were clearly soldiers from Ur.

CHAPTER 19 DUSK

For Ilene, seeing these Ursians at the door froze her more than the cold. The group was made up of around a half-dozen soldiers with their swords brandished at the helm of their hips as they were in Patricho.

At the center of this squad of fur clad warriors was their leader. He was wrapped in a rough cloak made from an albino deer, a stark contrast with his bald head. He had a fierce look about him.

"Did we have an accident with the window, gentlemen?" His voice was smooth, but aggressively to the point. "I hope that this doesn't mean that you're closed. My men and I just got into town, and we are most thirsty."

Isaac approached the Ursians with a nervous look at his fellows behind him. The merchant changed his obvious fear to his flamboyant penchant for polite business formalities that he personally liked to believe made him sound charming. "Honored guests of Omega's heart," he slowly said with a deep bow to the snickers of the soldiers, and even from Mr. Hound too.

Isaac continued his oration as he rose up. "We regret to inform you that our latest stock of beverages has been delayed due to unforeseen circumstances."

The man laid his hand tightly on his sword. He marched closer to Isaac. "You mean that you are a pub without anything to drink? Didn't I just tell you that my men and I are thirsty?"

He raised his sword. But he did not direct it at Isaac. He merely whisked and thrust it about the air. It was being swung away from the merchant. Yet the weapon's movements were inches from his face that began to spurt out sweat.

The warrior began to speak in relation to this action. "I've practiced with this sword for years before I even joined the military. Its hunger for striking down those who have wronged me is far greater than the thirst of my lips. I wish for all my years of practice to bear results upon those who work against Alpha's heartland, not upon useless louts that can't even fulfill my basic needs."

The growing threat evident in the lowering tone of the client's voice made Ilene hide behind Jake and wrap her face further into the covers. She was afraid of being recognized. The soldier that descended from the wave flashed in Ilene's mind. This made her tremble to think of how rapidly these soldiers could descend upon her and rip her asunder... as was done to Marlene.

Isaac was equally scared. Yet this was not his first upset customer. He had an idea. "Your men will surely get their drinks. Just not here. There is a pub down the street that has beer aplenty, though it is a tad expensive."

The man was not amused. He stabbed the sword into the ground in front of Isaac, who shuffled back by the time it already penetrated the floor. "So, you expect us to go back out in the whipping cold? It is turning into a blizzard out there."

"Of course not," lightly returned Isaac, "I'm not as silly as I look."

Before the trained killer could mumble that this could have fooled him, Isaac lined out a solution that soothed his ears. "As a free service of 'Royal Services' (our business) we'll send some of our top men out into the harsh elements with your money and bring you back drinks. In exchange, we'll let you not only spend the wintry weeks here with us at half-off our usual rate, but we'll also sell you our latest order of drinks half off when they finally ship in."

The soldier waxed happy with a hardy smile stretching over his face. "You drive a good deal, little man. I like it."

The warrior held Isaac up with a hug wrapped about him with one arm. "And if you don't return with our drinks," he darkly whispered, "we'll cut up the rest of your workers and take this place as a conquered post."

Cheering happily again, he announced to his comrades that, "This man is the savior to our thirst. Give him your cheers and list of drink orders. Have at him."

The burly man shoved the fumbling Isaac into the throngs of the crowd. Fighting to keep hold of his hat during the stumbles, he also grabbed a notepad and pen from the table to begin taking orders. Isaac then juggled with keeping track of each loudly given order mixed with four others going off at once.

Ilene turned to Jake. "So," she began with confusion bubbling in her mind, "this place is not only an exporter, importer, pub, and playhouse- but it is also an inn?"

Jake simply said, "For every new financial opportunity, we take up a new trade. That's our unspoken slogan according to Isaac. Makes for a real pain in the ass to keep track of during tax season."

"Allow me to introduce myself," broke in the Ursian commander. "Lieutenant Dusk Hawkskin."

Mr. Hound was the first to interview the militant guest, shaking his hand warmly. "Mr. Hound. Fine to meet you. What brings you to Princeberg, lieutenant? The view?"

Hound spoke as if he were joking with a stranger on the street rather than a newly promoted officer hungry for respect.

"We are in pursuit of a fugitive from Ur. Details on the suspect are still classified, but you'll be hearing about her soon enough once the proper policies have been arranged."

Ilene tightened the covers about her face. She knew that **she** was this fugitive, though she broke no law. Lida firmly established that she would pursue Ilene to the ends of the earth to exact her plans.

Hound talked leisurely on, "Any trouble getting here?" This talk should be causing as much anxiety for Hound as for Ilene. But he kept it casual.

"Indeed," affirmed Dusk, "we were nearly sunk by a giant last night. Thankfully, our men loaded up on the platform in time to escape its clutches. This rock must have orbited out of its reach by now too. But those poor devils that had to take charge of the ship were not so lucky."

As Ilene bowed her head in prayer for those who died, a laugh leaped out of Dusk. "Oh, well. The ideal of an Ursian soldier is to live like a hero or respectfully die for your people. In that respect, I'm very happy for them."

Ilene could not gauge the reactions of the others given her covering. She believed that they had as much scorn written on their faces against this vile man as she did.

Craigson said, "I thought that the giants were killed off by the people of Ur long ago."

Dusk replied, "We did. But there are still a few broods leftover."

Jake said, "Why, that must be the same giant who lost us our supplies when we picked up the prince-"

With a blink upon hearing this, Ilene found herself muffling Jake's mouth. This did not go unnoticed. Dusk walked toward Jake after he wiggled free of Ilene. Each of Dusk's steps doubled the steps of Ilene's panicking heart beats.

"What was that, jester?"

Jake just remembered that she was not to be found, especially by Ur. He had to watch such slips. "I said... I said..." he wavered in what to say as Dusk's presence seemed to grow larger and more supreme before him.

"I said that the giant attacked us too. That's why we don't have drinks. What you just said about the monster going after you was such a relief to me. I knew that if we handed out such an excuse earlier you wouldn't have believed us. What a load off my mind that is."

Dusk wouldn't let up. "Didn't you also bring up something about a prince? Or was it a **princess**?"

Ilene felt cornered. She didn't know what she'd do if they found her out. Her sweat doubled through her layers of clothing.

But Jake regained his wit. "Princess? No, sir," he said with a casually dismissive fluttering from his voice, "you must have misheard me. I said that: **afterwards,** we picked up a **Prince**berg newspaper. But before I could finish, I had to cough."

Dusk seemed satisfied as he pulled himself away. "I see. You know, I've seen many a strange sight in your town thus far. I'm not used to the weather changing so suddenly. So, you'll forgive me for my ignorance when I ask you about that strange woman in the covers over there."

Ilene was frozen, encased in dread. "Excuse me, miss? Why do you act so oddly?"

Jake was three for three as he cooked up another explanation. "I wouldn't go near her, sir. That cough that I have? It's going around. She is afflicted by it. The covers are meant to keep us from catching it."

Ilene worked up an ugly cough from her throat to encourage this.

"Very interesting," said Dusk.

"Okay," Isaac exclaimed just in time, "I have everyone's order. Now to send out my best men. Jake. Hound. You two will have to do."

With one dreaded look out the door into the snow pummeled wasteland, Jake said, "After you, Mr. Hound."

Hound snuffed grumpily as he snatched the order's paper along with a spare jacket from Isaac. "Some job so far. All I do is fetch like I'm some literal hound."

"And keep this in mind," joked Jake as he took his own coat from the racks, "they treat you like a lesser animal than that over time."

After they faced the biting breeze outside and began treading into the knee-smudging depths of snow, Dusk sent two of his men to go out with them.

"Just to make sure," was how he worded it.

Isaac wasn't worried. He had no reason to swindle these men. This venture was sure to be a good boon for the campaign of returning the princess, and themselves, to a luxurious life. Thus, happy Isaac offered the weary travelers a chance to repose about the dinner tables.

Isaac and Craigson together worked to re-kindle the fireplace with better care than they gave it a moment ago. Ilene stood afar off so that the flames wouldn't catch upon her blanket.

After ending this labor, the trio felt a sudden tension as they realized that they were being gazed upon by the warriors of Ur. They were terribly trapped with nothing to say or do that could come to mind. Ilene couldn't even move as she wrapped the blanket about her so tightly that it felt as though it would trip up her legs.

Isaac finally moved when he was jolted by a joyous idea as he turned to share it with Craigson. "Get your violin out and play these folks that old song for some merriment."

"What song?"

"You know: the one with the simple, but fun, lyrics?"

"You mean the one about the birds?"

"No. The one about the deer."

"Ah-ha! That's a good one. That will lift their burdened spirits."

With that, Craigson scuttled into the backroom and returned with his strings. He had to tune it for a moment. The rickety whine made some of the listeners antsy. Finally, he got the tune that he wanted and began to play. The melody hopped up and down in time with the merchant's childish skips about the place. Each note got longer with each step that he took until he reached the side of the bar. Then it took a heavily low tone that foreboded a darker message in the song's merriment. He repeated the same cycle, but with the lyrics, as he danced with similar loose kicks atop that bar counter to each humming note.

There was a deer
He was in great fear
He looked up from the bush to see if the coast was clear
There goes the deer
In greater fear
What is the fear?
Why the hunter, Pete of the frontier
He had his musket locked on the white-tailed rear
Run, my poor deer
Run through the great frontier
Past the rocks and trees, our friends did steer
As Pete ran, he had that hunter's leer
The hunter's pursuit could not veer
Woe to my sweet deer
You'll be cooked tonight is my greatest fear
But you'll never guess what did appear
Why, it was another deer
But it was not in fear
For a stampede of such beasts did trample Pete's rear
So with your friends, stay near
You'll have nothing, then, to fear
Or, like Pete, you'll be robbed of all cheer
So it was how did escape my dear deer

With the song done, Craigson held aloft his arms in preparation for applause. But there were none. Ilene confided to Isaac. "I don't think that they liked it."

"Deer hunting is our people's way," announced Dusk, proudly

beating his chest covered by deer skin. "It is a traditional rite of manhood, and you would presume to mock its practice to our faces?"

It appeared that the song about the deer applied here. For poor Craigson tried to lend but a silly song to each ear. But he was but one without a strong group to stand near. The men were clothed, warmed, and wrapped in pride by the deer. Craigson shook in fear. He didn't enjoy being the subject of their sudden leer. Craigson could only quake. "Oh, dear."

Isaac was about to step in to perhaps talk the restless crowd down, but a sudden cavalry did this for them as Hound, Jake, and their soldier-escorts burst through the door with the blizzard raging behind them.

Jake heard the cause of the commotion from outside. So, he spoke with a wry voice to grab everyone's attention. "Never fear! We have the beer!"

Rumblings of a riot turned into shouts of celebration. That, and the stampede of Ursian soldiers rushing for their drinks shook the pub to its foundations. The rest of the day went past smoothly as happy larks of drunken joy reveled together. The Royal Services crew gathered themselves into a corner table to watch their customers tucker themselves out that night. Between the journey and the drinks, each man eventually slumped to sleep in their own special stretch of floor.

When the last Ursian man fell to the liquid conquest, each of the crew drew a collective sigh. Ilene later cooed while looking over a few of them. "Aw. They are like big babies."

Jake said, "I'm **not** changing their diapers."

"Thanks for saving my performance, boys. It was getting too hot," said Craigson.

Isaac asked Jake, "What took you so long? The pub was only down the street."

To answer, Hound pulled out his knife that was colored with blood. He used his jacket to clean it before flapping it on a chair. "You never said anything about your business having rivals."

"Ah, yes," hem-hawed Jake, "I, er, I got a chance to introduce Mr. Hound here to the friendly competition."

"Friendly?" The gritted teeth of Hound spat out, "They tried to kill us."

"Well, usually they just talk rudely to us in bantering jest. We never broke into a brawl like that before."

"How'd it start?" asked Isaac.

"Well," began Jake, "they bantered rudely as they do. For example, they made some derisive comments about our mother that I don't believe is worth repeating in the presence of a lady."

Ilene frowned, annoyed. She was starting to get coddled like a child. She understood that she was young and royal, but this pandering was starting to be a bit too much. After all, even Marlene told her dirty jokes when she was of age. This princess was not as sheltered as people thought.

"Anyway," continued Jake, "you all know that I'm an expert at grinning and bearing it. But Hound didn't take to it as naturally as I would have hoped."

Isaac drew a withering scowl upon Mr. Hound. "Hound, if you're going to work here you have to learn how to interact kindly and mannerly-like with the public."

"It wasn't me," said the sea-mate as he pointed at two snoozing soldiers with his cleaned knife. "It was them. They were the ones that began to violently demand service, slamming the ends of their swords on tables and chairs. They didn't want to wait around until after the extended stretch of banter ended. They were impatient to simply have a drink after all."

Jake bit in, "But you were the first to stab at them."

Hound rubbed his eyes and yawned as if the subject was boring him. "Was just defending our guests. The owner was coming at one of the rowdy soldiers to have a go at them from behind. I only wounded the guy to stop him. Scared him more than hurt him. Then we all tussled around a bit before Jake flung the money at them and we made off with the stuff. You ask me, I should get a medal for what I did. I saved that soldier. That medal would go nicely with the one I'm getting for bringing you home, eh, princess?"

Ilene did not reply as she took off the spare covers. No need to hide herself since the men were asleep. She was starting to get a little too warm anyway.

"Look," broke in Isaac, "let's go get some sleep and we'll figure all this out in the morning. Late night worrying is only going to make it worse."

So, after delicately sneaking over the mine field of slumbering Ursians, they marched up the stairs for some rest.

Ilene did not suspect that one eye was open. It was the eye of Dusk. It watched her and recognized her as his mark that the empress sent him after. But his job wasn't simply to just capture her. The next part of his mission would start soon. Then the girl would be his for the taking once it was over.

Her sleep did not improve. The Ursian that she killed rose from the bloody ocean with his head attached to the body of a leviathan. She couldn't outswim it. She awoke with cold sweats. She kept panting and crying. Somehow, she worked up the courage to go back to sleep. No monsters this time.

CHAPTER 20
WORKING STIFFS

Over the course of the wintry weeks to follow, the building of *Royal Services* fell into a routine regiment. Craigson, being the first to get up early with a farmer's effortlessness, proceeded to knock on each worker's door to begin at 5 AM.

Like Hound, Ilene proved to be not much of a morning person. She slugged herself into work at the start of each day. After splashing some water on her face and getting dressed, Ilene attempted to tidy her hair some.

"Come on, young lady. We're waiting," was the impatient call of Craigson each day as Ilene took the longest to get herself ready. She was trying with all of her wit to straighten and pull back her bangs enough to fit within the hair net that was given to her.

"You need to shave that head if you want those clumps out of your face," said Isaac, the mop-headed original owner of the hair net from *R.S.'s* early days when he had to manage kitchen duties.

Dreading the idea each time it was mentioned, Ilene opted to ignore it as she proceeded to her work for the day. Not wanting to be seen again by the Ursian soldiers, Ilene volunteered for work in the kitchen rather than waiting tables.

"Those brutes almost recognized me last night," Ilene explained. "As long as they are staying here, I want to avoid them at all times."

So she did. She entered the back room via the rear staircase that led straight to the kitchen. This was so that she didn't have to cross through the main dining lounge at all. Upon beginning her first day, she got to leave the zone of being coddled as she had to get used to the rigid and heavy-handed work of chopped bread, meats, cheese, and vegetables for the restaurant.

Thankfully, there were not that many orders to make during the first few days as the place still had a low ration. So, she had time to get a rudimentary training and understanding of her work. Jake worked alongside her on the dishes. Since not many of those needed to be done, he worked to train her. Day three on the job saw Hound and Craigson come into the back door with new crates of food. The two had been searching for a local place to get such goods while Isaac stayed behind and worked on the company's paperwork as well as attending to the guests. As for how they got this great batch of products seemingly sprung from the air...

"We bought them for a bargain from that restaurant going out of business downtown," said Craigson.

Isaac gave grim commentary on this news. "You don't mean *Pesto's Place* do you? I liked it there. Lot of businesses shutting down lately. The only place where companies seem to thrive is in Pangea, or their outsourced businesses abroad."

Isaac could not help but sneak a look at Ilene as he said this. Ilene could not help but wear a little mask of guilt for that moment, though she had no say on her government's economic relations with the rest of the world.

Ilene learned the physical as well as financial burdens that such lower modes of living brought. For the place was starting to grow much busier. She started each day with prepping for the onslaught to come. Three-to-four odd boxes were made for each victual of food. Most were stored in a steam-powered coolant within a few trunks out in the snow. Then the orders would begin to pile up before she could finish such preps. This was the hardest part of the job.

Ilene lost track of time and sense in the mad scurry to keep up with each new order and compensate for un-prepped items. At the end of each shift, she felt as though she left her eyes sitting on that table where she worked at a sweaty grind. It seemed like the Ursians never stopped eating. Whenever she couldn't keep up, Isaac would pop his head into the back to grumpily ask for unfinished orders.

"Ilene. Lieutenant Dusk needs that turkey sandwich."

"Ilene. Where are those three hams that we need?"

"Ilene! You put the wrong cheese on that last one."

221

"Ilene! Could you slow down? You're dropping vegetables all over the floor! Clean it up if you don't mind!"

And so on.

When Ilene's worried sobs broke out, Jake ceased his scrubbing and said, "Give her a break, Isaac. She's doing the best she can. Better than you did."

"But I am a performer, not a kitchen worker."

"Neither is she."

"I know. I know. You are doing a great job, princess. I am sorry. Now clean that up, please."

Then he slammed the door.

Jake then assured her. "If he gives you any more trouble, I'll show you my recipe for the poison that I used to put in his lunch back when I worked the prepping table."

Ilene expressed thanks with a smile and bent down to her drudgery with a stronger heart.

The Ursian men would often make noises that broke through the walls of the kitchen. They varied from loud and rambunctious, to quiet and still. Ilene reasoned that the silence must have signified that they fell into a stratagem meeting discussing their search after her, as the room grew hushed when Isaac was not around taking orders or milling amongst their numbers. Isaac mentioned that they would check out of the inn once the blizzard passed.

Though it made Ilene's shrunken world colder and harsher, she liked the blizzard. She saw it in the back window. It was like a living painting. The snow piled beautifully in hills over the backyard's pulley-platform, creating a tent-like quilt.

Another grace in the harshness was Jake, or rather his whistling. The sound that really pervaded the room was not the rowdy soldiers a doorway away, but the musical twittering of Jake. He whistled every song that Ilene knew, and even those that she didn't know- picked up from different parts of the world in his time as a trader. Often, he chirped off-tune or he would awkwardly transition from one song to another. Yet Jake always got the melody and sincere spirit of each piece spot on, whether he was making merry with a foot stomping jingle or a somber requiem.

Since getting busy with the new supply of food, Ilene began to see less and less of Hound. "Where's he been?" The princess inquired one night while drying the last of the dishes with her apron.

"Him and Craigson have been renovating that warehouse that we're using for the play."

"The play!" Excitement washed over her as quickly as the water washed down the sink's drain. "I nearly forgot about that. I haven't even had a chance to study my role."

"Don't worry. It's not until the start of next month. We'll have time to set it up. Isaac still has to give some finishing touches to the script. Then he'll hand them out to everyone."

"But when will I find time to study my lines?"

"We'll have practice every evening. Meanwhile you can sneak a few looks at your script while on the job, if business is slow, or before bed. It should all smooth out with our guests gone."

Ilene hung her hair net and apron up with a giddiness that kept her from going to sleep for once.

One day, as the snow began fading away once the orb neared the sun, Isaac left his script sitting out in the open lounge. Dusk picked it up and read it. He grinned with the most satisfaction that he had felt in a while. This was precisely the spark that he needed to light up his plan. Isaac walked in on Dusk during the second read-through of the dramatic narrative.

As Isaac entered the room, he looked about asking aloud, "Has anyone seen my copy of the script?"

Dusk held it up. Isaac gratefully drew near. "Oh, thank Alpha. You didn't... read it, did you?"

Dusk smiled wider as he affirmed that he did. "And I must say, it has the makings of a play fit for emperors and kings."

Isaac lathered himself in his greatest weakness: his pride. "Rightly so. For you should know, I once performed for the king of Pangea himself."

"Is that so? That explains the, for lack of a better term, **royal** level of your **services.**"

"If you wish," excitedly proposed Isaac, "when you and your men want a break from your man-hunt, our production will be opening in a month on the corner of Inkle lane and Bash street."

"That is, if we haven't already caught the fugitive," corrected Dusk.

Isaac nearly forgot himself. "Of course. Yes. Perhaps after the show we can discuss trading services for Ur."

"Hm. You do run an interesting number of facets in your business." They shook hands in agreement to the possibility of the idea.

"Now, Isaac, I just remembered that I wanted to let you know that the men and I are checking out tomorrow. The snow should be all but gone and we can trudge through the rest."

"Excellent. I'll have the bill prepared by tomorrow."

Dusk added, "Not only that, but I'm giving you something extra for your production. Call it an investment in exchange for the perfect show."

After Dusk left, Isaac was content to see that the soldier was not so nasty a brute as he thought. Isaac then entered the back kitchen. The door that he opened knocked over a crouched eavesdropper to the floor with a light smack.

Ilene twitched to her feet.

"Are you okay?"

"I'm fine. I don't need your help."

She slapped the helping hand away.

"What?"

"Don't play coy. I heard you making deals with Dusk. Need I mention what they did to my best friend?"

Ilene unclenched as her voice weakened, "Because I've been trying my hardest to not re-live what happened every damn day since then, until it all comes back again anyway when I go to bed- making me cry myself to sleep. I hate to even imagine what they'd do to me if they caught me."

"And you didn't like the idea of having them come to the play."

"I didn't like the idea of letting them stay here to begin with."

"What was I to do? They happened to come in. I saw an opportunity for extra money to get you home and I took it."

"Regardless of the risks involved?"

"Look, we can cancel the play if it makes you feel better."

"No. I get it. We need the money. And the make-up that I'll be getting will help. Craigson even said he'll cut my hair and put a bright blonde wig on me so that I won't be recognized."

Isaac put his hand on her shoulder. "Then what's the problem?"

"I just don't like the idea that you're dealing with them in general. After all, isn't the reward that you're receiving from my family for helping me going to be enough? You really need to turn an extra profit on this venture? For what? When is it enough for you?"

Isaac let go of her and took off his hat to scratch the top of his hair. "Look, I didn't do it to betray you or anything. It's just business. I'm always trying to make money and deals at every turn. It's a habit- an instinct for me. This is how I've stayed afloat for so long."

Ilene turned scornfully from Isaac. This made the merchant angry. "Well, excuse me if we don't have an ivory tower to fall back on, 'your highness.' Here in the land of the lowly, we do what we have to so that we can survive. Never mind if it fits into your little code of honor. Chivalry is dead because, for all of its so-called virtues, it couldn't foot the mortgage to save its life."

Without turning back, she began chopping some tomatoes. She became such a natural at it over time that she was able to cut them with a violent purpose without losing control of her hold.

"I can't keep chatting with you, Isaac. I've got to make lunch for the men who murdered the woman who raised me."

She turned her head a bit to let one sharp eye stare down Isaac. "It's what I got to do to survive."

Isaac didn't know what else to say. "Craigson will see you about that haircut tomorrow. Play practice will begin too. I hope you've been learning your lines. I-"

He sighed, lost for words. "I got to go." He left. Upstairs he lost himself in his paperwork- calculating profits and losses.

Left alone, Ilene began reciting a few lines that came to her from the play. It was the scene in which the Goddess spoke out against Alpha's controlling ways. So went her portrayal of the Goddess, Omega: "'I created this world as much as you did. Don't presume to tell me what is right and wrong. I am not your pawn, but your partner. How would man respond to such manipulations that you bestow upon me?'"

Ilene paused, filled with the vehemence of her delivery inspired by her helpless dependence on those that don't even seem to have her best interests at heart. "Indeed," she said to herself with frustration, "why manipulate man or Goddess when woman is a pawn that is closer to your heels?"

Time passed. She worked numbly through the rest of her shift. She slept. She dreamed. But not of the Ursian she killed. She instead dreamed of when she felt most alive- as a child. She was talking to Marlene again. She was six. She was the most curious about the world as she had ever been. This was when

Marlene taught Ilene the most. It was a soft thrill for Ilene to question, and gain in knowledge. The hardest question that the princess would ask came that day.

"Marlene?" The question came on their walk home from the weekly rituals at the Alphite temple in the mountains by the shore, just outside of the city. Ilene held Marlene's hand. The pair trailed behind Ilene's parents. The king and queen were surrounded by guards, attendants, and debating policy makers as usual. "Does the story of Alpha and Omega mean that girls are bad?"

This has been a theory of Pangean theological scholars: that the pervading sexism and repression of women in society may have a connection to the creation story because the act of a woman rebelling was written as the first act of evil. But that is an overly simple as well as an obsolete theory. Though it was dismissed by other leading scholars, it began to spread in the tongues of the gentry. It was hard to explain all of this to the innocent mind of a child.

Marlene decided to investigate further before answering. "Why do you ask, little Ilene?"

Ilene recounted the story. "Outside my window, in the streets, I saw some boys playing. It looked fun. A girl wanted to join. They said no and called her an Omega lover. And they threw rocks at her. She ran away crying. It was mean. I stopped watching."

Some groups of women worshiped the Goddess while trying

to find a place in society on par with that of the male hierarchy. Some other women tried to live in equality likewise-refusing arranged marriages, leaving family homes to live alone, becoming Alphite priestesses... only to always become destitute as a result. But not all of them worshiped the Goddess. It was hard to distinguish between social descent and heresy.

So, they all got bad reputations. Their daughters got the bad reputations passed on to them by the sons of their accusers. Good girls, like Ilene, stayed in their place while getting patted on the head and taken care of- just as *The Holy Volume* said that it was meant to be for the obedient daughters of men. It was all so complicated.

The young maid's mind knew to keep her place. But her heart wanted more than what men let her have. She sympathized with the radicals. She prayed to Alpha, asking him to end this conflict of the sexes. But how could she explain it to Ilene when she was so unsure of the answer herself?

"Ilene... sweety... Omega was evil and wanted to take our freedoms. Alpha was good for stopping her. But that doesn't make all boys good and all girls bad. We were all still made by him that is good. And if you stay good, and not become bad like she did, he will bless you."

"But, then, why were those boys so mean to that girl for wanting to play with them?"

Marlene lovingly tightened the hand that she held. "I don't know. Sometimes people are being mean when they think that they're being smart."

Ilene looked up to Marlene's face. "Like when I ate all those carrots."

Marlene snickered, to her own surprise. "Yes, dear. Just like that. But you've learned never to do that again. And you'll try to stay good, won't you? For me?"

Ilene hugged her beloved maid. "I will, Marlene. Because I love you!"

Marlene held back the sob over her mouth. This was the first time that little Ilene ever said that to her. Marlene hugged her back.

"I love you too!"

The last sentence echoed until its repetitious echo finally woke Ilene. She placed her hands over her face. "I still love you, Marlene," she whispered.

CHAPTER 21 THE UNPRODUCTIVE AGE

Ilene got up and looked out the window. The snow was reduced to puddles, revealing the cobblestone street. The sun arrived visibly to Ilene for the first time in Princeberg. It shined over the hill of clouds, and it laid shadowy dominoes under each building in the townscape.

A peddler pushed his cart past. A dog followed. Although it was noticeably warmer, she still put on the blouse and overalls. It was still too cold for her liking. She tied the collar of the scarlet cloak about her. Then came the work on her hair as usual.

Ilene felt as though she was starting to get a handle on fixing her hair up. Marlene still would have critiqued it to death. But Ilene resolved to assume that her maid would have nonetheless been impressed with the effort of her progressive improvement.

Ilene went downstairs. Craigson stopped her halfway down. He invited her to sit down for some breakfast in the lounge now that the soldiers were gone. They sat down. Hound was seen on the other side of the room sporting an apron and sweeping up.

"Why did you groom your hair? You do remember that I'm cutting it today, don't you?"

Ilene chided herself with frustration as she smacked her napkin on the table. "I forgot."

She began rubbing her locks instinctually and softly. "It's just become such a habit, you know?"

Craigson shrugged in understanding as he took the last bite of his meal. "We'll be going into town soon. Do you want to get it over with now so that it will be safe to come with us?"

Ilene answered by getting up and un-loosening her hair band. The untamed locks flopped out, free from their bondage. She turned the chair away from the table-top and sat down. She leaned her neck back- ready.

As Craigson got out the scissors, Hound stopped sweeping to view the event. As the sharp metal grazed the flesh of her skull, each snip made her hair fall away like autumn leaves. A weight seemed to shower off when she closed her eyes.

It had been months since her last haircut. Marlene did it. It was before setting sail for the wedding. How much can change over the course of hair growth. Ilene felt as though she was losing something more than hair as it rained down under her eyes. She wondered if it was innocence, identity, or solely all of those vain attempts to hold on to Marlene by performing her hair styling duties.

The answer never came. Craigson was done. He wiped her neck clean of extra hairs pricking about. Ilene placed her hand on her head. The hand winced. She felt as though part of her head was gone. She imagined that she was touching a new part of herself- a deeper layer of flesh made bare.

Her fingers streamed through the tiny stubs that were left. Her other hand followed in traversing this landscape that made her head feel molded into a perfectly spherical shape. It felt as though she not only lost something, but also gained something too- a sense of windy freedom forcing her senses to be more alive.

Isaac came in as she finished wiping the excess hairs off her clothing. Ilene could not turn her continuing scowl from him, even though she wanted to.

Craigson stretched his hands over his work. "What do you think?"

Isaac stared at Ilene. Then he blinked at Craigson as he said, "Beautiful work. I thought that I was looking at a stranger for a second. Now, Craig, I need you to fetch Jake. And Hound, I need you to sweep this hair up before we go. We're leaving in a minute."

Ilene got up as Hound leaned toward her in a whisper. "I think it makes you look beautiful." He mouthed a small kiss her way.

Ilene returned a reluctant thank you. She skirted past him as he began his work. She stroked her head some more as she made her way out the door.

They waited out in the street. The wind was still a little chilling. Ilene tightened her cloak and put its hood over her head. Being practically bald made her sensitive to the frigid elements. The crowds were just starting to bustle out of their brief hibernation.

Jake and Hound got outside. Jake squinted at Ilene's trim. "Got the snips, eh? Too bad. I thought your hair was pretty."

Ilene questioned this. "Pretty what?" Everyone giggled at poor Jake.

He shined red and gave a frazzled answer. "Blast you all! You know what I meant. Pretty beautiful. There! I said it. Now shut up and grow up! Blast it all..."

His tantrum caused more laughter until he had to join in by at least smiling and coughing out a few chuckles as mutely as his pride could manage.

Only Isaac did not laugh. "If we're done with small-talk, let's proceed to Inkle Lane."

They began to walk off with Isaac in the lead. Isaac stopped. He abruptly blocked everyone with his arms.

"Wait!"

He jogged back to the door. He pulled out his keys and locked it. He then took the sign that was hung up by a chain over the door. It read 'open' on one side and 'closed' on another. He switched it to the latter. Isaac jogged back to his group.

"I'm always forgetting to do that. Okay. Let's go."

They trudged through the multiplying crowds. Ilene had to run to keep up, a task that she found a little easier in overalls and lessened hair. But this resulted in her bumping into, or being bumped by, the innumerable mob of many colors. As she began to fear that she lost her friends, she found herself bumping into the back of Craigson. The party's train stopped. They were standing in front of what looked like another pub down the street corner. The business's sign read: 'First Thirsty Resort.'

A burly man with the shadow of a beard stood before them. He was dressed like a fallen prophet of old. He wore white and stood erect with his husky arms bristling with hair. One of these arms had a white rag secured tightly about it. Though his apron was white, it was mostly blackened gray by over-usage. It flowed from his chest to his legs like a gown.

A cabal of other like-dressed followers stood behind him. He held his eyes harshly upon the merchants. He said even harsher words. "Thinking of coming into my place and making trouble again, my pack of whore-sons? Just because your ugly brood doesn't know how to run a proper business does not mean you can come in and ruin others. Perhaps you'd like it if we scheduled an appointment in which we come to your place and break some things, as well as your bones!"

Ilene's heart rang for fear of a fight. But Isaac handled it. "Ignore them, my fellow whore-son children," was his instruction as he led his friends past the competing rivals with a hand raised to their malicious eyes. "We've better things to do than waste our wits on Miles and his intrepid band of what he laughingly refers to as our competition."

As they made their way past, Hound rubbed on the indignant owner's bloodily damaged arm. "How's it healing?"

Miles pulled back and grabbed Hound by the lapel. Hound already had his knife over Miles' drooping throat. "I can make a matching set for you right here."

Miles immediately let go as his face scrunched into a sour ball. Ilene thought that they were out of danger when Craigson said, "Isaac. They're getting ready to do the rock throwing shtick again."

Sighing with an annoyed want for wise men in the world, Isaac suggested that they run for their lives- forgetting dignity. Stones rained after the fleeing merchants, followed by jeers jumbled together by the rest of the morning commuters.

One stone struck Ilene's head. It was a crumbling sting that crippled her senses for a second. Then there was an aching soreness that she would wear for the rest of the day like a hat.

"Those bloody-!" she began to curse as she held the back of her neck.

Jake pulled her back. "Let it go, little Ilene. You learn to develop a hard head going by that place. They're all talk when they're not playing one-way catch. Brush it off."

Ilene was struck deeply by his unexpected use of Marlene's favorite nickname. So, she got over her ill feelings long before the headache. After sticking close by for a few more blocks, the streets grew less crowded and the buildings more decadent as Ilene was presented the warehouse on the corner of Inkle Lane and Bash Street.

A man emerged from a nearby house to approach Isaac with open arms and a handful of keys. He was an old, baby-faced, and gangly fellow. His smile was thicker than any other part of his form. Giving the keys while heartily shaking Isaac's hand, he happily clucked, "Good luck with the place, Mr. Inklewood. You're going to need it."

Isaac shuddered. "What?"

Before Isaac could inquire further, the man backed away while pointing knowingly at the merchant with praise. "You enjoy yourselves. I'm sure your show will bring the house down."

He blitzed back into the house. Isaac stood there with the keys clinking in his hand. He stood there because he was busy with losing track of how many broken windows the place had.

Jake stood by his speechless brother. "Level with me, Isaac. Did we just get ripped off? Again?"

Isaac erupted into the faces of Craigson and Hound. "You two were supposed to check out the place to see if it met up with our standards."

Hound didn't bother with flinching. Craigson made up for much of Hound's lacking in this area. "But, boss, the place looked pretty good on the outside when we bought it. We didn't want to take too many trips to go see the place. We didn't want to get caught in the snow."

"You didn't even go through it once?"

"Well, yeah. Once. Just some dirt and cobwebs here and there. See all those windows near the top? That's going to give us some good lighting. The star's and the moon's light will shine through."

"Tell me this then, if your search was so thorough; was there any vermin? Grime? Weather damage? Good Alpha above, did you even examine the basement?"

"It has a basement?"

Isaac sucked a deep breath into his beat red face. He let out a shrill siren of frustration as he stamped the ground savagely and beat the building's walls with the fat ends of his fists. His next breath gave way to a soothing composure to process all this. He closed his eyes gently during this process.

When finished, he opened them. "Okay. Sorry. Just had to let out a little stress. Now, considering that we," his mouth blubbered sappily as if about to vomit, "put a lot of money into this, let's try to make the best of it and work with what we've got. We have less than a month to practice while getting this place into shape. It may take every bit of coin in our savings, but it will be worth it for the fortune that will benefit us as a result. So, let's not waste a minute."

Isaac put his key into the front door. The door fell forward instead of craning open. Isaac lifted the heaviest smile that he could manage for a barely formed smirk. "One more bump on the final road home," he repeated in a half-whispered mantra as he strode within.

In brief, the place was a big mess. A longer description would say that it was a four cornered coliseum on the edge of decay. The longest way to describe it would be to go into gory detail regarding the mud and mold accumulating on each end of the walls. Worn-out, rusted machinery hung over every step that the party took. Most of the warehouse's darkness was canceled out by the sun-showering light that made the dank sight of its inner parts visible.

While walking about, Craigson offered a little history lesson about the edifice's life as a factory business to perhaps show Isaac that he **did** do some research. "The old man told me that this used to be his factory for steel mills and crop-reapers during the 'Unproductive Age.' You know, back when upstart businesses and inventors tried using machinery to yield more crops and profits? This was when too many were against the concept of working with their hands. He and other mechanical businesses tried to compensate for the expensive machines that they wanted by decreasing worker hours and lowering wages. This eventually lost them most of their workers. So, lots of places like this died out."

"The old man always blamed Ur for this. They are the most populated nation set in the old, religious ways. Even the rise in global trade is currently frowned upon by the priests of Omega's heart land. Many like him believe that if Ur invested more into such ventures, perhaps they could have succeeded. Though under decay, the old man said that Ur, as the birthplace of all world cultures, still holds great sway over world affairs in many such subtle ways. He fears what this may mean for the future."

Ilene asked, "Despite all that, I've always wondered why I've still seen some machines being used- like the steam-powered pulleys and cannons."

Craigson said, "Those are devices promoted by the government of Pangea to use and sell for their own personal ends. It's kind of an ugly two-edged blade. One nation dismisses handy tools as irreligious evils and the other uses selective devices for their own profitable gains. Meanwhile, old folks like our conman were just trying to use the machines to make a better living off the farming market. But he gets left behind. Kind of sad."

"What I find sad," said Isaac with a grinding grunt, "is that you know all this history about the place and it didn't occur to you that it might be in shambles."

Craigson shrugged. "He said it was in good shape."

"And you believed him."

"Look, it's like you said, the deal is done. So, what are we going to do about it?"

Isaac got a rough draft of a schedule lined out for everyone. Isaac resolved to conduct everyone on a multi-pronged workload each day.

"Ilene, me, and Jake are to work at the pub during the day. Craigson and Hound will make trade and storage deals with local businesses during this time. Then the pub-workers will close early to go practice at the warehouse and set up the stage at night."

Jake questioned him. "Couldn't we try trading with passing ships down below again? That always yielded us the most profits."

Isaac refuted Jake's inquiry as he stated, "No. I read in the *Daily Pamphlet* that traders are noticing that Princeberg's orbit is being guarded by that giant. So, all the other ships are trading with different orbs out of fear. The giant probably knows that we'll orbit over him again. He may still want revenge on Hound and Ilene."

Ilene realized something as Isaac said this. "We're orbiting around the giant a second time? Couldn't we get off over Pangea before we do that?"

With a sliver of fear choking Hound's voice he asked, "How long before we're over Marl exactly?"

"...Who?"

Hound rubbed his hat with his hand. "That's the giant's name."

"Huh," said Isaac, "didn't know giants had names. Anyway, we'll be over him in a little past this coming month. We can't leave before we pass this Marl again. There is still much to do before we're ready. It's much too late on this current rotation cycle. But we'll pass over Pangea again, a few weeks after him on that cycle. Then we'll be ready."

Ilene grew excitedly unhappy upon hearing this. "So that means I could have gotten off days ago during this rotation?"

Isaac corrected her. "Not really, technically. For one thing, I don't think we're over it on this current rotation cycle yet. It may take a day or two if my compass-calendar is correct. Perhaps tonight even? I forget. But, even then, we still need money for passage-papers. Otherwise, Pangean soldiers would arrest us for sneaking into the country. So, we got to wait until the next cycle when we'll surely have enough money."

"Now wait a minute, if I simply told them who I was, they would let you-"

"Still too risky. Might not believe you. And they might still throw us in jail for not having the proper papers."

"For Alpha's loving sake, Isaac. I want to go home! I want to see my room, my family, and most of all: I want to hold a proper ceremony for my poor maid Marlene. And you're keeping me from it all just so you can buy your own way in and become a part of the pampered palace workers once more."

"Not to mention risking a second encounter with Marl," said Hound, siding with Ilene. "That beast will have probably devised a means to throw ships closer to the town. Worse yet, he might be able to find a way to get up to the town itself."

"And," Ilene said as her mouth quickened with the same rapid worry as her pulsating thoughts, "what if the Ursian soldiers find me in that time? It seems that you've traded the plan that's riskier for you for the one that is riskier for me."

Isaac tried to calmly, but firmly, talk the two down. "Peace, friends. It's not like I'm never getting either of you back there. I just want to make it worth my while. Besides, I'm just trying to work within the letter of the passage-paper laws that **your** government made, princess. Trying to enter a nation without one is a crime, you understand."

"Holding the heir to the Pangean throne against her will is a far worse crime than that. But you can explain all this to my parents when they ask why it's taken so long to return me."

Hound added, "**If** she returns at all. Make all the promises you want. But you can't guarantee that something bad won't happen."

The shrill yell of Isaac turned into a roar as he raged. "Enough of your complaints! I've done **nothing** but help both of you two ingrates from day one. I'm your only way back, whether you like my means or not. I don't like this warehouse, but I'm not leaving it. It's just like us. We're both in too deep."

He turned with a deeper focus upon Ilene. "And did you really just accuse me of holding you against your will? Really?? If you want to walk out now after everything that I've put on the line for you, go ahead! I'm not stopping you. Just don't come crying to me when everyone out in the streets starts to realize that you're the heir to the Pangean throne. You'd be beaten, robbed, and stripped within the hour. What's it going to be, princess?"

"It'd be a bloody sorry hour for those attempting that," stoically growled Hound as he shielded himself in front of Ilene, who was not scared but angered by the idea of such a scene.

Ilene bit her teeth down while imagining that she was gnawing out Isaac's lying throat. "Fine," she said with malice springing from her gnashed teeth. "But I'm making sure that none of you get back in the palace. I'll let mom and dad reward you for your efforts- a small fortune that will be enough to start as many businesses as you like. But I don't want to see you again. You filled my thirsty mouth with gallons of laughter when I was a child. But you've put away childish tricks and innocent slights of hand in exchange for dubious deceits. These mis-directions no longer amuse me."

Ilene's words echoed in the old factory.

This cast Isaac into an abyss of shame. The warehouse's echo ended in silence. Ilene was caught up in the silence and started to feel a shame in her harsh words too. She neutrally suggested that they go get some lunch in town to stop this morbid quiet. So, they locked the warehouse and left.

CHAPTER 22
UNGRATEFUL
CHOICES

They ate some sandwiches from a vendor on the street curb afterwards. This was done quickly, quietly, and without an iota of cheer from the group. Ilene still held the bitterness of her words fiercely beating in her heart. They returned to the warehouse, and they numbly exchanged wooden dialogue to each other for the sake of learning the script's lines.

With a yawn, Ilene read, "'This is not goodbye. I will see you again. Thou mayest bring me down to the depths, but your children of creation will stand upon my shoulders. And I will hold them up until, one day, they are strong enough to defeat even you. Then I shall rise again. Next time, it shall be you who falls by my hand. For now... the world is yours...'"

Before saying the last line, Isaac quickly suggested that they wrap up practice and get to work on sweeping up the place.

"Aw, come on, Isaac. It's getting late."

"We're doing this, Jake. Ilene may not let us into the court, but

I'll be damned if I let the money in this place slip away."

With that, Isaac said his last line and monologue.

"'Now she is gone. She was the great love and hate of my life. I hope, yea, even God can hope, that humanity will be made up of the best of her to thrive, and not the worst of her to die. Thus, the world began after its greatest war. Hopefully, this will be its last.'"

They worked on sweeping afterwards with little ceremony during the transition. By the end of this late hour's labor, they shuffled home. On the way, Ilene spotted a patch of white fur striding from the print shop of the *Daily Pamphlet.* Seeing Dusk linger closer gave Ilene a fear that suspends one motionless.

Dusk waved knowingly at his former inn-keeper. Wanting to distract him from Ilene, Isaac fought against suspicion by wishing Dusk a good evening and pulling him into conversation.

"Good evening yourself."

"How fairs the search?"

"Fair, but still unfinished."

"What were you doing in the print shop?"

"Working on a notice about the criminal. Further information needs to come about, but we should have it soon- hopefully before the press gets ahead of us with their lies. By the way," he leaned towards Isaac confidentially, "would you do me a favor, Isaac?"

"Certainly."

"Should this controversy get out, I'd appreciate if someone as honest as you could help set the record straight if it ever comes up in casual conversation. There is a rumor from Pangea that Ur is holding the princess, Ilene, hostage."

"My..." gulp, "word! I thought she was to marry Prince Jacques."

"She was. But she ran away during the ceremonies. Some men tried to stop her, but she commanded her soldiers to kill the emperor and his family. Only our empress is left to lead us."

"Good Alpha in the sky! It's the end of an era," Isaac croaked in a way that even Ilene could tell was fake. For an actor, he was spectacularly terrible at lying with his feelings.

Isaac carried on. "How could she do this?"

"We don't know. But her family is using this as an excuse for war, claiming that we're holding her captive. There have already been naval skirmishes about the sea."

"So she's the one you are searching for."

"My, my," said Dusk, 'impressed.' "You're a clever man, I must say. I didn't mean to connect the two subjects together. But, yes, you're correct. We believe her to be hiding on this very orb city since it was the closest to Ur during the time of its routine orbit. If we could only capture her, we'll promptly bring her back to Pangea to dispel the rumors. Hopefully, that Godless nation does the right thing for once and puts her on trial for her actions. I need not mention that there is a substantial reward for anyone that can help us."

Ilene did not like how lustily each man's eyes widened at this.

Isaac tried to hold up his heavy words. "I... will gladly tell others the true story should anyone tell me the contrary."

"I thank you, dear Isaac. I know that you are not obligated to take sides. The orbs have been neutral territory since they have been listed as trading posts. But it's nice to see one of its citizens standing by us in our time of need. I hope we find more like you."

"Should I see something, is there somewhere else in town that I may find you?"

"Aye. There is an Ursian base downtown by Mcferis Street. We couldn't access it during the winter's storms. By the way, I must be returning there."

Before a turning step could begin, Isaac halted it. "Wait. Before you go, I was just curious. You said you needed more information about the escaped princess before the press talks about her. What is it? Why not fight the lies by having the full story given out now? "

"Your answer is equal parts complicated and classified," Dusk said with a threatening smile.

"Don't worry. Things will be brought to light. I will say one good thing about this mess: the new empress now allows us to expand our trading, though it is hard to store all of our exports at the base."

Without even a turn to Ilene, Isaac bounced upon this new prospect. "Fortune of fortunes! We have recently purchased a building for the play that I invited you to. Perhaps we could work out a deal for supplying your resources?"

"Splendid. You can come to the base tomorrow morning at 9 AM, and we can discuss it further. I'm most lucky to have met such an agreeable business man in these times of equal growth and danger for our nation."

Isaac cordially tipped his hat to Dusk in flattered adoration.

"Also," asked Dusk, "who is your dear maid there?" He cocked his head to Ilene at the back of the pack. She couldn't help but cover her face with her cloak. "What was her name again?"

"Mara," blurted out Jake. "Her name is Mara," he repeated with a forced cooling of his tone.

"Is she still afflicted with that sickness? What was it? The flu?"

Craigson joined in, "Y-yes! She's still got a touch of it..."

"I must say that if she is well enough to go about town with you there's surely no reason for her face to be covered. I despise needless veils, even if I understand their necessity at times."

Ilene knew that she had to speak or die. She crumbled her voice. "Thank you, sir. But I've been left quite hideous from past experiences. I'd hate to reveal myself in public. My mother taught me to be modest regarding such matters. It's awkward to have such values questioned. So, if you don't mind..."

"Hideous? I thought you had a flu, not leprosy."

"It's just that the flu has left her red and swollen. Congestion and all that. Now, we don't mean to keep you from the base, and we must be off ourselves. Much to do."

"Very well. Farewell." Dusk departed around the corner. After waiting to see that he wasn't turning back, Ilene let out victorious relief.

"I believe that thanks are in order," Isaac suggested.

"For what? Pressing your advantages with manipulation?" Ilene huffed out, angry at the continued dealings between her hunters and protectors.

"Get used to the ingratitude," advised Hound to a disappointed Isaac. "She assumes that it's her right and privilege to be pampered and protected- never mind the sacrifices that men like us make for her."

"You're right, Hound," agreed Isaac, "and that's not how the world works."

Ilene stopped in front of the pub. Everyone else did too. Miles and his mates had been there. The boarded window was bashed asunder again. Inside, all of the drinks and food were splattered and smashed, encompassing every step like an overly colorful new carpet flooring. On the door was written in black paint: **Whoresons.**

"I'll get the mop," grunted Hound as Isaac slapped his hat to the ground while hanging an evil eye over the smirk of Miles taking in the sight from his own pub down the corner.

Running on steam-powered yawns, some of the mess was cleared by the *Royal Services* crew. Once the slosh of glasses, drinks, and food were discarded; everyone slopped their way into their respective beds. The day was supposed to be about profit- not loss.

Ilene could not sleep. She was too busy. She was preoccupied with keeping herself awake long enough to make her ears believe that everyone else was asleep. She fumbled about in her bed. She splashed a lot of water on her face more than equal to the amount that she used each morning during her long stay. By the still hours of the AM, Ilene developed bulging red eyes whose upper lids were gripping desperately to the top of her head to keep from falling asleep. The sopping bulk of the bags under her eyes were pulling against this force with much vigor.

By this time, the place was at its most quiet. No creaking or movement could be heard, nor shuffling outside her door. She had faith in the word of her ears that no one was up. She took up the scarlet cloak and crept downstairs, out the door, and into the cobbled streets. No one was out in the misty gloom of the night. It was like a ghost town that even ghosts wouldn't visit. Fear of her surroundings stroked about her. Staying on the sidewalks made her cautious of possible attackers emerging from the dark. So, she tried walking in the middle of the dead-silent street.

It was muddily rippled by the many carts that tracked their way through it each day. The residue of old trash and food was crowding into the pointy shoes that Isaac gave her. It mortified her, a lady of high standards, cavorting about such lowly waste. Yet she stuck with this path so that she could have extra time to run away if she saw a criminal. Unfortunately for the lack of the girl's street wisdom, this also made her an easier target to follow. A shadowy figure trailed after her, content that his prize would soon be his.

Finally, Ilene made it to her destination at the end of the street. It was a half-circle of sidewalk laden parallel to a tall fence of bars. Jake told Ilene about this one day at work. This was a popular spot for recreation back in the day. Many would lounge about to eat and play at the grassy park on the other side of the street. Ilene saw that this park was overgrown with bulging weeds.

Originally, the main attraction was a view of the orbiting skyline from the bars. One could see nations, oceans, and landscapes closer than ever. The novelty wore out after a few years. Not many frequented the park anymore due to everyone being preoccupied with work or the less profitable labor of trying to find work.

Ilene was not here for fun either. Looking through the rusted bars, the open sky greeted her with an on-coming cloud that splashed into her face. The source of the mist lining the streets was evident. When past the mist, Ilene could see her country below. It was a heart-hugging joy to see her home laid out before her again.

It wasn't just her country that she was happy to see again. It was also gladdening to see the Pangean capital: Elysium. Here was home to not just the seat of power for the royal family, but it was also where the princess spent most of her formative years under the care of Marlene. The first glimpse she'd always get of the city after a long journey's final horizon was the surrounding statues of history's Twelve Great Alphite Prophets. High, skyscraping obelisks adorned with matching granite robes stood around the city- ever vigilant with their hand-clasped prayers for the Alpha-loving Pangeans below them. They each marked the twelve gates encircling the great city's walls. Ethos, Numa, Amos, Phobos, Minerva, Minos, Ada, Sygar, Axios, Jerimiah, Mithra, and Shelby were all present- as if they were always there simply to greet Ilene. It was a comfort as always, now more than ever. As she got closer to the city, she could see the great spires within it too.

The rising spires were glimmering under the light of the Torch of Truth adorned on top of the Great Ziggurat at Elysium's center. It was the highest tower in all of the great cities of the Pangean Kingdom worldwide- even higher than the statues of the great prophets. Such towers were built tall enough to be just inches near the direct route of each orb for easier trade without needless ship meetings out at sea. The many other ziggurats in the city were part of what made Pangea an economic powerhouse among all other decaying nations.

Ilene hastily calculated that the orb was about to go past the top of the ziggurat. All she had to do was hurry back, hijack the pulley platform at the right moment, and she'd be home. She sprinted through the way she came.

When she got to the pulley platform in the merchant's backyard, someone was waiting in the darkness of the mists. His form was instantly recognized. "Hound?! What are you doing here?"

Hound was standing on the center of the platform. His smile was touching his hat's brim. "Nice night for a stroll, isn't it? Did you know that from the park down the street, you can see that we're directly above Pangea? Why, you could get off right now if you wanted to- nary a goodbye."

His horrible chunk of teeth seemed to brighten with his rising grin. Ilene stepped back and defensively whispered a demand. "You're not stopping me, Hound."

Hound picked up the musket from his first adventure with Ilene. Whether he had left it outside or kept it in his room since the incident was ambiguous to the princess. He looked at the weapon.

"You know, I think that I'll put this over the fireplace for nostalgia's sake when I move into my new abode in the palace with you."

Ilene stamped the fertile ground. "What are you talking about? You're not living in the palace with me!"

Hound's smile slowly evaporated a little. "That all depends on you, Ilene. You get one or the other. Two simple little options for an all too simple little girl. The first is that you let me escape with you. I get to present you to your family, and you will recommend rewarding modest me by letting me marry you. A leisurely lifestyle is the least that a hero like me deserves."

Hound glided to Ilene so that he could slide his arm around her hip while his other hand stroked the naked flesh of her skull. "Not to mention the... comfortable nights that we'll be able to have together."

Livid with discomfort, she squirmed her way out of his lusty grasp- mostly because he let her go to tell her the second option. "If that idea doesn't thrill you then, please consider the second option: I stop you. I call out and wake the merchants up. This Hound may normally be reserved, but I can howl with the best of them."

Ilene stiffened her shoulders broadly to entrench against his advances. "They are not stopping me either. I'm going home and that's that. I don't care if they get rough with me. If they do, I..." She faltered in her assertions. "I'll just have to get rougher back."

Hound dropped the musket as he could not help but sputter giggles as he tried to hold himself up with his hands slapping down at his knees. He sucked his outburst back in. "That's cute. You: rough. I mean... 'rougher.'"

This mockery made her face downcast. He was right. She was helpless. "Don't worry, little Ilene," condescended Hound while resting his hands on her loosened shoulders. "They won't have to get rough with you. No one ever has. All those clowns need to do when they come down is the same thing they've been at since they took us in. They'll talk you into their way. And you'll crumble to their persuasions as if you were paper. That's the cute thing about you, my sweet. For a person who is meant to be a ruler, a queen- you are pliable to everyone's will. You're the good little girl that was trained to obey everyone who is older and wiser than you. You'll find more such 'advisors' once on your throne. You have no will of your own."

She did not look up.

"Don't give me that. You should actually thank me. Not just for my saving your life, but I'm also giving you something that no one has ever allowed you in all your days. I'm giving you a choice. Now what's it going to be? Either way, you'll have to go back eventually. And I'll be with you to collect the goods for it."

Ilene cradled her confused eyes into her palm. She was given a choice once. The truth of having no freedom was almost as terrible as the offered freedom to choose one damnation over another: such as paths to alternate between getting friends killed, or nations betrayed.

She couldn't stay. There was too much risk involved. The Ursians, the giant, the rival pub, the merchants, and especially Mr. Hound, seemed ready to strike. But to go home would mean to give herself up to Hound, who was looking worse than Isaac's manipulative aspirations by each passing second of the mate's longing stare through the mist.

"I can't... I can't," she whimpered. Hound tightened his grip on her shoulders.

"Can't? Can't what? Make a choice! Or I'll make it for you. We're probably about to pass the ziggurat as you go on about how you can't."

She sniffled and crumbled under his towering anger tightening about her. "You know what? I was wrong. Maybe you do need physical force to move your will."

He pushed her into the pub's wall. With a whack, she was plastered on to the ground. Before getting up, he pinned her down again by her breathless neck using his arm or leg (she wasn't sure which it was) careening from the dark.

Ilene screamed as Hound pulled a fist back. His arm was ready to fire just as the back door swung into him and knocked him into the ground too. It was Isaac. It was all of them. Jake and Craigson's shapes hustled into the yard and charged into Hound.

The trio mobbed the sea-mate while yelling and striking upon him. But such blows were nothing to a man who endured the worst brutalities of the merciless oceans and faced down a giant with an empty musket. Hound dispatched Isaac first. He jabbed the merchant countlessly in the stomach until the winded trader slipped to his knees to tend to his soreness. Once there, Hound speared his knee into the jaw of Isaac. Isaac sailed flat on the ground.

Craigson soared his arm out with a vengeful hay maker. Hound rolled his eyes at how slow it was as he parried the fist's wrist into a severe twist behind Craigson's slender back. Cries of vengeance turned to cries of shooting pain stinging out as Hound shoved Craigson into the outdoor ice box. Hound used his free arm to open the chest's lid. Tripping Craigson into the vessel's open burrows, Hound then used his free hand to clap Craigson's clamped neck with the box's lid until Hound's adversary slumped down- unconscious.

Jake tackled his shoulder into Hound, who simply met this with a lightening back-hand. Ilene did not want to see the next blow as she activated the pulley during the fighting to escape. It was about to lower down with her on it. There would be no going back. She had no way of knowing if she was over the ziggurat, or even near it. But that unknown factor didn't stop her.

"Come what may," Marlene used to say during chance times like this (mostly while playing a competitive board game with the young princess during a desperate move to win). But Ilene could not help but notice Hound's intense blood lust distracting the sea-mate from her exit. He savagely bowled over his prey as he littered punches into Jake's face. Ilene hated hearing Jake's cries most of all. The kindest merchant shrieked more shrilly and childishly than herself. He was more like a wailing newborn experiencing pain for the first time. She was so close to coming home...

"Come what may."

Hound showed no signs of letting up. That is, until, the butt of the dropped musket was jammed into the base of his neck by Ilene. This screeched his attack to an abrupt halt. As Hound folded his skull forward, Jake flew both of his hands into a choice collision that boxed his foe's ears in. Made even crazier by the sudden offenses on too many fronts, Hound looked to see who was behind him.

It was Ilene who swung the end of the musket again, this time squarely bulldozing across his nose. Jake secured a hold over Hound's neck as he pushed his way behind the mad man. Isaac and Craigson were somewhat recovered too. The two returned each punch and kick to the trapped Hound with sincere interest. Despite the dramatic flow of blood and multiplying of bruises, Hound never lost consciousness.

"Enough!" he finally cried. With that, Jake pushed Hound out the fence-door held open by Craigson. Mr. Hound was sprawled about the front lawn. He lost his hat when he was being held by Jake. Ilene saw Hound's eyes in full this time. The moon's glow spotlighted his eyes, glaring with animalistic resentment. He heaved a furious growl to take in what was lost of his breath.

"Never return," said Jake with the least mirthful of all his voices.

Before Hound could cough a reply through his swollen lips, Jake slammed the fence-door. Before anyone could see Ilene during the aftermath, she was already slamming the door to her room. After locking everyone out, she cradled herself into

264

the corner. Now she really couldn't sleep.

"Alpha... no more nightmares... please..." she whimpered in pathetic prayer.

CHAPTER 23
VULNERABLE

Ilene's trembling died down to a mute stillness. She was set to stay in this corner for the rest of her life. It was the cruel world's next move. The move was a knock at the door.

"Ilene?" It was Jake.

"It's been hours. It's nearly morning. Do you want to come out?"

"No," Ilene abruptly answered.

She was weary, but not so weary as to keep herself from snapping out in fear and anger.

"We just want to know if you're okay. I think me and the rest of the boys got the worst of it from that thug. I never did trust him. If you can believe it, we're all now uglier than ever from our injuries."

Ilene voiced her contempt in response to hearing this. "I'm

sure you do care. You wouldn't want your precious princess to become damaged goods. That might get in the way of your big break."

"What?"

"You heard me."

"Ilene, you can't stay in there forever. Can't I just come in there and talk to you?"

"No," she repeated.

He sighed so quietly that she did not hear him from her side of the door. Then he voiced his heart. "I understand that you're scared. I get it. No one should have to go through what you went through. And I don't blame you for wanting to leave us after we kept you from home. But I'm out here on my knees, begging that you'll let **me** go back if no one else. Please. I've a reason beyond luxury that makes me want to go back. Mine is the reason of a broken heart. The woman I love could still be in the palace."

He spoke with a depressed sincerity that paralleled her own sorrows. She was moved by her heart strings that took her to the door. The open door presented the jester with a bruised and swollen face disfigured by Hound's beating. He was flat on his legs.

He grinned through his blood smeared lips. "Told you I was on my knees."

Ilene could not help but smile too. "Come in. It's a cold-hearted world out there."

He got up and went inside. He joined her on the edge of the bed. Once seated, he poured out his heart as if he were confessing to an Alphite priest.

"My brothers and I were exiled from the palace because of my lust for one of its maids there. Yet some notion within me has me thinking that I might have loved her too. For you see, when an-"

He coughed stiffly.

"-article of her clothing was found in my room, the queen gave me the option of revealing who she was. They knew it had to be one of the lady-servants. For no one was permitted to breach the palace walls without an invitation. If I gave out her name, we would've only been lashed. If I didn't, I was to be kicked out. But I would never let her get hurt because of me. I think it was something liken unto love that kept me from doing it. For I've never stuck out my neck for anyone before. How do you think I got so far in the jesting business? Plus, I couldn't even bear the thought of ruining and humiliating her like that. So, you know the rest of the story. I was banished instead because I wouldn't kiss and tell. And so were my brothers for standing by me."

He scratched his head during the silence that the two shared. "I don't know. Sometimes I don't know if I did it because I loved her. Maybe I was tired of stepping on others. Maybe I felt like I deserved punishment for my vices. That's why I want to see her sweet face again. I want to be sure about how I feel."

He became quiet again. Ilene's sorrow was a distant island that was overshadowed by the cloud of grief from this story.

"I mean, I eventually stopped thinking about her over the years. But then I met you. In convenient concordance with Isaac's plan, I knew that I could be reunited with her. And I was surprised by how much the prospect excited my very soul. If nothing else, I'd like to resolve what my feelings for her really were: love or lust. But your denial of our return is based on Isaac's dishonesty, alone. You didn't know that you were blocking my heart's desire. I just thought you'd like to know what you're cutting me off from. Possibly true love, if anything in life can be so true..."

Ilene rubbed a hand under her chin. Jake seemed sincere. Yet Ilene began to wonder if he was telling the truth. This could be another deceit by Isaac, to manipulate her naïve romanticism into bringing them along. Yet the poor jester was clearly broken up about this. Hard to fake. She had to be sure. Ilene asked, "What was her name?"

"I've tried to keep it secret, even from my comrades. I'd do anything to keep her honor safe."

"Tell me. I won't say a word to anyone."

"Okay. But, please don't repeat it. It was Marlene. I believe she was one of your primary maids, yes?"

Ilene got off the bed and retreated to the window. "I'm afraid you can't see her again, Jake."

Jake got up to make her understand. "Please, Ilene. I don't care if I live in that palace again. You could just arrange a secret meeting for us. I just wish to know how she has been getting along."

"I just can't do it!" exploded Ilene while slamming her palms on the dusty window's sill.

Jake scoffed, "You can't be **that** mad at us. You won't even help an aging old boy see his sweetheart again? What excuse could there be for such heartlessness? It's not like she's dead, is she?"

He beheld Ilene's reflection. The dust particles fluttered around like lost bugs. Her face was drenched in tears. Her mouth was blubbering with sobs. Before Jake knew it, his reflection matched hers. "Is she?"

Nothing.

"Is she??"

Still nothing.

"Please, Ilene..." he moaned as he clawed his fingers over his face. He tried to slash away each tear into nothing.

"I was just joking," he whispered with a sob. "Tell me the truth. Why can't she see me? Tell me anything. Tell me that she forgot me. Tell me she is happy with another. Tell me that she hates me! Just don't tell me that she's-"

Ilene's tears stopped long before his. "It was the Ursian soldiers," she reported coldly. "They got her during the wedding party. Empress Lida killed Marlene because I wouldn't join her plan for conquest. Marlene is dead because of me."

She wouldn't leave the window even long after he left.

Jake sloppily made his way down the steps. He motioned his view to see Isaac and Craigson sitting at the bar. Isaac had a wet towel wrapped, dripping, around his neck. Craigson had such a dabbed rag over his sprained arm's ache.

"Well?" asked Craigson.

Jake's lips were drooping with grief as well as pain. He rubbed at the end of his skin-ripped bruises. "I don't think she's coming down, boys," he murmured regretfully. "I still can't believe it…"

The weight of this statement did not fully hit until Ilene appeared behind Jake in full attire. "I wouldn't say that," she chirped in with surprisingly happy joy on her smile. "I thank you all for the pains that you had to endure to protect me. And so, with that," she took in a soothing breath with closed eyes, "I've decided to let you all return to the palace with me. I'll see to it that your old positions are restored."

Isaac and Craigson would have jumped and shouted for joy had their aches not suppressed them into keeping their seats. So, they were content to thank her with applause while loudly repeating, "Thank you, thank you, thank you!"

When the jubilation subsided, Craigson's penchant for the curious shined through. "But, Ilene, our saving you from that brute can't be the only reason that you've changed your mind. What was it?"

Isaac slapped into Craigson's wounded arm. "Silence, knave! Never look a gift horse in the mouth, or it'll bite you."

Ilene knowingly looked at Jake, on the verge of recovering his wayward tears. "I have my reasons," she finally answered.

"Okay, troops," blustered Isaac as he hobbled happily to his feet. "Since we've now rid ourselves of the traitor in our midst and have become more united than ever: I believe that it's time we proceeded on with our original plans. Since Hound is out, I'll join you on the search for clients, Craigson. Jake, Ilene: you'll both have to stay here and run the place. We'll meet at the warehouse tonight at 6 PM and practice for the play. All clear?"

A customer walked in before they could gladly agree. "Excuse me," said the middle-aged stranger. "I'm unclear as to whether you folks are open or not."

Isaac then said, "Very well, sir. Our best will be provided to you. For now, my companion and I must be off."

Ilene and Jake took the man's order after Isaac and Craigson were on their way. Before going on, Isaac had to stop Craigson. "Wait," he said with a block to Craigson's path. "I forgot the you-know-what again."

He turned the 'closed' sign back to 'open.' When Isaac turned around, he saw Miles standing by his store. "We're still here!" yelled Isaac with triumphant glee. Then, with a mocking tip of Isaac's hat and a flourish of his cape, he went down the streets with Craigson past the gaze of the scornful Miles.

Ilene and Jake worked in the kitchen as they always did. They spoke not a word about Marlene to each other. Jake did not even so much as manage a note for a whistling tune. Thankfully, the stifling quiet was broken by Jake occasionally going out into the lounge and taking orders from customers. He gave the orders to Ilene and brought the finished food out with little fanfare.

Isaac and Craigson journeyed the bustling streets in search of clients. They went to every business that they could stop at. Most kicked them out. They also had ads for their play printed in the office of the *Daily Pamphlet.*

After this, Isaac began to talk frankly with Craigson. "You do know what Mr. Hound being banished means, don't you?"

Craigson nodded with understanding. "Aye. **Someone** will need to provide the musical accompaniment."

"Are you up for it? I know how you feel about playing for non-royalty."

Craigson rubbed his sore neck. "Give me time to think about it. These sudden changes are a lot to take in. That incident with the Ursians really shook me up."

"Of course."

They wandered on through the crowds of Mcferis street. They had their 9 AM meeting at the Ursian base to honor.

"Maybe Ilene was right," cautioned Craigson as they neared the walled gate of the foreign base that doubled the size of a city square. "Maybe it is too much of a risk to deal with Ur. What do you think, Isaac?"

Isaac did not answer as he walked closer to the main gate as if he didn't hear Craigson. "Isaac?"

Isaac approached the imposing guards. They were girded with their large shields, larger spears, and beige tunics. Isaac walked up to them with nary a hesitation. Craigson walked nervously behind. "Lieutenant Dusk has invited us for 9 AM," said Isaac with stern assurance.

CHAPTER 24
MEETINGS

On the other side of the gate, another visitor was being escorted out. This visitor's escort gave brutish hospitality. Isaac saw him from across the yard of soldiers marching their drills. The guards locked both man's arms up in theirs as the prisoner tried to fling himself out of their hold. Isaac and Craigson were shocked to see who the other guest was. It was Mr. Hound.

The fresh morning light made the bruises that he endured last night terribly visible. He lost his hat, which meant that his normally covered face was naked with pulpy swells and dirty looks all about his eyes. His mouth flashed snarling teeth. Some of them were gone. One tooth was hanging by a gummy thread between the bite of his lips.

"What's Hound doing here?" openly asked Craigson.

One of the guards roughly hanging on to the raging Hound explained, "This lunatic has been stalking the outside of the gate all night and all morning, insisting that he enter to see the lieutenant. He claims that he knows him. We finally got tired of him. We decided to let him in, but not without a good beating for his insolence."

Upon saying this, the guard flogged Hound about the neck with the butt of his knife.

Through the pain, Hound pointed to the merchants and railed, "It's them! **They** have her! It's them!" Hound was dragged away to another part of the base before he could continue.

The merchant's own guard patted them along. "Sorry you had to see such a vulgar sight, gentlemen. This way."

They went within the base's compound. They walked through a series of torch-lit hallways. They passed through a large hall with the Ursian mark of repeating pillars confounding the whole of the room.

"How does one not get lost in such a dizzily designed room?" asked Isaac before bumping his head into one of the pillars.

The great hall was finally crossed as they were brought into a comparatively smaller room that acted as an office for Lieutenant Dusk. The window-less room of rough granite had parallel shelves, a great spear adorned on the back wall, and a desk occupied by the lieutenant.

No longer cold, he did not have his white wrap on. This revealed that the man himself was not as muscular as perceived but had a slender build. He was still great in height and filled his tunic like a tall drink of intimidation to sedate any foe. He was working at his table with a fan that he waved over his head to help him concentrate on a distressing report that he had to write for his empress.

He put the fan down and welcomed his guests. "Just in time," he said. "Now let's get down to business. I was admiring your warehouse property on the way back yesterday and I believe that we can store one-fourth of our weapons within. For that, we'd be willing to pay-"

Isaac put out a dismissing arm. "I apologize for interrupting, lieutenant, but my brother and I came here with something to say."

Dusk tightened his manners. "Then by all means, say it. We have business to get on with."

Craigson peered curiously at Isaac. The head merchant gave Craigson a look to assure him that he knew what he was doing. "Your honor," Isaac began with a well-hidden gulp, "it has come to our attention that we're unable to store your weapons for the time."

Dusk's voice grew grim. "Is that so?"

Isaac kept on firmly. "Yes, sir. Sorry, sir. We've gotten many clients recently. Many of them will pay very well. I've done the numbers and I've discovered that it'd be disadvantageous to use your supplies over our other clients, financially speaking of course."

Before Craigson could process what was said in time to say that this was not true, Dusk walked close to Isaac. Craigson slid behind his brother- who was keeping his feet from the edge of backing down.

"These new clients," questioned Dusk, "they wouldn't happen to be of Pangean ancestry, would they?"

"I don't discriminate, sir. I just worry about who can meet my rates."

Dusk reeled in Isaac by the collar of his cape. "And isn't it convenient that the Pangeans think that they can simply buy this world's resources over Alpha's chosen people? Their land is literally made up of Omega's devious mind after all. As for you, how dare you waste my time! If this embassy were not on foreign soil, I'd have you executed for breaking your dealings with me!"

Dusk dropped the fearful Isaac to the floor. "Guards, take these filthy merchants from my sight." Isaac was then scooped up by the guards and rudely shoved out.

Isaac got the last word in before his abrupt exit- a questioning one. "Will I still see you and your men at the premiere of my play?"

An answer was not given as the door was slammed. Alone again, Dusk sat back at his desk. He fluttered the fan softly over his face. He planted the fan over his face in disgust of all that he has seen of the world. The door opened again. He slapped the fan back down.

"What is it now?" The guards flopped Hound to the foot of his desk.

"This vagabond claims to know where we can find the princess that we've been looking for. We had to work him over to make sure that he wasn't a spy for Pangea."

Hound got up and brushed the dirt from his clothes. His eyes bulged before the cool skepticism squinting from the brow of Dusk. "I **might** know where the little brat is- depending on how much that reward is."

Dusk crossed his arms. Lida taught him everything regarding negotiation. "You're one of those merchants, are you not?"

"Not really. That was just a temporary position. My job before that ended after some of your boys sank the Pangea ship that I was working on."

Dusk walked around the table to size up this possible adversary or ally. "So, you're of Pangean birth?"

"Pangean born, raised abroad by my sea-legged old-man. 'You'd be surprised how many whores you can find in even a Pangean port,' he used to say to me whenever I asked about mom. He took up every mariner job out there: from trader, to smuggler, to the Pangean navy itself. After so many years glued to the blue yonder, I'm very sick of it. I think it's time I got my feet on dry land for a living."

"And," Dusk asked sternly with investigation, "you're absolutely comfortable with betraying your nation of birth for monetary gain?"

Now Hound was crossing his arms. "Don't see why that would matter to you. You want the girl, don't you? I'll lead you right to her front door just before lunch time."

Dusk halted Hound's assertions with hardened words. "Ursian culture does not recognize money as the final absolute in life. Our values are measured by the virtue of the divine Alpha and not the lusts of Omega's world. So, when I see one who has no reason to turn against his own based on nothing but money, I find it suspect. So do enlighten on a deeper reason for your casually traitorous acts. You would hate to see what would happen if you were planning on crossing me as you do your friends."

Hound uncrossed his arms and clenched his fists.

Hound speared a finger forward as he let his anger out. "They are not my friends! Friends… please." He winced at the idea of the notion.

"A fancy word that cowards use as they're all huddled together against the rest of the world, if you ask me."

"A fine claim. Perhaps something more material could convince me."

Hound reached into his pocket. "Very well."

The guards laid their hands on their swords, half-unsheathed. "Make another move and we'll bury you where you stand!" one said with ferocity.

Dusk put his hands confidently behind his back. "Please, gentlemen. I hardly believe that he has come all this way to make his final resting place in my meager office. Let him proceed."

Hound tauntingly asked, "Kind of jumpy, aren't they?"

Dusk did not reply. Hound pulled out a medal- a Pangean medal of valor.

"For a lieutenant," said Hound while twirling the bauble about before putting it on the table. "I've yet to see any of these pinned on you. Consider this the first one that you've earned."

Dusk picked up the medal to examine it. "We Ursians do not recognize the childish notion of medals. Our accomplishments speak for themselves in our society. We don't need trinkets to signal our greatness."

He was done examining the Pangean medal. "Where did you get this?"

Hound smiled, revealing his broken teeth. "Peeled it off my C.O.'s body right after I killed him."

Dusk fingered the medal some more as he stared into those grimy teeth. "After the shipwreck that I can thank the dear empress for, Captain Crock and I were the only ones left. We grabbed on to a weapon's case. But it couldn't hold us both up. Desperate to live into his twilight years, Crock knocked me off. Then he picked up a pistol from the case and pointed it at me. Told me to back off. 'This is my raft,' he barked. Years I've spent getting barked at by him and other C.O.s like him. The last order that I could take from a C.O., especially from him, was the order to die. I swam off only to find my own weapon's case. A musket was inside. I was just far enough away that he couldn't see me load it. When I drifted close enough on my case, I fired my only shot before he could see that I was armed. The shot must have hit his collection of pins. Because this medal floated right toward me as if it were a dog submitting to its new master."

Dusk was not impressed. "What does this prove? That you're as ruthless in matters of blood as well as matters of trust?"

Hound shook his head. It seemed that his grin couldn't stop growing. "You don't get it. I could've floated to safety on my case and not bothered with Crock again. I did what I did to Crock not to survive, but out of pleasure. Because I hate the Pangeans with just as much passion as you- maybe even more."

Dusk still did not trust him. But the sincerity of his Pangean hatred satisfied him for the moment. Dusk waved a signal at his guards. "Leave us, men."

The door was shut.

"So? What are we waiting for? You know where they are. It's obvious that the girl in the cloak is the princess. Let's go!"

Dusk eyed the spear that he kept on the wall. "Don't be foolish, Mr. Hound. I've always known."

"Then why not act now?"

Dusk picked up the spear. "You seem to hold a special hatred for this particular girl."

Hound backed off. "Let's just say that she showed me that the Pangean women are just as scornful as the men."

"I'm sure that the Pangean royal family would've rewarded you for her safe return. How else could she have escaped the giant?"

Hound clenched up. "Trust me. I'm your confirmation. The Pangeans are scum. Never deal with them and drop them when you can. So why aren't we doing some dropping?"

Dusk began practicing with his spear away from Hound-training his thrusts and parries. "As a boy, I used to go fishing with this spear in a stream outside my home. Father taught me an ancient Ursian proverb. 'Don't go after only one fish. Let one live, lay out some food, and soon: many will gather. Then, you'll have the entire stream under your net.' I'll soon have the entire net over not only Ilene, but the whole of Pangea itself. There's a war coming. And I've a means to make sure that none of the other peoples of the world will even consider siding with Pangea when it begins. On that day, money will be meaningless and only Alpha's righteous people will be the voice of authority to be heard. So, it was written, so shall it be."

Dusk swung the spear over his head and slammed it back to its post on the wall. Hound pinned Crock's medal to his shirt. "Whatever happens, I want to make sure that I get my reward, as well as the first shot at her throat. Also, I'm going to need a new hat."

CHAPTER 25
PREMIERE

As the days rambled on, the princess and the merchants grew closer to their goal. Isaac and Craigson got some storage clients that didn't quite measure up to the profits that would have been gained by dealing with the Ursians.

"I've been meaning to ask you," queried Craigson, "why did you turn down the lieutenant? And out-right lie to do it?"

Isaac put the cash from the day's meager, but steady, profits back on his desk. "I've been doing some thinking since the night Ilene was attacked by Hound. I couldn't quite sleep before the incident. I began to consider that maybe we were exploiting her. But this was our big break too. I happened to hear her scrambling in her room around this time. Mr. Hound didn't drag her out there. She was trying to leave. And I had no heart for stopping her. It was her home, and she had a right to go there. Hound was far stealthier. I would've stopped him and let her go. But thanks to that moldy filth of a man, she missed her chance. I still want to go back, no doubt, but I felt as though I had to make it up to her. In order to take the edge off poor Ilene, I cut the deal with Dusk. And I obviously couldn't give them the truth."

"But," wondered Craigson, "now we may not have enough for

passage down to Pangea."

Isaac went back to his counting. "I guess that means we'll have to work a lot harder."

"I must say, Isaac. You're turning into an honorable man."

Isaac looked down while pausing to himself. Then he looked up and scolded Craigson. "Enough of this small talk. Go mop the floors or something. Without Hound, I suppose you'll have to do for that job."

Craigson could not help but smile as he left the room. "Aye, aye, boss."

After Craigson left, Isaac could not help but smile and feel a little better about himself for once.

As the days went on, their skill with the play's script grew sharper and sharper until they were nearly perfect. Ilene and Jake kept up their duties at the pub. They each agreed to not speak of Marlene. The carpentry needed for the stage was set up, while deliveries and supplies were managed by Isaac and Craigson.

At last, opening night arrived. Live entertainment outside of street performers was rare in the run-down orb-town. So, ticket purchases were plentiful.

A large section of the cheap, folded seating belonged to the Ursian soldiers. They were dressed in their finest deer skins. These cloths were of the darkest shade of fur. Their hair was also finely pulled back. Isaac was so excited about the coming performance that he only gave out a worried glance to his cast once.

He lit the two hanging lamps on the stage as he addressed the crowd. "Ladies and gentlemen," he began with an echo, "we will be starting our show in five minutes. I hope you enjoy our performance tonight. Thank you all for coming."

He proceeded to the backstage behind the curtain. He looked up. The moon light through the upper windows would give the performance the right amount of cosmic ambiance. He kissed his compass-calendar for helping him time his premiere during a full moon. He then looked to his crew. Their prepping area backstage was situated under some girders and catwalks. Craigson was tuning his violin with twitching agitation. Isaac swiped it from his hands.

"No, no, Craigson. We're tuning it in D. Not C."

Isaac adjusted it accordingly and just as suddenly handed it back.

Craigson would not take it. Isaac was concerned. "Are you sure that you're up for this?"

Craigson put his hands over his neck. "You know how we started out, Isaac. We were abandoned at an orphanage that abandoned us to the streets. All those years of learning to play there were used over and over to peddle pennies from those nasty, ugly faces in the streets. We only survived because of the reluctant pity in people, made gross with an obligatory compulsion to help the poor boy that couldn't even tune right. When I... we got work at the palace, I was so happy that people appreciated my playing- especially the princess."

Ilene spoke from behind her changing screen. "And you haven't lost your touch, Craigson. You're still the greatest violinist that I've met. Hound may have been a beast, but he wrote a good piece that I'm sure you can improve on with your talent."

"That's just it, Isaac," Craigson protested, "I don't want to go back out there and have to see their faces, all ugly... just like when I was a child- just like they gave me in the bar."

Isaac flicked Craigson's sensitive nose.

"What was that for?"

The taller of the brothers rose to shorter Isaac. "That," expounded Isaac, unafraid, "was for acting like a child still yet. It's a play, genius. They'll hear your music, yes. But they'll be watching **us** on the stage."

"But I'll see them. That's the thing. And if I get to thinking back, I'll mess up a note and ruin everything."

"Then do this: just play behind the stage, facing away. Problem solved."

Craigson was still not convinced. His hands quivered.

He was rusty and unsure of himself. Isaac knew it. "Look," said Isaac pointing to Ilene as she emerged from the screen in her heavenly garb of white and glitter. "That girl over there loved your music. She still does."

"I sure do," said Ilene as Jake painted some make-up on.

Isaac pulled Craigson closer to his shoulder. "Now she needs your charity to get her home. The question isn't whether that audience out there is going to be like the rough crowds from the old days. The question is: what are **you** going to be like? Are you going to make ugly, reluctant faces when you should be helping the girl who appreciates the heart and experience that you've put into your art?"

Craigson's mind wandered back to see the little girl that danced about her throne room whenever he played the song of, "The Gentlemen's Romp." It was a court of very few. But her enthusiasm in tapping to each repeated note made it the best performance of his career. The performance to get her home would have to trump it.

Craigson graciously took the violin. "I'll face the crowd. I'll face anything for her."

"Hey," came a brave cry from the back row of the audience. "When's this play going to start?"

"Damn," Isaac cursed. "My pep talk made me lose track of time. Jake, throw my costume over me."

"Over your clothes? But you'll get hot."

"Never mind that. It's been starting to get a little cold again anyway. I'll be fine."

After Isaac fumbled on his heavenly robe that matched Ilene's, he began to rush out on to the stage with hurried words upon his parting. "I'll stall them with some kind of preamble. Touch up her make-up, adjust her wig and she'll be fine. We've magic to make tonight, people. Fail me and I'll have your leg lobbed off."

"That's how he says good luck," sniffed Craigson. "Everyone always said that he was the odd one. I'm going to go take my place by the stage."

Craigson left.

As Jake applied the last vestiges of make-up, he gazed with admiration upon his handiwork. Ilene's lips were painted with violet that popped out of her skin that was slightly colored tan about the face and hands. Her eye lids were given a matching shade of violet. The long bangs of her blonde wig were adorned around her brightly sprinkled dress. Ilene looked like the Goddess indeed.

"At the risk of making a boyfriend at home awful jealous," admitted Jake with playful caution, "I'd venture to say that you look very beautiful, Princess Ilene."

Ilene grinned as she slapped a bang of her golden faux hair back. "You're just complimenting your own skill with the make-up, Jake."

Jake snapped his head away in a mock show of wounded insult. "Figures for me. Admiring a fine young lady seems to always get me in trouble."

What this alluded to stopped their mirth.

Ilene stepped closer to the face-fallen jester, who began to frown for real. "Before I go out there, I want you to know why I decided to let you all come back with me."

Jake sat down on a stool and listened to her. "I want you to come back so that you can give testimony at Marlene's funeral."

Jake seemed to slightly shrink in his seat. "Me? No. No. I couldn't. I want to preserve her honor. No one must know that we-"

Ilene stopped his agitation with a caring look twinkling brighter than her glittering gown. "You don't have to go into all that during your testimony. If you truly loved her, I'd wish to hear the kind words that you'd have to say about her."

"Why do you want me to do this at her funeral, though? I don't know if I'd be able to handle how I'd-"

"Because," interrupted Ilene, "I was the only one left in her life when she died. She'd have sporadic dealings with my parents and others, but other than that... she had no one. I want all of Pangea... no: all of the world to know that Marlene was the most kind, helpful, spirited, and-"

"And clumsy," Jake broke in.

Ilene was soaked in a good round of snickers. "Yes. Once she dropped soup all over daddy-king himself."

Jake stopped shrinking and held himself up with staunch

pride. "Why, I must be on par with royalty. For she has anointed me with that honor thrice."

When the joyful nostalgia sputtered out, Jake was sternly resolved. "I will do it, Ilene. I'll do it for you and her."

They hugged and held on. "Thank you," she sobbed out. "I miss her so much. And-" she lost her breath for a second. "And I wish that I didn't have to bring the news to you. How I wish that I could have done something."

Jake whispered, "It's not your fault. Don't do that to yourself. Bad things just happen. And it's best not to make yourself ashamed of that. At least that's what she told me when I was blaming myself during our final night together before my exile."

Out on the stage, Isaac was finishing his preamble. "And so, this drama will be the first play to portray Alpha alive. We will marvel at his mighty dominance over the wretched Goddess. Yet keep this in mind as you watch, dear friends. For tonight, you will have pity for more than just a fallen Goddess, but for a starry-eyed dreamer."

"You better go out there." Jake sucked away his tears as best he could. "I'll be on the curtains. They are waiting for you."

Ilene exchanged one last, brief, hug before entering stage left. Craigson played the first long, haunting notes of the play. Hound had composed a most cosmic sonata. It gave musical atmosphere to a vast nothingness on the verge of creation by the God and his dear Goddess.

CHAPTER 26 THE TRAGEDY OF OMEGA

The play had many low points. Isaac could feel the grievous eyes of the audience prick his skin with each delivery of his lines. Isaac conceived the idea for this play about a year ago. A play about the revered deity Alpha really has never been done before. Isaac believed that the best plays pulled in a crowd based on a collective interest. He was sure that many would consider his idea of representing the almighty on stage very interesting, as it essentially breaks the religious law of not creating images of heavenly bodies. No matter how people stood on this issue, the existence of the issue itself would make tickets sell.

And he was right. Unfortunately, as he found himself going about his performance, he felt a twinge of fear with every spoken syllable. These micro-seconds of passive sacrilege made him worry whether he bit off more than he could chew in angering the religious gentry. This stress over-powered what could have been an effective performance as he rushed through his lines like a nervous twit, and not the father of all the universe.

His opening line that he squeezed out indicated this by the sputtering tone of his voice. "The world began because the God and the Goddess worked together. We are made one flesh so as to make one world. I now call on her loveliness to begin this work now."

He harkened his hand out and called her. Ilene straightened her blonde wig and said a silent prayer to the actual Alpha for the favor of no one recognizing who she was. Then she entered stage left. Before even opening her lips, the audience could tell that she would be the high light of the play. *The Holy Volume* does not go into detail regarding the Goddess's appearance. Artists usually favored forming her as an ugly serpent or leviathan in the shape of a woman. Ilene's character was in every way contrary to each evil that people thought that they knew about Omega. She spoke reasonably and kindly to Alpha at every turn in the first act. "Here am I, lord. How may I serve thee?"

"My beloved woman," bellowed the false God with softened murmur, "I have loved you for countless eons. Yet now, we must cast off the pleasures of our infinite domain in space and strap into a most divine work- creating the finite and the beautiful. We shall create a world and our own children for them to dwell therein. We shall call them: humanity."

Thus, the first act went on. The two gave colorful descriptions of the world being formed off-stage by the will of their minds and the passion of their hearts as they gazed and gestured to the creation taking place before them. Their 'creating' was interesting as it was equal parts scripturally accurate with some artistic license added on.

For example, Ilene admired the orbiting isles being created, just as Omega did, but only from a distance off-stage. They alluded to the earth only being a pool. But it was never physically on stage. Thus, they could not bathe in such a pool as their 'characters' did in the volume. Isaac grew flushed with ungodly disgust to think that some audience members might have expected such a scene.

Craigson's work on the violin really carried the scene. His lofty variations of high and low tones impressed the epic and majestic feelings that something like the creation of the world would evoke.

The first act then ended ominously as Omega asked Alpha if they would be worshiped by their children. This was foreshadowing Omega's wish to force all the world to worship her. In the play, Isaac's character gave out the same viewpoint in opposition to this. The God is great without the worship of his people. They may do so of their own thankful free will.

Yet the character on-stage explained this with more aggression than what is commonly thought to have been found in the benevolent creator's tone within the book. He yelled and rejected the idea of such a foolish notion in the head of Omega. This outburst saw him stomp off stage left. Left alone, Ilene's character gave off an interesting counter argument in the form of a soliloquy.

"My heart is fatigued from hearing my lord strive against me in such a way. But my eyes are in greater pain. For since we began shaping the physical plane, the meta-physical plane begins to shine before me, and I can see the pre-destined fates of our world shaping even now. My eyes are salted with omniscience.

I see the ages to come in every detail. The divisions of nations, our children abusing each other for their differences, and the schism of worship are all pains that I am beholding a thousand times a second. O! The horror of these visions! My beloved and I could help our children if we can somehow twist the fates. Even if by force, our children could be safe under our thumb. This way, they cannot hurt themselves or each other. How can he not see these visions too? Is he ignoring them? I must convince him, or I'll live in anguish over the world that we may bring about."

Jake let the curtain go down. Ilene and Isaac moved into position for their first scene of the second act.

"I think that it's coming together marvelously," she whispered to Isaac within the dark of the curtain.

He muffled a cautious grunt in thanks, uncertain if she was correct. Isaac knew that they usually clapped after the end of an act. None of the faceless masses in the dark made a single sound.

When Jake raised the curtain for act two, it opened in the middle of an argument. The first line was Alpha's response to Omega. "So: you believe that subjecting our children to forced worship will prevent much sorrow in our future world, do you?"

Omega was unsure of how strongly she must press against her lover, so she hesitated in saying, "Y-yes. Surely your grace has seen the world to come."

He yelled while her guard was down. "I am Alpha! I am the omniscient omnipresence! Do not assume that I am blind to all that is and shall be!"

Omega cowered from his rage. "Then," she quivered, "surely you see the harsh realities awaiting your offspring."

Alpha drew a heavy breath and turned away from her. Then he turned back. "Woman, I've weighed it all in the grand balance. If I enforce worship and paradise on everyone, they'll be safe. Yet they'll never know the heights of joy that far exceeds paradise if they know not the meaning of mere suffering."

"Mere suffering?" Omega grew upset, gulping in angry air hysterically. "Mere suffering? My lord, they are going to hurt each other, and even kill each other! You mean to tell me that allowing this is better than unhalted serenity?"

Alpha stomped his foot down. Thunder sounded a hard note. This was thanks to Jake catching his cue to wave and strike a thin metal sheet to simulate thunder caused by the lord's wrath. "Only I know what is best for humanity. Only the good will have paradise at the end of their small lives. Those whose vices outweigh their virtues will be locked in the icy depths of hell."

Omega would not back down. "But why make them go through proving such a distinction when you could let them all remain in harmonious paradise under your power? That is, if you really know what is best for them."

"Hold your tongue, woman! Do not presume to judge God!" Isaac's portrayal of Alpha waved his fists wildly in furious whirls.

Meanwhile, Jake had a line of metal sheets stacked over cans like drums. He randomly beat them with a stick to highlight Alpha's rising rage. Jake then slipped some open jars of non-flammable and odorless smoke under the curtain. Their growing vapors made the mood more haunting than ever. Craigson's violin notes also added to this mood by hitting scratchy single notes with each snap of thunder.

Despite the wroth words, gothic atmosphere, and hard sounds; Ilene's Omega still refused to back down. "I created this world as much as you did. Don't presume to tell me what is right and wrong. I am not your pawn, but your partner. How would man respond to such manipulations that you bestow upon me?"

With these words came more thunder and new vapors from Jake, now colored blue in contra to the whiter vapors of Alpha. The God seemed ready to back down too, but he instead slapped her. The blow crashed the violin into the impact of a quiet halt on the edge of a fine echo. This knocked Omega back to the end of the stage where she had cowered before.

During the weeks of practice, Isaac taught Ilene the art of rolling with the punches. Isaac was all for making the scene with the blow as realistic as possible. So, Ilene learned how to follow the telegraph of Isaac's hand and time it so that she could fall back before actually getting hit.

Isaac liked to joke, "You never know. This might come in handy during a real fight someday."

With Omega struck down, Alpha yelled, "Enough with you, insolent wench! We are proceeding with our creations soon-just as I planned them! Now... I shall be examining the earth below. Pray that I find you in a more subservient attitude when I return."

Alpha exited stage left. Omega wiped away the imagined blood from her unblemished mouth. Omega grimaced darkly at Alpha's exit.

"You won't."

Down came the curtain. End of act two.

Isaac sharply whispered to himself. "Damn, damn, dee-amn!" He repeated this as he lifted his robe while running to the other side of off-stage. Isaac made this trip to give the audience the impression that Alpha had gone a great distance between the earth and his woman. As for the motives of his cursing: "They're hating it! They would have at least made a peep if they were invested."

Ilene's ear followed him as she stood back up. She was ready for the final act. The curtain rose.

Omega was sadly gazing at the stars and heavens about her. Omega's thoughts were sealed as she remained silent. Then she pulled out a knife that was hidden in her wide sleeve. "I don't want my unborn children to suffer under the hands of a confused father who runs them ragged between joy and distress. With him gone, I will encamp the peace of the heavens upon them all and draw them to my grace so that they will be safe and happy. But, hark!"

Footsteps in space (off-stage). "The father approaches. May the mother's blade be swift, and her soul be strong. This one cut of blood will be the first and the last. It shall paint a perfect eternity and happy infinity for all."

Alpha entered. "Now is the hour nigh for the cradle of humanity to be filled. Come, woman, that we may go about it."

Instead, Omega thrusted at him with her blade. "The first thing that it shall be filled with is your corpse!"

Alpha stepped out of the way. "What is this? Betrayed by the hand of my own lover?"

Omega doubled back but was poised to strike again. "Didn't see this coming, oh 'Omnipotent Omnipresence?'"

"We are only able to see into the earth's future. As for the heavens, nothing like your filthy treachery could ever be predicted."

Omega gripped the dagger tighter, preparing for a second strike. "It was you that was treacherous from the start. You planned on chaining humanity to a life of misery. You rejected reason and compassion so that you could avoid responsibility. That's all it is, is it not? You fear that you don't have enough power to care for them all. Some God you're turning out to be."

Thunder rumbled with each step that he made unto her. "Whereas you'd take the active approach of holding them in literal chains."

Alpha stepped dangerously close to where she could lunge out. He held out his hand. "Give me the dagger, Omega. Eternity is a long time. We can forget about it between now and then."

"Never. You mistake the shelter that I would offer for a prison. And you mistake a true cell for free-will. Since we ultimately decided their fate between the two of us, that surely means that they have none. And if you will leave them outside of my care, then you must die."

"I see that there is no way to change your insane mind. A mad Goddess cannot be left to her own devices in the world to come. Especially if I cannot predict her erratic behavior. Forgive me."

Alpha bounded in place with both of his feet. This made a tremendous thud upon the stage floor. Awakened from a small nap by the impatient second thud of this cue, Jake struck the largest of the metal sheets. This resulted in the largest of all their gongs. The simulated quake that this sound emitted made Omega fall to her feet again.

Alpha then tried to wrench the dagger from her hand. Alpha was slashed in the side of his lower leg. Isaac was glad that it was only rubber, though it did smart a little. Alpha still managed to get his hand on the knife, and he freed it only to drop it. The weapon slid over to the stage's center.

Omega kicked Alpha off of her. Joined in equal footing, both began to grapple. Their hands collided while attempting to over-power each other. Their struggle flew back-stage. Jake released more blue and white smoke. As Craigson's strings rose in frantic pacing, the jester then raised the extra curtains to reveal an opaque screen of paper spread over the stage as the new background.

The lamp lights displayed the shadows of the battling Gods behind the white paper to the wonderment of the audience. Craigson's hustling notes reached a fever pitch during the climactic battle. Jake followed the instructions by Isaac to, "go wild during this part," on the rest of the metal sheets. Jake tossed and abused them like a soldier in the depths of a mad battle- clanging and crashing thunder for the battling Gods.

Alpha finally pushed Omega off of him. Alpha rushed back to the main stage's foreground. Omega's murderous feet were behind him. He made a rolling dive for the dagger. Omega was hot on him. With the weapon in hand, he turned and stretched it right into her on-rushing charge- stopping not only her, but the music, and the last echo of the metal thunder. Omega had been vanquished.

Adorning the implement under her arm pit, she swooned and dropped to the floor. Omega fell back with her hand about her brow to give out the last lament. "I am dead. Can a goddess die? Where can she go? Heaven or hell? No. I will live on. In some other form I will live on. And in that form, I shall take this world back."

Omega looked up to her killer with ultimate disdain. "This is not goodbye. I will see you again. Thou mayest bring me down to the depths, but your children of creation will stand upon my shoulders. And I will hold them up until, one day, they are strong enough to defeat even you. Then I shall rise again. Next time, it shall be you who falls by my hand. For now... the world is yours."

She passed her last breath out slowly.

"My love and my light," sobbed Alpha. "This shall be our last farewell. For I will assure that you do not rise again to confound my omniscient predestinations of freedom for all. But, soft, even now your reasoning does begin to prove my words contradictory. Freedom under predestination? It maddens me to think that I may have been wrong. Maybe... but no! I must be confident in all that I do. No turning back."

Alpha got up and surveyed the damaged galaxy, unseen by the audience about him. "We have destroyed the asteroids that we were to use for land."

These asteroids being planned were mentioned during their creation sequence back in act one. "Though I could create more asteroids, I shall prevent Omega's rebirth by breaking her body parts up into the future nations. Her legs that pursued me and sat with me shall be the lands of Kenorland and Rodinia. Her arms that struck me and lovingly embraced me shall be Pannotia and Vaalbara. Her mid-section that boiled with passionate hate and love shall be Ur. And her head that directed these evils and considered love her motive shall be Pangea."

Isaac turned to the audience. Some were already getting up, almost intuitively sensing the up-coming resolution's line. "Now she is gone. She was the great love and hate of my life. I hope, yea, even God can hope, that humanity will be made up of the best of her to thrive, and not the worst of her to die. Thus, the world began after its greatest war. Hopefully, this will be its last."

The curtains closed. The applause was only a couple of polite claps. Isaac went from being the God Alpha to a lowly mortal, feeling even lower. Jake and Craigson gathered near Isaac and Ilene backstage. Everyone was happy that the play went off as well as it did. But any cries of joy were cancelled upon seeing Isaac's sullen face.

"Isaac," asked Craigson, "what's wrong? Everything went off perfectly. I even got every note right."

Isaac sat, downtrodden. "Not everything. They hated it, for starters. They used to give my plays encores in the palace. Now they just sit and gawk at my works as if they don't mean anything. Maybe they don't…"

No one could make him feel better. They could only gawk in curiosity at this sadness. Isaac finally got up and ordered everyone to get dressed. "We're going back to the pub. I don't feel like giving a bow."

As the crowds gathered in shuffling droves out of the warehouse, Isaac and his crew lost themselves amongst the masses. They made their way out uncelebrated, unbothered, and most of all: unrecognized.

Only one man out of the whole audience seemed to have been pleased by the play. He was leagues away from Isaac's crew on the other side of the crowd. This was Lieutenant Dusk, who was found exiting with his head and smile held above the smog of weary people trudging from the mediocre play. For Dusk, the play was everything that he hoped that it would be and then some.

CHAPTER 27 CRITICS

The next day, Craigson woke up and remained laid out in his bed. He stared at the ceiling thinking of how miserable Isaac was last night. Then an idea sprang into his head. Craigson got up earlier than usual and ran downstairs into the street. He picked up a copy of *The Daily Pamphlet.* The play's review would surely cheer Isaac up. Craigson began to read it as soon as he was back inside. This made him instantly regret this idea just in time to see Isaac rocking his way down the stairs.

Isaac was on to Craigson- judging by the look condemned on his poor face. "That's the review, isn't it? Let me see it."

Craigson tried to keep it away, but Isaac nearly tackled into him for that paper. "NOW!"

Craigson released it. Herein is what Isaac read as Ilene and Jake gathered about the bar area with the distraught playwright:

"On the outset, I find that this review is a mistake. As you know, this paper has advertised the attraction that came to the corner of Inkle and Bash. So, this recent update regarding the play came as a shock. We were asked by local merchant and former performer for the crown of Pangea, Isaac Inklewood, to provide a review while informing us that his play *The Tragedy of Omega* has been scheduled for only one show. No further performances in Princeberg are to be made according to him. Thus, a review is moot as no one reading this will be able to watch another upcoming showing of this slop. Yet this update is so last minute that we must add this review into our paper to fill up space. But on the bright side, it is a good thing that the play will not appear again. Initially, it sold out handsomely."

"This is given that the premise is a bold one that could grab the attention of even those casually familiar with creation's history. Instead of seeing the Goddess Omega as a devilish schemer and tyrant, we see her as a beautiful woman wishing to protect humanity by putting us under, as I understood it, 'harmonious paradise,' in contradiction to Alpha's will. But Omega in the play does not want to do this out of lust for tyranny as is canon, rather, to help humans avoid the sorrow that pervades our history within the omniscient eyes of both Gods. The tender and sincere delivery by the unknown actress made this nigh-blasphemous idea almost believable."

"As for the many aspects of this drama that do not work: the themes are too heavy-handed, the dialogue is flat, and then there is Isaac's portrayal of our beloved Alpha... Where do I begin? His performance was so dull-witted and oafish that I'd call it total sacrilege to bring about such a vision of our creator-beyond making him appear as a villainous brute. I suggest that this small troupe at 'Royal Services' repent to Alpha and the viewing public for such a sinful and poorly executed piece of work. Most of all, they should also get their muddied heads into the source material of *The Holy Volume.* They could stand benefiting from Alpha's blessed wisdom rather than casting judgement on God."

Ilene felt Isaac's shoulder as she saw the first of his tears trickle from his head. "Don't cry, Isaac. I really liked the play. I thought that it was some of your best work."

Isaac sealed his face into a static cocoon of aggravation equal to that of the wrathful god that he played. "I'm **not** crying, and I'm **not** going to be pandered to. What do you even know of my best work? This was just an 'oafish' re-telling that I knew wasn't going to work and it didn't. So..."

Isaac trailed off his tirade as he became lost in the many words that he wanted to use but couldn't organize. Jake placed a hand on Isaac's shoulder too and said, "Come on now, Isaac. We made out all right. We got enough money to get those passage papers back to Pangea. Once there, you can make some more plays."

Isaac fought off the hand as if it belonged to his worst enemy and not his sympathetic little brother. "Off with you! What do you know about entertainment? You just waddle about telling foolish jokes that you hear children say in the streets, only to randomly fall on your arse! I'm an artist! Yet, I don't know if I can replicate my past glories. This play shows me that I'm past my prime. How can they keep such a hack like me in the palace of Pangea? More the fools, all of you, for trying to convince me otherwise. Fools!"

A painful pause emerged from the awestruck group witnessing Isaac's gasping after this traumatic blow-up. Isaac asked, "How many days until we're over Pangea?"

"About a couple weeks," murmured Craigson.

"Craigson," he bellowed, seeming ready to yell at him too... only to give an order. "See that you get the passage papers before the lunch rush this afternoon."

Isaac then ordered Ilene and Jake about as if nothing terrible had occurred between him and his friends. "You two: we'll be packing up and closing the store. I'll be getting my things together if anyone needs me."

Like a haunting wraith, he went up the stairs, fully embraced in his despair.

Ilene and Jake began to clear some tables. "We'll have to sell the place too," mentioned Jake. "He didn't think of that. Who will take it?"

"Doesn't matter," said Craigson. "We'll ask for it cheap. We'll probably be more accurate in its value that way. In the end, we'll have more than enough for safe passage."

Sullenly, Craigson gathered up the money from the previous night, the weeks of supplying storage, and the pub profits into a bill fold. Craigson went out into the streets without a goodbye. Outside, Craigson turned around to move the open sign closed. But it was already in the closed position. He began to clamber morosely about his way. His head arched low, and his pockets were filled with his limp hands during the whole of his march.

This was it. He was heading back to the palace. He was heading back to the place of his glory days. Yet a serious sadness clouded the edge of this happy return, stubbornly becoming pinned to him. Craigson couldn't understand this sudden depression.

Because of this melancholy, Craigson was caught off guard by Miles taunting him as he went by the rival pub. "Hey, Craigson! Nice play last night. I had no idea that Isaac was Alpha himself. I'll be careful not to bother him from now on. Wouldn't want him to smite me or anything."

Craigson froze at this confrontation. He was so used to hiding amongst his brothers. Though Craigson was the tallest, he usually considered himself the shyest of the trio. He silently mused that the words of the foolish Miles were of no use minding. So, he resumed his melancholy meditation as he tried to continue his walk by darting past the brute.

But new words only stung harder. "If you're going to be that way, maybe you should have that Goddess of yours strike me down instead. Where'd you get her, anyway? That whore a friend of your mother?"

Craigson snapped out his fist at Miles' face- blackening his eye. Craigson's fist bled profusely. It was worth it. "Whoredom," rasped Craigson over the body shrunken from brute to bug, "was the last resort of our mother after father died. Even then, she still worked two other jobs before also dying of disease. I don't know how Isaac tolerated these rumors from scum like you, but I'm not him. I catch you spouting such dribble again, I will smash your throat so badly that pronouncing words like 'whore' will be excruciating to the utmost degree."

Moron probably wasn't worth it. But even reserved fellows like Craigson need some catharsis every once in a while, especially on days like this. Thinking of his sordid childhood made him realize what had really been bothering him this whole time. This was the unknown of the future ahead of his road. If events such as the happy return to the palace could do things like shake the bold Isaac out of his confidence in his creativity, what worse could lie ahead?

Instead of cowering from such changes on the way, Craigson walked on towards them. This didn't mean that he had to like it though. So, he straightened his overall's straps and went on down the street- glimmered by the morning light of the sun that seemed to be living at the very end of the town like a big attraction for all to behold. He went on, ignoring every other curse and insult that Miles sent after him. For Miles was but the hallow echo of the past better to be forgotten to make way for the new hardships to come. Kind of inspiring. Kind of depressing.

This new road at last brought our melancholy friend to the Office of International Travels. There, he bought the expensive passage papers after a relatively short line. He also received a new and ugly twist on this road of life before exiting the building.

"She is risen!" read the poster on the wall. "Omega has come in the form of one whose influence stretches across the earth. Not only has she murdered the Ursian royal family in cold blood, but now she flees from our justice to rally the world under her evil will."

"As it is written regarding the ill-omen in the final book of *The Holy Volume*: 'And she shall come as an exiled killer. She'll gain the hearts of all men via her charming ways. But harken! For she shall wish to only deceive so as to gain the souls of this world. Her heart may follow human virtues, and she may yet believe them herself. But the great traitor dwells within her. The Goddess dwells within her. Omega shall rise again through and by her.' Beware Princess Ilene of Pangea!"

Ilene was pictured below the text. It was a copy of her famed royal portrait, laced in a sparkling dress with diamonds about her ears and a tiara over her silk hair of old. Craigson almost didn't recognize her. The proclamation continued below the picture.

"Report her to the Ursian forces, for she is rumored to be in the city. Together we will end her evil reign in the holy name of Alpha."

"Oh no!" gasped Craigson as he sprinted his way back, driving and pushing past the crowds. He heard the rumors flying into his ears as he shoved past each civilian discussing this revelation.

"Can't believe that of all the possible vessels, it was that nice

Ilene and I- hey!"

The posters lined the walls of each street. Craigson cursed himself for not noticing them when he was walking by that morning. "The Goddess has risen? I never thought that the end of time prophecies would occur in our day, I mean- whoa! Watch it, you dolt!"

Craigson had to get back. He couldn't believe that this was happening. "You know... that girl playing Omega last night kind of looked like the princess. You don't think-? We'll excuse you!"

Got to get back, got to warn them! his mind screamed upon each strained trod about the cobblestone. Craigson even streamed past Mr. Hound and Lieutenant Dusk without getting a good look at who they were. Mr. Hound, however, recognized the frightened merchant.

"That boy sure is in a hurry," chuckled Hound as he adjusted his new hat. It was like his old one, except that it was deer-skin beige and not black. "You'd think that the big, bad Goddess herself were after him."

As Dusk planted another poster over the glue that his soldiers just painted on the wall, he said, "Indeed. For soon everyone will have that superstitious fear plugged into their hearts."

Hound patted the poster down to make sure that the glue wouldn't wrinkle the parchment. Ilene's face on the poster was rubbed by the cusp of Hound's hand. "One thing I still don't get. Why don't you just tell people where she is instead of asking them to report her in themselves?"

"It's all part of the majesty of Empress Lida's wisdom. If we simply told people where she was, trust between Ur and the rest of the Princeberg populace wouldn't be as complete. The more skeptical people would question why we didn't just capture her ourselves if we knew exactly where she was."

"But you knew that she was in Princeberg the whole time."

"We tracked her here, but that doesn't mean that she couldn't lose herself amongst the populace. No one reporting her to us will think that far ahead anyway. All that matters is that the lucky pawn who does will feel special for finding her and that makes our propaganda all the more convincing."

The thespian performance from the previous night inspired a dramatic lamenting woe sarcastically from Hound. "The poor crusading Ursians are unable to track down the Goddess hiding in human form. Now we need your help, **you** the people."

Dusk completed patting down the last of the posters for the morning. "You get the idea. It is all a performance. We're tricking them," he emphasized with a nod to the crowds walking about their business.

"We're tricking all of them," continued the Ursian warrior,

"into thinking that they're each of individual value in this war. It lifts the esteem of the lower classes up-"

"-While bringing down the name of Pangea," summed up Hound. "What better way to destroy Pangea's reputation than to make their sweet daughter into the embodiment of evil?"

"With that, no one will ally with Pangea when we face them in combat. The war is ours before it even begins. Now all we have to do is spread the good word further and watch as the sheep lead us to the slaughter as every bum in Princeberg will drag Princess Ilene through the streets in chains. Then the rest of the world will follow in bringing down the Pangean Empire- for we have effortlessly built it up as the harbinger of the ill- end."

"So long as I get my money in the end, I don't care if you call Pangea the harbinger of the common cold."

"Enough. I must now personally get the trust of the people."

Dusk stepped atop the cart that they rode about town in. He raised the Ursian flag: an orange circle surrounded by three crescent shapes of the same color spiraling about it on a bright yellow background. He then raised his voice.

This is how nations rise and fall. Just get the right man to raise his flag and voice.

"People of Princeberg! As a humble soldier for the humble nation of Ur, I implore you to lend an ear. Pangea sent their princess to kill our royal family under the pretense of a peaceful marriage, leaving only our poor empress left to fend for our crumbling country. But we have learned of a worse danger that has emerged from these events. Our Alphite priests have learned from divine visions that the Goddess has risen through this beastly child's raging spirit. We have tracked her here. And she could be out on these very streets plotting to strike and cut apart your own family to ensure her ascension to power. Are you going to walk on and ignore the monster of old trying to kill your beloved spouses and innocent children?"

"NO!" shouted the people who were only a moment ago murmuring in confusion over the developments. Now they were united under an umbrella of common reasoning by an authoritative figure.

"Join my men and I," he railed on, "as we rally the town in search of the evil Goddess. For we are the human race. We are all Alpha's chosen people. In his name, we shall conquer even the Goddess. For we know that Alpha was more powerful than her. If we are for him, how can she stand against us? Who's with me?"

The passion of Dusk's rabble rousing was so sure and powerful, that even the most irreligious of the gentry dropped their work tools and cancelled their day shifts to ensure the safety of their families.

Thus, the mob continued to grow from the chosen few into the many wishing to be counted in their number when they came marching in. For the mob grew ever larger with each assembling speech made by Dusk down every street using similar rhetoric. Soon, a verifiable army was made. Dusk and Hound were marching at its head.

CHAPTER 28 THE OMEGA RUMOR

Ilene was the only one who had nothing to really pack. Ilene lived the past month with nothing to her name. She only had the clothes generously provided by her hosts. She took in a good look at her room's mirror. Her face had become rougher, and older looking. Yet Ilene's eyes were still filled with a youthful gleam despite her hair growing back in clumsy patches. From a distance, she still had a head seemingly made large from her pronounced baldness- highlighting her forehead and skull. Ilene was still dressed in one of Craigson's overalls with a blouse of Isaac's as a shirt.

Ilene could not help but wonder if her parents would recognize her if they ever saw her again, and if she could ever restart her old life after the horrors that she saw.

A clatter from downstairs broke her from this melancholy. She rushed down to see that it was Craigson back in record time. He was panting with every word that he pushed out. "We need... to get out... they're coming...!"

Isaac and Jake interrogated their fatigued brother. "**Who's** coming?"

To answer, Craigson handed them a copy of one of the posters that he snagged on the way back. Isaac sped through it. "He's right. We need to get out of here."

"Why?" asked Jake.

"Dusk is trying to convince everyone that Ilene is the Goddess risen again in human form to conquer the world."

Jake could not resist the temptation to make a jab at this claim. "Ilene? The Goddess?" He flashed a surprised look at her. "She's a nice girl, but she's no Goddess. She only plays one on stage."

"All bad jesting aside," interluded Ilene, "Dusk must have been letting us do the play to bide his time for the opportunity to use its contents to initiate this slander against me. My performance helped make a public suspect out of me, no doubt."

"But," questioned Isaac as he tried to help tired Craigson up the stairs, "why discredit you in such a roundabout way? Why not just call for your capture based on getting blamed for the Ursian family's death?"

Ilene thought about this as she and Jake grabbed the bags of their fellows. The latest snow's descent was making the windows white. Then she recalled the mad ambition for world encompassing power on the part of Empress Lida.

"Because if I'm villainized as Omega, more people will side with Ur. They're trying to start a war against Pangea."

Isaac gathered the remaining bags together by the door as he wiped his head. "That's just perfect. Now here's what we're going to do. It's still a few weeks before we're directly over Pangea. Let's exit the building casually. No storming out in blind panic. We'll hold ourselves up in a cheap inn, lay low, and we'll come back to our platform lift in the back yard when the time is right. Perhaps the dead of night. Craigson, do you have the passage papers? Otherwise, Pangea's border patrol is booting us into the slammer as soon as we arrive."

Craigson, reinstituting his normal rate of breath, held up the documents. "All right. All out. Nice and slow. It's not like everyone has figured it out and found us yet."

Before Isaac led everyone to the exit, a thunderous series of knocks assaulted the door and windows. "I think they found us," stated Jake.

Ilene drew near the head merchant. He looked even more scared than she felt. Still, she asked, "What do we do?"

"What needs to be done," gulped her friend. Isaac proceeded out alone. "Stay here."

Outside, Isaac squinted to see through the expanding stream of snow in the air as he faced a mob of hundreds, fenced inches from his door and stretching from each end of the street as far as he could see. Miles jutted an accusatory finger at Isaac. Isaac wondered where Miles got the black eye. Jake would've probably joked that the look was an improvement.

Dusk and Hound were standing by Miles as he shouted, "That's the place, lieutenant! I recognized the girl from the play!"

"May I help you, gentlemen? I'm afraid that the pub is closed due to certain..."

"Silence, Isaac!" barked Hound. "You know who we're here for. Just let her out and we'll forget that this happened."

"Perhaps," interceded Dusk, "we'll allow you some of the reward money for assisting us, Isaac."

Hound's eyes followed Dusk upon hearing this.

"Better yet: Ur too could use performers for the new court of the empress. Perhaps your troupe could join us? It's all you ever really wanted, yes? That's what Hound tells me. All you want is a comfortable place in which to concentrate on your thespian craft. Given your most recent show, I could see why you'd desire the chance to improve it."

Isaac's eyes were flooded by the sea of people before him. Stage fright. They gradually stepped closer to him. There was no way out and his reversing feet knew it.

"Very well," he said while raising his hands. He finally remembered his lines. "I'll give her up. Girl made lousy sandwiches anyway."

"He wouldn't," whispered Ilene as she watched through the cracks in the boarded window.

"I'll be right back with her." He entered the door. A hush. Sounds of tumbling struggle broke through the shut walls of the pub.

"The feisty little lady isn't going easily," said Hound to Dusk. Both chuckled slightly at this satisfaction. At last Ilene would be theirs.

The door was kicked open. "You wanted Omega, huh?" Isaac loudly queried on his way out with his burden clenched in his hands. "Well, you're all saying hello to Alpha instead!"

Isaac swung and aimed Hound's discarded musket at the alarmed crowd. Everyone was backing off, anticipating a shooting. That is, until the empty click was heard. Isaac stood there- dumbfounded at this awkward beat.

"I'm afraid it's still empty, Isaac," jovially noted Hound. The mob reversed their fear to merriment as they began to rain laughter upon the dud of a threat. But then came plan B.

Jake leaped from the door with something in his hand. "If you folks thought that was funny, wait until you see what this jester has in store for you during the second act."

Before the guffawing could stop, Jake tossed a spare smoke jar from the play at Dusk. It exploded in a brilliantly powdered vapor of white that seemed to match the increasing snow fall. This sudden illumination left the crowd confused. Thus, the crew had enough time to put on their cloaks and scurry out the back door.

"That was an insane plan. You know that, Isaac?" said Ilene as she ran apace with the thespian across the back lawn.

"Hey," he puffed, "it worked, didn't it?"

They were about to jump the fence when Ilene heard the flood of feet trampling through the pub. The people poured out of the door as plentifully as the gobs of snowflakes. "There she is!" one Princeberg throng member cried.

"Don't look back, Ilene! Quickly! We'll pull you up from the other side of the fence!" yelled Isaac as he encouraged her to hurry up.

Ilene turned away from the fire of hate in the mob's eyes as she sprinted for the fence- igniting the mob's chase faster.

With the crowds right behind her, Ilene leaped for the brother's outreaching arms from the other side of the fence as they yanked her just out of the mob's clutches. Once everyone was over the fence, they ran into the open street before them. Craigson worried aloud, "Won't they boost each other up the fence like we did?"

"Nah," sneered Isaac as he glanced behind his run. "Too many of them pressing each other up against the fence it looks like. From here, it looks like they're just trying to push it down with their sheer numbers. What sheep…"

Jake scurried closer to everyone and asked, "So where to?"

"Anywhere but here." Isaac began to run opposite his pub that he could still see from his side of the block. The others ran after from behind. Isaac waved at his pub without stopping his race.

"Farewell, my pub," Isaac said to his business. "May those jackals drink you dry until they're too slow to follow after our flight."

While apace with Craigson, Jake asked him, "You still got the papers?"

Craigson saluted them over his head before pocketing them.

They kept sprinting. Everyone was heaving grunts with each step. After a while, Ilene felt like she'd fall over and burst into a pool of defeated sweat. Jake, wasting away likewise with each lunge of his lungs, offered his hand to Ilene so that they could help usher each other on. They took hands and were linked to keep trudging on.

Just when Isaac was smiling while feeling assured that they lost them, an arrow narrowly whizzed past his ear. The thwip of the projectile was like a bell's death tone to him. Turning about, he could see the mob on their track again, just down the street and stampeding closer. Ursian soldiers brought their bows and were firing after them.

"Keep going!" Isaac wheezed with a dry and breathless mouth.

The crowd was gaining on them. As they got closer, hope of escape grew thinner than their shortness of breath. They managed to gain some extra distance around a wide corner.

Jake pointed around another corner. "It's the warehouse! Let's lock ourselves in and hide."

Isaac tore that idea apart. "Are you crazy? We'll be sitting ducks in there."

"Well it's either that or try to outrun them and I don't think-"

"Fine," broke in Isaac. "Maybe if we hurry before they round that corner, they won't know where we went."

They ran into the quiet of the warehouse. Each door was locked. They then huddled into a dark crevice under the old catwalks. They hoped that the enemy would pass them by. The tension was silently crushing Ilene's vibrating heart to her core as she tried to catch her breath.

She whispered to Craigson. "Do you think that they…?"

But a slam on one of the doors stopped her query. Indistinct but clamoring murmurs yelled from the citizens, demanding their prey outside.

"What do we do, Isaac?"

Isaac didn't say anything. Ilene looked to see him crouched up in his own fear.

"Isaac?"

"I don't know!" He snapped bitterly. "I don't know…" he melted as he sobbed into his knees.

His brothers trembled at the sight of this. They put a hand on each of his shaking shoulders. Soon, they were hunched over in their own despair as well.

Ilene looked at the man who loved Marlene almost as much as she did. Jake was breaking down and weeping, "This is the end..."

Ilene knew that they were good men. They've proved it time and again by helping her, but these were not strong men. Ilene always knew that life was no fairy tale. She knew from the beginning that a prince could never ride in to save her. Yet for the first time, she experienced this truth as the world outside was ready to tear down the walls.

So, she went to the remnants of the stage and kicked down the outer space background of the play that gave a vision of Omega to the public. Once the several metal poles that held up the background toppled over, Ilene pulled off the suction connecting one of their halves to the stage-floor.

The half-pole was now a weapon- a staff that was just a hair taller than Ilene. The princess was not trained in using such a device, so she commanded everyone to grab their own staff and get ready to fight.

"It won't work, Ilene," said Craigson without looking up from his knees. "They have us. There's no point."

Ilene's head grew light upon hearing this. Maybe there wasn't a point... They were sure to die. Her head grew so light upon thinking harder about this that it felt as though it would slide off. The only way she could hold on was to grit her teeth down. This held her head back down to her shoulders. Her hold on the pole also became more tightened the more she thought about how much she still wanted to live.

"All my life," she said, "I've let people take care of me and tell me what to do. I guess I was hoping that this would always keep me safe. But not anymore. I'm taking a stand for myself this time, even if it may be for the last time."

With that, the surrounding windows were broken open by the claws of ladders penetrating their seals- bringing in the cold snow as well. The carpenters of the mob suggested the usage of their ladders in hopes that this would give them the most credit and reward for the Goddess's capture.

The Ursians were given passage to go through the windows first as they swarmed every square inch of the above catwalks. They unsheathed their arrows and gave aim unto Ilene, who was centerstage in their firing range. The military drummers outside were beating at an aggressive speed in time to the arrival of each soldier and their taking of positions. This left her too surprised to move.

Dusk and Hound emerged from one of the windows on to the catwalks with the rest of the regiment. He put his hands on to the catwalk railing to look down at her below them. "Well... hello again, Ilene," scoffed Dusk. "I'm sorry, I meant: Princess Ilene, the fair maiden of Pangea. Or would it be more appropriate to call you the Goddess Omega come to us in human form? Quite a legend, isn't it? It's like you've actually turned into one of those romantic fantasy tales that you've been famed for liking so much since you were a child. The only question now is, how shall this tale end? What are we going to do to you? Kill you, do you think?"

Dusk tutted this idea away with a wag of his finger before discerning the thought further with the same finger holding up his thoughtful chin.

"Too easy," agreed Hound.

Dusk offered, "When we take you in, I'm sorry to inform you that we must put you in a deep, dark Ursian prison hole recently reserved for murderers, animal feces, and corpses. I know, my dear. It's not exactly a palace suite. Upon that, we shall tell the world that Alpha's chosen people have driven your evil Omega spirit away and then your country will become a bigger target than, well, you at this moment."

Ilene's eyes raced around the room. What could she do? One twitch would equal a hundred arrows railing into her.

"And don't think that you can pull off martyrdom here by proving your mortality to the people by, you know, dying. We'll simply change the story to suit the same end. So, which will it be, Ilene?"

Hound laughed like a mad wolf as he leaned over the catwalk rails with joy. "Yeah, little Ilene. I'd be delighted to see you finally choose your fate. Here I am, again giving you a choice. I told you that I was a fair man. Maybe you'll even make the right choice this time. Go on, girl. This story isn't going to end itself."

Dusk then caught sight of a Pangean naval ship's mast flying from the snow's fog at a comet's velocity into the warehouse's widest window. Dusk couldn't believe what he was seeing. A... **ship** was **flying** towards them?

"What the-?"

All the Ursians jumped from the catwalks. Ilene and her friends ran for the exit. But the ship crashed into the building before they could get out. Every brick and mortar crumbled like bread in a child's hands as the ship barged through the structure. The snow, now in a flurry, ran about the place in sprinkling madness. The shards of glass hailed furiously. The wads of bricks rained mercilessly.

Ilene's ears hurt trying to discern between the screaming and the wailing of the careening walls crashing into each other. A great dust mingled with the white flurry, washing over everything about her. Ilene could then only see the snow-white haze before she passed out into darkness.

CHAPTER 29
THE BATTLE OF PRINCEBERG

Ilene smelled ash before opening her eyes. She coughed as she found herself outside with the flurry pelting her face. "What...?"

"Oh, thank Alpha," rejoiced Jake over her body. Ilene was flat on the ground. She felt his hand holding her head up like a pillow.

"She's okay," Jake told Isaac, who was bending over to vomit. But that sight was not the one that sprang her to full consciousness on her feet. It was the heap of the fallen warehouse's desolation spread and sprawled about with the living and the dead.

"How'd we-?"

"It was Craigson," Isaac informed her after wiping off his mouth. "He used the metal sheets from the play to shield us from the debris as we got out of there. Not for lack of turbulence," he whined as he held up his aching stomach.

Craigson walked into her line of vision. He had blood racing and freezing about his hand. "Holding on to those thin strips of sharp metal, they..."

He winced. The pain... it...

"I don't know if I can ever play again. Oh... Isaac... it stings out in the cold."

Isaac removed his cape and tore it to wrap around his brother's trembling hands. "No," advised Craigson. "That's your favorite cloak... knitted from fine Kenorian cotton."

Isaac gulped with his puke sickened throat. He felt blood in it. He still smirked. "I don't think so. The Kenorian who sold it to me said that it was highly durable. Probably another fake on the market."

Isaac tied up his little brother's hands.

The unspoken question from the survivors of this strange onslaught was: *what caused a ship to fall from the sky like that?*

The answer cast a shadow over the helpless. A great tower rose over the city. No. It was Marl. His plan to get on to the orb when it cycled by again worked. He managed to ascend to his goal at last. The blurred tint of the flurry made him seem like a great spirit come to steal souls. There was only one soul that he was after.

"HOUND!" Marl was louder than a legion of thunderclouds. Ilene huddled her friends close to her as they stood in awful awe of the giant's vengeful return.

Craigson whimpered. "Is now a bad time to say that I lost the passage papers?"

Princeberg was a boiling white scar in a matter of minutes. The Ursians engaged Marl with arrows and gun fire. The giant raced behind buildings and began tearing about the town in search of:

"Hound!"

The singular fugitive also ran for cover behind a building with Lieutenant Dusk after the ship fell. Both, especially Hound, resolved to stay there when Marl appeared out of the chaos. Hound looked around the corner to see that he was just out of Marl's view. He couldn't hide for long. Hound confronted Dusk.

"Give me your pistol, Dusk," demanded Hound while reaching to grab it out of the Ursian's holster. Dusk parried the hand and kicked Hound off. The slippery slush did the rest to lay Hound flat on his back.

"You've done your part, Pangean," Dusk said with contempt that croaked his voice lower than usual. "Your quarrel with this giant made me lose my prey. But I won't let her escape this time. You're on your own."

Dusk was about to march off at this when he heard the familiar unsheathing of a blade. "I'm a crack arm at throwing knives," said Hound with his drawn piece arched back. "You owe me for all the help that I've given you in finding the princess. I like my deals resolved. If you stab me in the back, I'm returning the favor. Now give me the gu-"

Gone. Dusk's dusting kick of snow over Hound's sight blew off his hat. Hound's reflexes went for the hat. Dusk rolled out of range during this brief interlude. Reassuring a strong stance, Dusk fired his pistol just as Hound launched his blade.

Marl stepped on a building that muffled the blast with equal thunder. Hound was down again. His crying shoulder made the snow a scarlet target for giant eyes. The flying blade came upon Dusk too. But he merely caught it by the handle after tilting his head out of harm's way.

Dusk stood over the trembling rogue. "I only hit your shoulder and not your chest so that you can run from the giant. Should be a fine distraction while I collect our princess."

Hound could only growl as the wound left him as speechless as a rabid beast.

Dusk crouched to Hound in a condescending whisper. "Did you really think that I'd reward you when I already had everything in motion for her? Please, boy. You're just another member of the ignorant mob to go after the girl while believing that your part in it really matters. The only difference is that you came lynching for her first- the first ignoramus in the lot. But now you've your own sins to answer for. Do your part in Alpha's grand scheme. Run. I need that giant diverted, and I assume that you need to live. Run. Run…"

Dusk departed. He tossed the knife back to Hound. "You might need this."

Hound struggled his way back up. Hound took up the knife, but Dusk was already faded into the fog of blizzard. All of the breaths that he could manage were blown away by the rushing winter breeze. After re-pocketing the knife, he stuffed his hat into the hole on the shoulder of his shirt to stop the bleeding. The roar of the giant in the distance made him run faster every time he heard it. Hound's blood drops followed, and later, Marl's street-encompassing strides did too.

With the giant out of the main square, the Ursians searched for Ilene in the gray fog beyond the whipping blizzard. Ilene led her group to the fallen Pangean ship, planted in defeat about the square. The ship creaked in sporadic spurts under the heightening weight of the snow fall.

"That's a Pangean ship," observed Ilene as they ducked under some snowbanks to avoid being seen by a wayward Ursian in the distance. Only Ursians remained in the street after Marl arrived. The storm got worse too. Everyone else returned home.

When the Ursians were out of sight, Ilene moved towards the ship. "I don't know what they are doing out here. Still, if there is any refuge that we can find…"

Isaac cut her off. "Then let's get to the ship and cut the chatter."

So they waded through the waist high snow. They shivered the whole way in suffering silence, save for Craigson's chattering teeth. They were near the imposing vessel. A wide crack was torn on the side of its hull. One unstable crack on it broke into pieces to make way for an armored figure.

He wore the blue-hued uniform of typical Pangean soldiers. He was adorned with white tassels about his belt, shoulders, and masking helmet's back. This signaled that he was but a private in the army. He was short for a soldier too. Ilene was even a bit taller than him.

After stumbling from the wreckage, the soldier approached his guests. "Greetings," he echoed from his shell. "I represent the Pangean army. A spy informed us a week ago that Princess Ilene was not kidnapped by the Ursians but has actually escaped to here. We assembled a fleet to find her, but it was attacked by that awful giant. He slaughtered them all and piled each craft into an elaborate pyramid with many of the other ships that he had destroyed as a buoyant foundation. Only our ship survived. He used the tip of our mast to stab a hold on to the orb when it went by. After climbing his way on, he threw us. Our losses are great, but I recall the motto of the Pangean military: 'Always overcome!' Thus, the mission continues. Where is the princess? Talk! I'll not rest until I find her."

Isaac, Jake, and Craigson raised their frigid fingers to Ilene. The soldier tried to bow, but he stopped with a surprised slouch. "Forgive me, my lady. I didn't recognize you due to your... haircut."

Ilene had to smile as she plumped one hand on to her head.

The knight took that hand. Its metal bit Ilene's skin when mingled with the poison of the cold. "Come with me. I'll protect you in here as a base from the storm."

Isaac and his brothers followed behind. The soldier whisked his sword towards the tip of Isaac's runny, red nose. "Away, ruffians! You have no business with her grace."

Ilene finally slipped from his hand. "And you have no business threatening the friends of her grace, **private**."

The soldier looked over at the desperate merchants. "As you wish. Come out of the cold then, the lot of you."

As they came into the shelter of the fallen ship, the soldier leaned over to Ilene. "I need a full report of your experiences during this last month."

Ilene looked to her friends. She looked back at the soldier. She sighed, shaking her head. She straightened herself up. "Let's just say that I've been getting by with a little help from my friends. As of now, I'm being pursued by Ursians."

The knight's armor chimed in abrupt startle. "By Alpha! Where are they?"

"Outside of the ship," said Ilene with a wave of her hand. "Only the blizzard protected us from being seen. They were about to capture me before your... timely arrival."

"It was verily worth it in that case," he said with another bow.

Ilene raised an eyebrow at this while looking down at him as she wondered, *Does chivalry really look this foolish up close?*

"Now then," grumbled the knight as he proceeded to matters at hand, "it won't take the Ursians long to assume that you've taken up shelter in the ship once they identify our colors. I'll set the men about the perimeter of the deck with fire power. Hopefully, they can hold the enemy off."

Craigson broke in. "How can you order that? You're only a

private, aren't you?"

The soldier briefly moaned out, "Many perished in the fall."

He shifted to sternness in his voice to save what little face he had.

"Why do you ask?"

"Because," Craigson said with fortitude hiding his blistered hands. "I'd like to volunteer."

"Me too," said Isaac.

"Same here," said Jake.

"Count me in," broke out Ilene.

The knight shuddered harder than an alarm bell with jingles of agitation. "We could certainly use more men. But you need to stay below the deck, princess."

Ilene was ready with her retort. "Is it not my life that you men are fighting for? I would like an opportunity to take part in the same cause. I would even venture to say that I care about my safety more than any of your soldiers care for theirs."

"That's the point, my lady. We don't want to increase the odds of your getting killed. We'll hide you down here."

Frustrated, she replied, "What if the Ursians breach the firing line and go through the hole?"

"We'll leave a man down here with you," the soldier quickly returned.

Ilene felt lost for defense.

"Until then," bowed the soldier one final time, "pray to Alpha-most-high for our victory."

One more note of worth made Ilene wish to halt the man's march upstairs. She grabbed his hand.

"Yes?"

It was at that moment of this halting that Ilene decided not to tell him. So what if the Ursians were trying to convince the rest of the world that she was Omega? It was a scheme that Ilene was earnestly sure that the Pangean soldiers were about to put an end to. Why bother this warrior with so frivolous a bit of knowledge that will soon be quelled by the killing of the Ursians here?

But she had to compensate for this interruption. She knew just the diversion as she looked into the eyes peeking from the rivets in his visor's helmet.

"What is your name, sir? I wish to report your bravery to the king and queen when this business is done."

He softly patted her hand with the hardness of his gauntlet. "No need to know my name, my dear. I'm just another soldier of many who live and breathe just to serve you and die for you. I've no desire for accolades."

With that he was up the steps.

"Well, little Ilene, looks like things are about to get serious," stated Jake as he nervously jingled the bells on his collar. "You know how bad for business that can get for my line of work."

Ilene did not answer as she sat next to Craigson on a nearby crate. "You shouldn't go up there to fight," she lectured plainly. "Your hands won't be able to stand the cold, let alone hold on to a gun."

Craigson stubbornly moved his face away from this advice. Isaac lectured him too. "Ilene is right. You stay here and watch over her."

"Very well," gave up Craigson. "I just want to do what I can for you, princess. Sue me for altruism."

Ilene patted his shoulder. "Never."

Outside, Dusk gathered his forces after locating each member that was wandering in the formless drift. Dusk was used to walking with obstructed vision. He trained for it his whole life.

"That ship is of Pangean design," he explained. "They must have arrived to help Ilene, only to be thrown up here by the giant. Fence the men around. Once we surround the ship, I will fire a signal to make siege for it."

CHAPTER 30
SURVIVAL

So, the Ursians formed a circle with the ship at its center. The snow fall began to steadily end. When it ended, everyone on deck could see the Ursians surrounding them. The green soldiers (Isaac and Jake) were so scared by the stand-off that their guns shook in their trembling hands. Seasoned soldiers merely gripped their weapons tighter as they coolly exhaled.

With a snap of Dusk's trigger, snow fall was replaced with gun-smoke being traded between both sides. Both sides also took heavy hits from the first volley. The smoke amongst the snow turned the world dismally gray while decorating it with colorful splashes of red.

Ilene and Craigson had to cover their ears. Craigson's hands were still so raw that they stung sharply when he pressed them into his ears. No one above had that luxury. Even the shots that didn't fatally land still hurt their ears. The blast of each gun made Jake's hearing turn into an endless chime.

Isaac had to re-load after his shot with the musket. He was having trouble packing in the ammo when a ballistic went through the rail that he was laying under for cover. The splintered chards rained on him just as the shock of this hardened his nerves to a stand-still.

When the last crumb of wood finished trickling down, he went into a wild tirade of repeating, "I hate this! I really hate this!" almost childishly, to himself.

Jake didn't quite hear him. So, he raised his voice to ask, "What?"

"I wasn't talking to you!" snapped back Isaac as he fired and missed the Ursian that he supposed was just shooting at him.

"What?"

"Never mind," grumbled Isaac, upset that he missed his mark.

While the fight raged on, so did the legs of Hound a few blocks away. While looking for a place to hide, Hound found the ominous shade of the large figure's shadow over him. Marl found him.

Hound bolted off. Hound hurled himself around many corners to out-race Marl's blood lust. Hound rounded one icy corner at such a speed that he stumbled sharply on to his side. Hound scrambled to his feet after the titanic footfalls quaked the ground enough to spring him back up. Seeing this, Marl lunged for Hound. Hound lunged out of reach.

Two buildings were knocked down by the giant's stampede. Hound then rolled down a flight of stairs on the side of a bridge that he was on. When he took this roll, he let himself go limp as his descent commenced. During this fall, Hound lost his new beige hat. There was no going back for it before he landed with a thud from the last step.

Hound got up a bruised and weary man. Marl skipped the stairs and jumped, soaring over his enemy, prepared to crush his vile blood upon the frosted street. Hound doubled back by going into a tunnel arched under the bridge. Hound thought that he was safe for a spell until Marl's arm rammed its way through the tunnel's mouth. The fingers were clawing just inches from grazing Hound's foot.

The sight of this in his peripherals horrified his sense of safety and caused him to roll further away. Grimy thunderclaps festered over the tunnel's mouth. Marl was pushing his way in. The cement sprinkled into Hound's matted hair. He wished that he still had his hat as he simultaneously got the idea to get out his knife.

With another grope from the enormous hand, Hound timed it so that he could slice one of the giant's digits with his dagger. The hand promptly exited as Hound ran out of the tunnel's other side.

Once outside, he turned left. Citizens began wandering the streets again to see if the danger had passed along with the snowstorm. But they were met with a grisly sight. The beady eyes of Hound glowed out of his matted hair. The ensemble of a giant's finger blood upon him did not help make his impression any better as many cleared from his savage path.

Only a little girl stood still in utter awe and confusion of this curious excuse for a human. Not wanting to lose his escape, Hound pushed her out of his way.

After pushing the kid, he saw Marl coming down the street. When Hound saw this, he knew that a new diversion was in order. The girl that Hound pushed grabbed on to him out of fear of the incoming giant. Hound bolted her movements to the spot with his bloody knife dancing before her unblemished face.

"Come here, sweety. I'll save you from the giant. I'm a good guy."

"June!" It was the mother. She lost track of her daughter in all the confusion. She found June just in time to see the terrifying display just out of her reach past the crowd. "Get away from that man! He has a knife!"

"June, huh? Come on, June."

He saw the princess doll gripped in her arms. "I'm a knight- a hero. That monster stole my shining armor. Trust me."

Her trust was put into his hand. That hand was then made into a lever for Hound to lift and fling the child before the stomping path of Marl.

The mother was crumbled into a wash of weeping, unable to bare the sight of her little girl about to be trampled to pieces.

"Excuse me, ma'am," casually said Hound after passing the panicking mother.

Marl's eye was singular in his desire for revenge. But his ears were not deaf to the high-pitched wailing squeaking below him. It reminded him of the funny way in which his son cried when he was born. Stopping upon hearing this oddity from beyond time and the grave, he saw the child crawling on her knees just a giant step away from his big toe.

He opened his hand down to the small babe. She had some reddened knees from where she fell. She held on to her dolly the whole time. Marl's hand felt sticky from her knee's blood. His heart felt cleared when she cried. The mother's cries broke over this as she got pieces of fallen bricks to hurl at him.

"Give her back, you monster!" The remaining citizens joined in. These flying specks didn't hurt. They only annoyed him. To stop the annoyance, Marl put the girl down into her mother's rejoicing arms.

Marl was brought back to how much his wife loved his son before Hound came. His heart was singular again when the specks continued to spew after him. Being careful not to step on the others, he continued down the next street that Hound entered.

The crowd and the mother cursed the giant as he ran off. The smallest voice amongst these bitter people could only faintly whimper, "Thank you for not stepping on me, Mr. Giant."

This voice of gratitude and understanding was ever unknown to Marl as he sprinted on.

The orb trembled with hard beats as Marl chased Hound closer to the square again. Ilene could feel the quakes of Marl's bounds as they made her stumble into a crate behind her. Craigson was too distracted from helping her up to see a figure rise from the snowbanks outside of the ship's broken hull.

It was Dusk, using his albino deer's coat as snow cover to get the drop on Ilene during the calamity of the gun fight. Ilene's stumble was the moment that he was waiting for. After brushing the snow from the seamless cover of his coat, he pulled the sword out of his scabbard. Craigson had yet to turn around.

Ilene was about to yell out a warning when Craigson whipped around with his gun out. The look that flashed on to her face was enough for Craigson to sense danger. The gun fired. The burst of pain that blared upon Craigson's hands during the feedback made him drop the gun immediately. The shot got Dusk's hip. This stopped him for only a moment as he kicked the fallen gun away with his other leg. Dusk then got past his hip's throbbing as he thrust his sword into Craigson's throat.

Then he sliced it thoroughly.

Craigson made bizarre clicking sounds as he could only stand there twitching. The final click of his throat released a flood of blood on to the floor. This overflow bore down the gravity for his twitching limbs as he dropped to the ground. The red pool that developed made Ilene squirm away. Dusk's approach made her shrink off even more.

"Poor girl," Dusk cooed. "Her hero wasn't quite up to par. Maybe you shouldn't pick them off the streets. Now come along. I've got a country's good name to run through the mud with you."

Ilene screamed for help. Only further volleys of gunfire could answer her.

"Sorry, but they're a little busy with the first battle of the war- the war that will make Ur a great empire once more."

Ilene backed into something that fell- a broom. The pool of blood drew closer. She picked the broom up, not knowing what she was going to do with it.

"Are you joking?"

Suddenly knowing what she was going to do, she dipped the broom deeply into the blood between her and Dusk. She drove it diagonally forward with a rough jerk. Doing this flung the contents of the pool into a littered spray through the air and into Dusk's eyes. He winced.

With the lieutenant blinded, she darted up to the main deck. On deck, she looked in every direction for Isaac and Jake. When she caught sight of them, she clutched her arms between each of their shoulders. They saw Ilene's haggard eyes. They were startled by this sudden cameo.

"Ilene, what-"

Ilene heaved for air. She was forgetting to breathe. "Craigson, he-"

Hound ran out of a nearby tower at that moment and dashed behind the ship. What followed was Marl demolishing through the tower in pursuit. Seeing Hound make his way around the ship, Marl proceeded to grab the vessel again and push it over his enemy before he could get away. Everyone stopped shooting for fear of becoming the giant's next target.

As this shift in the deck spiraled everyone off-balance, Ilene managed to get it out. "Craigson is dead!"

Anguish for their loss and fear for their lives washed bold wrinkles over the faces of the brothers as they buried themselves into each other's arms. Ilene's skull was forced by the subversion of gravity into the ship's rails. The wood slammed her head back, followed by a gnawing headache.

This also happened to the brothers. But their turbulence off the rail threw them from the ship entirely. Isaac's raw hand locked upon the end of the rail to hang on. He could barely hold on to Jake. He was slipping.

CHAPTER 31
CROSSFIRE

Ilene watched in awe as Marl's face eclipsed the snow while he glared mercilessly down. His fingers were crushing the wood on the up-turned side of the ship. What was mercy to someone who was always hated and hounded? Even when he gave mercy, none was returned. This new creed weighed darkly in his breast as he neared his revenge, casting the shadow of the ship over the futilely fleeing Hound. Marl relished in this.

Many items slid down the diagonal deck during this time. An anchor bulldozed a mate straight into the ground. Ilene learned from this horrid sight, dodging the assorted crates and chests that nearly hit her too, as well as other falling human bodies. These fallen were trying to reach her hand for salvation, but she knew that they were only going to take her with them.

One item that Ilene had to let hit her was a rope. It was still attached to the mast. It dangled just out of reach from the desperate soldiers. One soldier got a grip, but it didn't last long. It seared through his fingers until he succumbed to the mass of dead below.

Ilene wrapped her hand in the cloak that she was wearing. She reached more and more for the rope until she got a handle on it. Ilene reached out to Isaac.

"Grab."

Isaac returned, "We'll never make it. You're not strong enough to hold on to us, let alone yourself."

Ilene secured a hold on his hand anyway. "Well, I say that I **am** strong enough!"

She really wasn't strong enough. But she held on anyway. Her left limb felt ready to snap off, holding the arms of the merchants clutched about it. Her right limb was hurting even worse. She could feel her hand bleeding through the confines of the cloak. The rope was blistering through.

As the final decline made the ship give out, Ilene could only hear Jake screaming through her pain to hang on. The pain grew greater while Jake ushered her on louder. Isaac was weeping loudly into his arm. He couldn't watch as the ground spiraled closer.

Ilene kicked the side of the deck with all of her remaining strength. This allowed her and her friends to swing away from the deck's destruction. The ship was demolished as it flattened into the ground. Wild swarms of broken boards and bodies erupted through the air.

She sailed over the holocaust below her. Mounds of dead and dying bodies lay before her. Ilene knew that this was where she had to land, least she swings back into the ruinous carnage of the broken ship. She just had to hang on until her swing's arch was on-point.

Ilene was weighed down to the point of slipping. Yet knowing that the lives of these men were her responsibility somehow gave her enough power to hold on until they swung close enough to the mound of bodies for her to finally let go.

Before a sense of falling could be felt, they already crashed into the decaying heap. To land in a mess of fallen bodies as if they were objects was a shame and a torment to Ilene as she felt herself getting sucked into the muddle of limbs cracked out of joint, twisted torsos, disfigured faces, and blood- more blood than should be inhaled.

Getting up to face her sores, Ilene hurled down her head to vomit on someone's snapped neck. After whispering sorry to the dead, she tried to grind her eyes shut to wish this nightmare away. Ilene slipped and laid her hand on another body. The body moved. She darted off it. It was Jake.

He had tears, blood, and vomit drenched over his jester's clothes. Not very funny. He sealed his arms around her and melted into sobs until they both fell to their knees. Isaac emerged from his landing spot. He came out with the least gore on him, but his limp suggested that his ankle was badly sprained from the fall.

Isaac joined them in their crying as he lamented into Ilene's ear. "I'm sorry, Ilene. I'm so sorry. I should have let you go home when we had the chance. Forgive me. Forgive me, Craigson. Please..."

None of them could guess how long they lay there in the pile of corpses- bound to each other. They mourned Craigson by only whimpering his name continually. It was all that they had. No one was there to provide musical accompaniment.

Out of the quiet of the aftermath's gray fog came a supreme command to fire.

Gun shots and arrows galore were released, but not for Ilene and her friends. Marl appeared from the gray fog, but not to attack. He was falling like an idol being tipped over. Marl's fall was heading straight for Ilene. They broke apart and ran. They pushed each other along as the towering shadow became darker with every second. With a final leap, the trio got ahead of Marl's skull by a breath.

What they did not miss was the cataclysmic aftershock from the great fall. The cobblestones shattered like shrapnel. It turned the gray fog beige, as if the atmosphere were permeated with human skin. When this fog began to die down, the arrow-punctured head stared blankly before them like an ancient Kenorian totem with a curse upon it.

Marl abruptly began tossing and turning in his death thralls. The arrows were poisoned tipped. He made pathetic yowls of thunderous drones. He went on as his haunting twitches kicked up more stone about him.

Soon his movements slowed down. His yelling quieted. He straightened his back, and he stopped moving.

"The giant is dead," said an unknown voice echoing in the distance.

"We got to get out of here," said Isaac to his comrades. More of the dust cleared up as they went off. One cloud opened to the victorious band of Ursians with Dusk at its helm. Dusk had Craigson's blood stained on his face like a sloppy mask.

"Gentlemen," he brashly said whilst addressing his soldiers. "I have grown very frustrated with merely capturing the vessel of Omega. We're killing her nice and slowly instead."

The trio turned and ran from the troops. Dusk sighed. "Nice and **quickly** then. Men: fire your arrows on my mark..."

Ilene bumped into another soldier. But he wore armor, not deer skins. It was the Pangeans. "We won't let him take you," said the familiar voice of their leader.

A series of arrows were halted by strong shields that each nearby knight lent to fence a safe barrier over the frightened three.

The head knight drew his sword as he rallied his troops with the Pangean motto. "Always overcome!"

"All will fall before the people of Alpha!" returned Dusk during his call to arms.

The stampedes from both sides clashed into each other with eager speed. The Pangeans seemed to be winning. Their superior armor and weapons fended off the Ursians. Sturdier swords blew down the poorer Ursian weapons. The Ursians may have had guns, but they mostly had to resort to their bows. The Pangeans had more guns with more ammo and used this to their advantage.

Yet the grossly outnumbered Pangeans were slowly overwhelmed despite their successes. It helped that some Ursians were still far off from the battle. The cabal of distant Ursians opened fire on the Pangeans with a blizzard of arrows. Even with the newest model of guns, the Pangeans were too far off to get a bead on the snipers. Thus, most of the Ursians survived because of Dusk's clever strategy. Only a few Pangean soldiers of the original force remained to face the endless odds.

The Pangeans carried on the fight. Some others were not so lucky as some were immediately killed as the poisoned arrows pierced the cracks in their armor. It began to bode awfully when even the wall of shield-wielders commissioned to guard Ilene was attacked.

The enclosure began to shrink with each slam by the enemy. The Ursians were not seen from Ilene's side of the shields, but their presence was felt when each protector was bludgeoned with a fury that made their resolve weaken.

A dropped sword slid under one of the shields into the trio's dwindling sanctuary. Isaac picked it up.

"We're going to have to fight when the shields fall," he told Ilene and Jake with nervous reluctance.

"You don't know how to use one of those," stated Jake. "You can barely hold it up."

Isaac failed at trying to look more confident with a shrug as he hoisted the sword by the side of his hip. "Maybe not. But I've learned a few tricks from my acting career. Remember the sword practice that we got from that expert for *The Ship of Nightmares*?"

"That production was a flop. You kept dropping your sword on opening night."

"I got better. By the last night, you would have figured that I was born to fight with one."

"Isaac. This is serious. Just because you used a sword well in a play does not translate to the actual battlefield."

"I know this is serious, Jake. Don't you think I've known that ever since we lost-"

He couldn't finish saying the name.

"I know this is serious, okay? That's why I've got to give one last performance. I'll hold them off while you two get away. I'll catch up."

"I remember your last performance at the palace," said Ilene, nearly shouting as the beats upon the shields were growing louder. "You died at the end."

"Yes," said Isaac. "I remember that. I believe that play was called *In His Lord's Service.*"

He paused to shutter at the name. "Craigson composed his finest sonata during my death scene... I hear it even now."

Isaac looked at Ilene and Jake. "Lady and gentleman, I give you: the greatest performance of a lifetime."

Just then: the first of the soldier's legs buckled as the shields were broken through by the enemy. Isaac sprang past the falling Pangeans to face the Ursians. He fought valiantly. Ilene and Jake held on to each other as they huddled behind their brave friend.

Isaac parried many thrusts that were slung his way. He was surprised to see that he was better than he thought he was. Only, his attackers began to gather on every side. Soon a sword ripped across the back of his shirt. An Ursian's shoulder tackled into Isaac, and he dropped the sword.

Before Isaac was beaten to his knees, an Ursian blocked Ilene's view of her fallen friend. This tall soldier looked down at her and Jake while widely smiling. He lifted his sword to bear down on Ilene. Both she and Jake shuffled away from him. But there was no escape.

CHAPTER 32
HELPLESS

Ilene's assassination was interrupted by an extra group of Pangeans piling into the fray.

The Pangean leader himself shot the smiling Ursian with his pistol. With the ground cleared of foes, Ilene and Jake made their way over to Isaac. His injury was wetting the back of his shirt.

"Oh, Isaac," lamented Jake.

"I'm okay," Isaac kept muttering as they each helped him to his feet by the end of each arm.

Ilene felt something scratch at her leg. She thought that she was being cut by an enemy. It was actually Isaac's sword. It was still in his hand, dangling down to her leg. She was wary of the implement now that she could see it.

The sounds of the battling throng growled behind their fleeing backs. A great figure jumped in front of their path. It was the Pangean leader. "Get out of here! Now! Hide behind the giant's dead body. Go!"

They heeded his command and made their way to the dead carcass across the field, wherein the knight believed that they'd be safely hidden. They caught the decaying stench on the wind before even reaching Marl. Jake pulled his collar over his mouth and nose to protect himself from the approaching musk. Ilene made a similar precaution with her cloak.

Ilene felt badly for the man who originally loaned her the cloak. Isaac couldn't use his current cloak since he gave it to Craigson. So, Ilene used her spare hand to cover his nose. Then, they got to the corpse.

They first arrived near the head. Marl's strands of gray hair were stiffened on end. His mouth hung open. His eyes were fixed to the sky. They cautiously made their way around him once satisfied that he was really dead.

Once they revolved around his skull, they proceeded to hide by the tip of his moldy elbow. Then they sat down. The sounds of battle were only a faint muffle at this point. They were not sure if the distance or its nearing end was causing this decreasing volume.

"We got to dress these wounds," said Jake as he took off his jester's collar and stuck it into Isaac's flooding back.

"You'd better," grumbled Isaac like his old self. "I'm starting to lose feeling back there."

Ilene likewise sacrificed her cloak to stop the bleeding. The smell barging into her mouth made her cough. She nearly puked again. She managed to barely hold it in.

With this work done, they waited for things to die down. Jake spoke. "Now what?"

"Wait I suppose," suggested Ilene.

It wasn't a bad idea until a series of nearby steps were heard clomping a steady tempo on the cobblestones. Isaac nearly jumped to his feet. He was stopped by his cut. "Who is that?"

"It's coming from around the head," said Ilene.

The footstep's tempo picked up until it reached its peak. Dusk slid out of his run from around the head, sword drawn. Craigson's blood was dried with crust over his face.

"It was him," Ilene said without control. "He killed Craigson."

With no more words, Dusk charged upon his prey. This time, Isaac was able to fight his way up. He charged for Dusk. "You killed my brother!"

Isaac was ready to swing as he ran closer. Jake couldn't stop him. Too late. Dusk side-stepped Isaac's bull-rush and side-swiped his flying fist back into the merchant's throat. With a fleeting cough, Isaac fell like dead weight. Ilene didn't know what to do. Then Jake began ushering her to climb up the giant's arms.

"Lose him over the other side. I'll hold him off."

"Jake, I-"

Jake would not hear any of it as he pushed her into the gigantic arm. Ilene grabbed the bushes of hair dangling from the arm and roughly made her way to the top. Jake and Isaac's cries were clearly heard. Ilene didn't want to look down to see what Dusk was doing.

Once on top, Ilene balanced her way across the arm. Relief actually began to sink in a little when she was on the chest. A serene view of all the town square was dwarfed under her. She could see the rubble of the warehouse and the ship. She could spy the dead and the fighting. Even the most horrible of sights looked beautiful from on high, almost like she was a Goddess who-

But then she turned to see Dusk climbing the arm twice as fast as she did. Dusk climbed towards her.

The arms of Jake put a stop to that as they coiled around Dusk and ripped his course away from Ilene. She got further away until she heard Jake growl out when Dusk backhanded him off the edge. Ilene stared at the edge while praying that her friend wasn't dead. Then something was thrown to the top of the chest's edge. It wasn't Jake latching on safely as she hoped, but Isaac's sword getting tossed up.

Isaac's voice joined it from below. "Take it! Defend yourself!"

Ilene sprang for it. Dusk made it up. He was already wise to her. He slashed at her spot of retrieval. She ducked under the whisk that blew over her back. She had the sword. Dusk slashed down for his second attempt. Ilene jumped back just in time. She had a weapon- her only chance. It was heavy. She was weak. Dusk was strong. This one sword had to be enough to save her.

Ilene stuck to the defensive. Dusk jabbed in unexpected places, only to have Ilene swipe them away. Dusk's face of red jabbed into her eyes as it kept wildly following her. As the red face followed her, she slowly realized that Dusk was telegraphing all of his attacks so that Ilene could block them. Dusk was toying with her.

What made Ilene's mouth run dry through all of this was the question of how much longer before Dusk got bored of his game. The answer came when a quick slide of his leg reached behind her knee. With a jerk of his leg, and a thrust of his free hand, Ilene fell into the hallow of Marl's collar bone. Dusk was veiled by the fleshy cove's exclusion of light, making the man look like a shadow standing over Ilene. Ilene couldn't get up. She felt like something was twisted in her leg.

The shadow could not help but boast from his perch. "Poor Princess Ilene. Life's not fair, is it? You were locked in your castle for so long that you must have started to wonder if life was actually like one of your little fairy tales. Not quite the case. If it were so, a big strong man would have barged in and saved your dainty life."

Dusk girded his sword over his head. He was preparing to leap upon Ilene to finish her. "Take comfort. You'll join your lost maid soon enough."

Ilene embraced the idea as she closed her eyes in anticipation. A final prayer: *Alpha, please weigh my virtues over my vices. I just want to see Marlene again...*

With a momentous snap, her eyes were bolted open. Dusk was no more. In his place hung a fist the size of a carriage dripping profusely. Marl was not dead. He merely lost consciousness from the poison. Dusk was immediately killed like an insect bloodily crumpled in a mighty vice.

Marl sobbed happily, making his throat bounce along with Ilene. "Did I get him? Is the man who killed my sweet boy gone?"

Ilene was still panting and trying to process what happened.

Marl must have only been half conscious- not fully aware of who he just killed. Feeling the slowing exhales from his throat under her feet, Ilene could tell that Marl was going to die at any moment. So, Ilene gave him the answer that he wanted to hear.

"You got him, Marl. You killed Mr. Hound."

"Then," bellowed the shrinking voice, "I can die happy. My son has been avenged. Now I can face him without shame in the next life. Thank you… thank you…"

He breathed his last. The fist wilted open to drop Dusk back on to the chest. Dusk's body was a mangled corpse. His flesh and bones were fused into a shapeless mesh with pierced bones at its fringes. Only his mouth and one eye were the facial bits that could peek out from this mess. The eye was fixed on the princess, as if still alive enough to fulfill its mission of seeing her suffer and ultimately die. The mouth was hanging open, drooling blood.

Normally, Ilene would turn away from such a wretched sight. But as her panting finally subsided, something about the macabre abhorrence drew her closer. Ilene had seen so much death. Marlene, Craigson, and many others. An invisible link to death manifested in her. At this time, Ilene no longer could be repulsed by the dead. Their company had become a part of her. This force pulled her in like a curious animal. When Ilene's steps brought her face in front of the angrily fixed eye, she could only stare back as she took her finger and shut its lid closed.

Ilene kicked at the dead mass. The form twitched a little. Ilene did it again with screaming vindication. This time her kick tipped Dusk over. The mass of flesh rolled off the chest and down to the legs before crashing to the ground. It was shattered to pieces, with only the head intact to floppily roll away. Ilene felt the same satisfaction that Marl died with.

"Craigson," she whispered, "you're free. Play your beautiful music for all time."

Ilene could almost hear the sonata that Isaac mentioned earlier echo in the wind. Ilene looked down to see the sword that Dusk had dropped before getting crushed. She took it. The blood that it had reminded her of Marlene's death.

Ilene whispered to the dead again. "Fear not, Marlene. You will be avenged as well." Ilene then began speaking to the future dead. "Empress Lida, you may gain the world from this war, but by the end I will make sure that you regret ever starting it."

Ilene heard Isaac call for her. She climbed down the side of the arm's hair. Isaac and Jake were lying by the wall of the arm. "We saw Marl's hand jump up there. Scared me."

Jake asked, "Is Dusk dead?"

"Yes," Ilene coldly said, trying to hold back a grin that she knew only villains in her old stories gave out at the thought of another's demise. Ilene turned it into a deformed pout instead.

"It's all over now," exhaled Isaac.

"No. It's only just begun," said Ilene.

"Maybe," said Jake cautiously. "But it is for you. This violent world is not for you."

Ilene made a snapping turn to Jake. "How do you know? I've only had a small taste of it."

"That's more than anyone should have."

Ilene pointed to the many dead, including Marl. "Then what about them?"

"They're soldiers." Isaac gulped sadly. "That's their duty."

"It wasn't Marlene's duty. It wasn't Craigson's duty."

They stopped talking.

Ilene held a vow in her heart. *No matter how many wars stand between me and her, I will learn how to fight to protect myself and others. And I shall kill the empress herself. Then no one else will suffer at her hand. This I vow in the name of your love, Marlene.*

Ilene kissed the handle of the sword. Jake could not keep his eyes off the blood that was all about Ilene's foot. Jake was about to inquire on this when the ground shook again as if a legion of giant's had just landed.

This was a quake like no other before it. Ilene felt her feet slowly levitate from the ground. The air became like a warped gust.

A citizen was heard yelling. "Some Ursian ships have arrived under us and are firing at the orb."

"Princeberg is falling!" someone else cried.

CHAPTER 33
DISASTER

Ilene needed to ground herself. She stuck her sword into the ground made fertile by the explosive events of late. It stayed put, but she had to hang on or the falling orb's gravity was going to throw her into the sky and drop the princess to her death. The impact of the cannons was heard blaring into the seams of the orb's surface. Isaac and Jake held on to her legs.

Many people were not able to secure a hold on to something to get grounded. Hundreds began to ascend to their doom as if they were in a hurricane. Ilene's hands were burning and ripping into her core. She could no longer hold on.

This made her want to hold on all the tighter, but gravity's force caused the sword to be plucked from the ground. Ilene's horrible ascent began... only to abruptly end with the orb finally landing into the ocean. Ilene and the merchants were smacked into the ground after only being aloft for a few inches. They were sore from the hard touchdown all the same.

Isaac asked, "What was that all about?"

As Ilene cranked herself up from her sore knees, she hypothesized, "Those ships must have been reinforcements for when Dusk was late bringing me in."

Isaac helped her back up. "Looks like they wanted you dead rather than alive this time."

The world became dusty again. This time the world had a dirty brown hue. After they helped each other up, they began to walk the streets. Many buildings were demolished beyond repair and turned into sloshy garbage piles. Some were still finishing up their total crumbling. Many citizens wandered the streets as well. Women were holding on to their babies. Others were weeping for their lost children. They could not help but turn from these sights.

The trio tried to climb through the jagged wreckage. During this part of their trek, they saw some people digging others out of the debris- if only to retrieve the bodies of their beloveds. Others were in search of lost riches, like one gleeful man abandoning the circle of scavengers with a jewel in his hand. Isaac accidentally walked in front of the man to see that it was Miles.

Isaac turned away in disappointment as soon as their eyes met. The three looked to each other to silently decide whether they should help. The thief swayed their opinion as they decided to pass the rummagers by. Jake sobbed the name of Alpha into his hands until it sadly quieted with each step that he made.

Isaac saw a great gathering ahead, near the edge of Princeberg's fringes. Isaac gestured to the large congregation's objective.

"Pangean ships are evacuating survivors."

Jake asked, "Now where did **they** come from?"

Ilene replied, "We must have orbited near a Pangean colony. These ships must have been on their routine rounds near the harbor. When they saw Princeberg fall, they decided to help evacuate everyone."

Behind them a series of explosions rocked the remaining debris to pieces. The Ursian ships that originally assaulted Princeberg were beginning their bombardment again with renewed zest on the opposite coast of the orb-made-island. Ilene and the merchants ran away with each step unbalanced by the blasts upon the town.

They got to the crowds for the Pangean evacuations. They couldn't get through. With the cannon fire falling closer, no one was willing to give up their way on. If anything, this made people more desperate to fight through. Some people even got knocked into the water. The knights of Pangea from the arriving ships could barely keep order. Some of them were almost knocked into the water as well.

Then a shot rang out. It was closer than the cannon balls. So, this got everyone's attention. This gave the spotlight to the leader of the Pangean troops that saved Ilene. He and his remaining men marched closer to Ilene's end of the crowd.

"Listen up," commanded the leader. "Women and children shall go first. An orderly line will be formed and there will be no fighting, or my men and I will execute you on the spot."

The critics began their rounds.

"What if there's no room on board?"

"I can't be separated from my daughter. She lost her mother."

"Tyrants- the lot of those Pangeans!"

Ignoring these complaints, the armed soldier turned to Ilene and gestured to the coast of Rodinia- whose misty mountains she just then noticed on the northern horizon as he said, "You will join us on the next ship, my lady. You'll be safe once we get you to the Pangean embassy within the hills of Rodinia."

Without a word, Ilene followed the soldiers with her friends bringing up the rear. One of the more zealous soldiers noticed the two merchants tailing Ilene. He confronted the two with an unsheathed sword.

"Away, vagabonds," he ordered as he believed that they were more refugees trying to sneak in a free ride.

"Wait a minute," protested Jake with a stomp of his foot. "We're with her. She said that we could join her."

The stomp was taken for an attack. So as Jake debated with these words, the soldier jabbed into the jester's stomach with the butt of his sword. Jake was shattered into the ground before he could react.

Isaac was ready to fight this bastard for mistreating his little brother. This commotion possessed Ilene's attention. Ilene saw the abusive soldier raining kicks on poor Jake while also keeping Isaac's fists at bay with his threatening sword. Ilene approached the scene as she lifted the heavy sword still being dragged at her side.

Normally, Ilene would have resolved this conflict with patient, diplomatic reasoning. The anger that boiled from the troubled woman's teeth grinded these ideals to dust.

The soldier was at the height of his revels atop the heaving fool's chest when he felt something. A rock was lobbed at the side of his helmet. He couldn't recover from the sudden vibrations in time to turn and face the interloper. There was also a fear that the fist-ready brother of his victim would turn on him once he lowered his guard.

Instead, his head was torqued around for him by a hand's fingers arching into the ridges of his helmet's visor. This stomach-churning twist put him face-to-face with the vengeful princess. The soldier was about to push her off when he felt an uninvited poke on the front of this neck. His eyes looked down to see Ilene's sword. Her hold on his metal veil kept the helpless grunt too unbalanced to move away from the weapon.

"Ilene," gasped the leader. "What are you doing?"

Ilene didn't answer. She was too busy enjoying the pathetic whimpering of her victim. She stopped enjoying his sobs when they began to remind her of her own cries after Marlene died. Yet she did not release him. She decided to finally answer the question so that she could drown out the horrid mewling.

"These men are coming with me."

The leader looked at the merchants, confused. "With you?"

"Yes. They were once performers in my palace. My unhappy lot has brought us back together. They've shared each of my trials in kind. So, they've surely earned their place at my side. If your thugs even think of standing in the way of their just reward-"

"You'll kill him? That would make you a traitor. We'd..."

He tried to break this as calmly as he could manage. "We'd have to hang you."

Ilene looked deeper into the cracks of the helmet's ridges that she still clutched. He was breathing heavily in the echo of his helmet's metal chamber. The sun finally began to penetrate the blotch of gray clouds. Winter was no more for Princeberg. This illuminated the man's face, but mostly his eyes. They seemed so small, so afraid- like a child's eyes.

The commander spoke more sternly. "You've made your point, my lady. We're always at your command. We'll take these fellows in. Just let the boy go, and we'll forget the whole thing. We understand that you've been through a great deal, so-"

His dealings were shut up when Ilene gently released the fresh-faced recruit. Ilene stared into the sun's golden rays bathing over his face. His face was bewildered, but no less hardened by the trauma. Ilene bowed respectfully. This was done with the polite elegance that she was raised on, as if she had just performed a mere social embarrassment. Unsure of what to make of her, he merely bowed in return and then hobbled away.

Finally calmed down, she held her hand out to the leader.

"Lead us to our ship, commander."

The commander nodded and he led her on. Ilene looked to

see Jake and Isaac, who both looked equal parts shocked and gladdened by her words and actions on their behalf.

"Perhaps," she began while rubbing her neck, "I over-did it just now."

They nodded dumbly. Ilene lowered her reddened cheeks down in shame as she scolded herself as Marlene would have.

"One must consider every drop of liquid that one pours, or it may overflow and overwhelm your cup. So too must you consider every action that you take, little Ilene."

The departed maid used to say this to the impetuous girl, who did not understand this saying until it was compared to how Alpha weighs the virtues of people for the afterlife. At this moment, she felt that she understood this idea even better, in a more material sense.

The ship that they departed on gave the party their own exclusive plank to enter upon. It was guarded by more members of the Pangean guard. They kept the begging multitude away, barely. Ilene could not help but stare at some of their faces. Some were in sorrow beyond her ability to stomach. Luckily, she passed by these faces with a few steps. But then she saw more. The wrinkles of their faces were rolled into a distorted mush, like masks. Yet these were not masks. They were the masks of humanity at last torn away to reveal the animals cringing for survival within. Their ashen hands desperately reached out from the wall of guards.

Their smell paralleled their looks. They smelled despairingly ashen and bland. How many of these refugees crawled out of or into a fallen building to save themselves or a loved one? Their sound was the worst of it. Every voice was a trumpet of pity.

"Please help me!"

"The giant destroyed my restaurant! I can cook for the royals! I can! Take me in!"

"I'll starve without my job!"

"Down with the Pangean tyrants!"

"You fools have ignored the suffering of the common people for the last time!"

"I'll protest! I'll lead a revolt! I'll do whatever I have to so that I can see justice done."

"Listen. I'll pay you to let me on. Every cent I've got. There's nothing here for me. I lost my whole family. I've nothing. Look, I've even got money from their... bodies... Oh please... just... just..."

He was cut off by the pushing wall of soldiers. They had to be indifferent to perform their duty. Never mind a tear or two that might have passed from them. Such small tears didn't provide enough weight to bring down this great wall.

Though it was much calmer aboard the ship, the world did not look much better. Besides, the roaring of the people still echoed to the top of the deck. The tense stillness on the ship is what impaled Ilene's heart with each trod to her chambers. There were blanketed passengers that the crew had to navigate around to go about raising the sails and retracting the planks from the coast.

These people were more wrapped up in their own misery than the cloths that encompassed their chilled bodies. Their sadness did not make them ugly so much as hidden in shame. The deck was mostly made up of women and children. Most of these groups had one or two too few a husband or father around. One of the few men who managed to get on-board rose when Ilene passed by him. He pointed vengefully to her.

"It was you! You're the reason all these people died! The Ursians were right! You're Omega come to tear this whole world asunder! Well, I'll spread the word. I'll make sure that the whole world knows of your evil, along with the evil of the rest of the Pangean Empire! You hear me, princess? Your reign is-"

The man was dragged away by the attending Pangean guards. "Take him to the brig."

"I'll not be silenced! I **will** be heard!"

He was never heard from again.

Ilene could not bear to turn around during this episode. The other passengers held their peace as well.

"Don't listen to him, Ilene," said Isaac with his hand around her elbow. "It's just more of Ur's nasty propaganda. These hard times have a way of getting to people."

"Yeah. These hard times are getting to me too."

Ilene walked from the loving grasp.

Only the Pangean commander remained after the rabble-rouser was taken away. So, the soldier led the trio down the stairs to the lower decks. They stopped at a door.

"This is the captain's quarters. This is the finest room on the ship. He'll be on the deck during this short trip to Rodinia. You'll find plenty of food and a bed to rest in with his compliments. Any questions before we embark?"

"Yes, commander." It was Jake. "Perhaps I could volunteer to lend a hand on deck? You boys seem to need all of the help that you can get."

The soldier looked at the tattered jester in contempt. How dare he speak out of turn when it was in fact Princess Ilene being addressed. Still, the man did politely offer some help.

"Very well, jester. Follow me."

"Call me Jake." He turned to say his farewells. "You both get some rest. You've been through enough for one day. I'll see you again when we hit Rodinia."

Ilene and Isaac were too tired to argue. The room was an oval with sparse decorations and furniture. Its carpeted floor had ample room as a result. Isaac went for the bed with his last stretch of energy. Ilene kept her place at her end of the room. Ilene became invested in a window. She saw the needy of Princeberg shrink away after a shipmate's above command to pull anchor.

"Ilene? Are you coming to bed? I can sleep on the couch over there if you wish."

Ilene shook her head without looking back. "That's okay, Isaac. I'm not as tired as I thought I was. You go to sleep without me. I'll wake you when we arrive."

Isaac did not need to hear anymore. He slumbered. Isaac gulped up sweet rest as he melted into the covers. This was the first time that Ilene was alone for what seemed to be ages. Ilene spent that time looking into the port hole as Princeberg shrank into a speck. She could make out some ships with the yellow Ursian flags drawing closer to Princeberg. These were the same ships that fired upon the orb. They just missed an engagement with the Pangean vessels if not for their exit.

"The beasts have come from their shadows to devour their prey," Ilene noted hatefully.

"But they won't find her," she quipped in reference to herself.

Ilene spent the rest of her ride staring into the window, but she was mostly looking into her reflection. Ilene was wrapped up in her anger and sorrow.

"Forgive me, Marlene, but I'm going to kill them all."

CHAPTER 34 THE EMPRESS IN THE FALLOUT

Empress Lida was not happy.

When Monote failed to send a letter regarding his mission after half a month, she knew that something must have gone awry. Thankfully, as planned, the Pangean council was duped into giving a good portion of the princess's 'ransom' to Ur (this being back before the fools realized the truth of Ilene's whereabouts that were later informed by an unknown source).

So, some semblance of a financially stable treasury was being formed for the government of her people again- her first triumph as ruler of Ur. She was thus able to afford bringing a fleet of ships with her to take care of any interference that may have stopped their plans, whether that interference was big or small- army or assassin.

One captain in her fleet had misunderstood her orders. For as soon as they found the orb of Princeberg, one ship began to immediately open fire. The others followed suit. Lida got her own ship's captain to light the signal torch to cease fire. The empress saw no need to fire before assessing the situation on the orb itself. But it was too late. Most of her ships were destroyed in the orb's fall.

Lida's ship, and some select others, survived. A naval battle was avoided with the nearby Pangeans as the empress's ships creeped to the other side of the new island, just as Ur's foes were out of range with Ilene aboard. Lida ordered her vessel to lower anchor after seeing the Pangeans making for the coast of Rodinia in the distance.

The empress enlisted some Ursian warriors to follow her into town to find Monote. The Ursians fanned the crowds away, with a ferocity to match that of the Pangean's, to make a path for her excellency. Lida didn't even turn an eye to the suffering about Princeberg's rubble. Eventually, Lida found the giant laid out in the square. She was astounded by this sight.

"It is as if the end-times were really being brought to truth before my eyes."

Lida began quoting *The Holy Volume*. "'And my people shall be assaulted by the giants of Omega. But my people who are faithful shall smite them down as was in days of old.'"

Lida walked closer to the large carcass. A smaller carcass paralyzed her- this being what was left of Lieutenant Dusk. Lida panted in barely controlled hysterics as she drew closer to the dismembered head and twisted chunks of limbs. This broken pot of bone and flesh was gathering many flies that took off upon the empress's approach. Lida thus panted until she reached the dead lieutenant. Then she fell before him, on her knees. Lida gazed on at the lifeless head with nary a word nor a tear. She pulled something out of one of her pouches. It was Monote's veil.

Lida spoke to the dead. "The plan was to let you lead a group into Princeberg, find and defame Ilene along with the Pangeans while capturing her in order to bolster the rest of the world to our nation's cause. I didn't think that there would be a chance of you-"

Lida was plunged back to the words of the cruel past- ready to torture her worse than any enemy could. Lida recalled Monote's final words to her before he left Ur forever.

"What better disguise than to simply remove my veil and change my name, mother?"

"What would you call yourself?"

"I'm thinking of a verse in *The Volume*: 'I am the shadow in plain sight, the dusk to spread over the lusts of the damned Omega's hateful designs.'"

Lida approved of this. "Indeed, Monote. And with your personal combat training that you've subjected yourself to since your youth upward, it will be easy for me to get you a command position."

"I look forward to serving our nation, mother."

"I as well, Monote. Now remove your veil. I'll keep it and return it to you when your work is done."

Monote took it off and handed it to Lida, but she could not take it. Something held her back.

"Empress? Are you all right?"

Lida finally remembered to blink. "I'm fine. It's just... you look an awful lot like the last empress if..."

"If she were a man instead of a woman?"

Lida nodded solemnly. "It comes with being the heir. They say that all Ursian royalty is born with the face of the mother instead of the father."

"Do I still have your trust though I have the visage of your former rival?"

Lida ceremonially placed both of her hands on Monote's shoulders. "Monote, I know that you've yet to hear a kind word in your life, so here is the first: I don't take what you have now just done lightly. I know that I am the first pair of eyes to see your true face since you were born. I thus know that I can trust you with my life. Although you are not of my flesh, you are still my dearest son, and all that you have suffered will be worth it.

For my reward will be plentiful upon you."

As they embraced, Monote said this into Lida's ear: "I had my doubts as to how this venture would go. But now that I know that there is at least one person in all the world that believes in me, I have the confidence that I can do anything. Thank you, mother... thank you."

It was the first and last time that he called her mother without a tone of sarcasm.

Lida was brought back to the present by a startling sight. A mound of nearby bodies was stirring. A wry vagabond freed himself from the pile of the dead. He was dressed in bloody shreds of clothing. He was shambling closer towards the holy empress after he stumbled free. Her guards were at the ready to mow the stranger down with arrows, but he wouldn't stop approaching. Lida gestured them to disarm.

"Tell me, survivor: who are you? And what happened to the lieutenant during the battle?

The man chortled past a series of obnoxious coughs until he regained his voice.

"Excuse me. I must seem so terribly under-dressed. For you must be the new empress of Ur that everyone is so excited about. Congratulations on moving up."

The man chortled in a smoother fashion after his statement. Lida pounced upon him when he was a couple steps away. She held him in a death grip with her sword sharply lying in-wait below. Monote's veil was scrunched into the same hand as the sword.

"When the empress questions, you answer her, boy."

She felt a disturbing prick over her hand that was on his throat. He had swiftly removed a knife from his sleeve and held it to her wrist.

"You can kill me for my lack of posturing, but I'll make sure that you bleed out fast. For I cut deep. Then you'll never get your answers."

Lida squinted, crushing his head between her eye lids. Lida tossed him back to the ground.

He got up and dusted himself off as he said, "I was born with some nancy's name that I don't care to remember. But my friends and enemies call me Mr. Hound."

"Why do they call you that?"

"… I'm loyal like a pet hound."

Lida faced away from him, looking over the dismembered head while also examining the veil in her hand as she asked her second question again. "What happened here?"

Hound recognized the dead man's face as he got closer to it next to Lida. Hound noted the stilted emotion that she held in the faltering balance of her gaze.

"I was trying to report the princess to the Ursian base... for fear of the Goddess. I knew that if anyone could stop her, it was the chosen people of Alpha. A fight broke out- no, a battle... a great battle. It was a battle between Ursians, Pangeans, and even that damn giant-!"

Hound got too worked up over mentioning the one who almost killed him. He almost yelled as if to spite the dead Marl ahead of him. But he calmed himself.

"But the battle came at a cost. Guys like me were caught in its center."

Lida glared over the man whom she dwarfed. "What about the man here? What about Lieutenant Dusk?"

Hound could barely push off his tempting desire to smile. After Marl knocked over the last ship, the dust that it created provided Hound with enough cover to nestle into the stink-hole of dead bodies until the chaos blew over. A few vomits were a small price to pay. He briefly recalled Ilene screaming while in her flight from Dusk. Hound would know that scream anywhere. But that was all that he had to go on. Some exaggeration was thus in order to meet his ends.

Hound pushed off the smile and feigned sobering pathos. "During the fight, I saw him get captured. The princess ordered her soldiers to hold the lieutenant down while she took a sword and... well, you know the rest."

Lida listened intently. When he was finished, she drew a heavy breath. The veil was still in her hand. She knelt respectfully to Monote. Lida softly covered the veil over his face.

"Rest easy, Monote," she whispered. "May your veil now cover you in peaceful honor and no longer in shame. Though you were born out of iniquity, you have earned your place as one of Ur's greatest heroes. Goodbye, my son."

The wind picked up. It made everyone's capes and clothes ripple in the long note of its flow. With this gust came a piece of paper that smacked into Lida's leg as she stood up. She peeled it off and looked at it. It was the wanted poster for Princess Ilene. Lida looked at the woman who killed her son. Lida gave the poster to the head guard.

"Make sure that posters such as this are put up in every orb, isle, and city of every nation out there. Inform all who would spread the word: fellow soldiers, travelers, town criers, and leaders. The Goddess has risen through her vessel- the princess of Pangea. She must be destroyed, along with the rest of that

Godless nation. They must all burn in the fire of justice, as is Alpha's will."

Hound's hand fell on her shoulder. "Sorry to interrupt, but I must ask: is the Ursian army taking recruits?"

"The more help that I have getting that miserable wretch into my hands the better. Princess Ilene will die, and over her body... Ur will rise again."

Ilene did not hear this vow of vengeance that mirrored her own. Princeberg was completely out of sight within the hour. The ship was almost to the coast of Rodinia when she heard a far different sound. At first, it was only the sound of Isaac tossing and turning within the bed. Then he began to groan out horrid sobs.

"Craigson... Craigson..."

Ilene abandoned her meditation to see Isaac's still sleeping, yet unrested, face washed in sadness. Isaac kept repeating his chant for the one he lost. Ilene made a step towards him, unsure of whether to wake him or not. Then the tossing caused him to fall from the bed and crash into the floor. Then the real crying began. Ilene shot her way to the down-fallen man trembling.

He shouted out in utter dejection, "Craigson, no... I can't believe you're gone! I just can't. You were my brother, my friend..."

Ilene went to her knees to pick Isaac's arms up for a tender embrace. She was barely holding him up as he didn't even want to hold himself up. For he was weighed down by the thought of life without his brother. Ilene popped out a few tears of her own as she tried to soothe him.

"It's okay, Isaac. You're okay."

After whispering this, Isaac began to hold himself up as he adjusted his own knees and rested his trembling sobs into the cleft of Ilene's shoulder.

It was within these muffled confines that she heard and felt Isaac say, "Why did we ever help you? He's gone now because of it."

He cried on without ever mentioning what he said, as if it never happened. Ilene did not know how to react to this. Before she could decide on a proper reaction, she heard a yell of triumph on the upper deck.

"Down anchor!"

Ilene then looked away from the miserable fellow to see out the window that overlooked the bed. The army of shrub-shaped trees that dwelled on Rodinia's mountainous coast appeared before her. A family of birds flew from these tremendous hills into the distance of the sky, whose sun was ready to set upon the grave day.

Isaac got up after patting Ilene on the back one last time. As he reeled in a final sniff, Isaac said, "Thank you, Ilene. I needed that. I… dreamt that he was disappearing before me. If only we could have…"

Isaac stared out at the port hole in which the distant Princeberg was last seen.

"Well," he stopped, "never mind. Let's go find Jake."

Ilene agreed, although it was hard for her to dismiss the blame that Isaac placed on her for Craigson's demise. Part of Ilene actually thought that he was correct.

CHAPTER 35
NOSTALGIA

They joined back up with Jake on the upper deck. The laboring jester was just finishing with helping another shipmate push a cannon to the side of the ship, no doubt preparing for a possible Ursian invasion. The three refugees were about to exit the ship with attending guards when a chattering round of familiar drums were heard by Ilene. They were rumbling in the distance with feverish fruition until they stopped with a sudden quiet.

"The king and queen are approaching," said a voice among the refugees.

It was true. It was the well-known musical overture for every place that they went. Ilene knew it well from her constantly forced attendance to royal proceedings during her innocent days. When the drumming ended, a new rumble began. The building volume of hooves permeated the air. A great row of horsemen broke from the gateway of foliage down a rocky path to the coast that was seated below the ship's hasty landing. The drummers were one of the last to be seen riding down. They had their instruments strapped to their chests and their drumsticks sheathed. Then the king and queen of Pangea followed them.

At their appearance, whether for delight or anger, the refugees of Princeberg began to clamor for a chance to get off the boat. The Pangean guardsmen struggled to keep up with the gentry's descent off the lowering planks. Through this riot, some guards managed to break up a way for the princess to walk through. Ilene walked a relieved, but nervous, beeline to her mother and father who stayed on their horse mounts in silent beckoning for her present audience. Isaac and Jake followed behind her.

They were as unapproachably imposing as she recalled. Her father, Jericho, wore his traditional robe of Pangean blue with white striped sleeves. He also wore his favorite Pangean crown. It was his crown of 'service to the people.' It was a traditional farmer's cap, a straw one. Yet, this one was more ornamented than the traditional head wear of the common man. It had tassels of many colors decorating its back, like tails, signifying his rule over every rank of the Pangean military and the nation's governors. Jericho wore the cap in the untraditional fashion of leaning it to the side so that he could see better out of it. Thus, only one elderly eye was seen.

Mother, Barda, wore the same robe. Her leader's uniform followed the traditions strictly, never deviating even slightly from the proper norm. Her leader's cap was a golden crown, wildly made colorful with gems dug from the soil of each colony under the Pangean Empire. It overruled her head, even over her finely tied hair. The crown stretched all the way down to her neck like a swollen skull. Atop this crown was a short spire with a trident at its head. Within this crown was the face of a beleaguered ruler and a disappointed mother.

Despite the bitterness on their faces, Ilene was almost happy to be seeing them after so long. That is, until they spoke. "Daughter, we sent you off to get married in the name of allying ourselves with Ur and instead, you return to us with a war at your back."

King Jericho denied Barda's accusations. "Barda, you know full well that the Ursians were plotting to kill her from the outset. This is not her fault."

The king turned to Ilene. "I'm just glad that you have made it back to us safely, my dear."

"Yes," sneered Barda, "at the cost of many expensive ships and possibly hundreds of other yet to be counted lost lives. The spoiled child cannot possibly comprehend the resources that have been wasted on her when they should have been used for other areas in the war effort."

Jericho tried vainly to reason once more with his short-sighted wife. "Preserving our daughter was a great victory for morale. Now that she is safe, we can focus on other matters of this conflict."

Barda directed her horse to walk closer to Ilene so that she could shadow over her child. "All I know is that I was pulled from my palace in the capital to be brought all the way to Rodinia simply because my daughter has spent her whole life as a liability to Pangea. And now that liability is coming at a heavy cost. Stay in our country estate, daughter. You'll be safe there."

Despite all of the dangers that Ilene had survived, she still held a fearful respect for her parents- especially for her malicious mother. "Yes, ma'am."

After the berating, Jake and Isaac approached Ilene sadly. They looked like men with something uneasy to say. So, Jake let it out as quickly as he could to avoid the agony of it.

"Isaac and I were talking, Ilene." He gulped wearily. "And we now see that we cannot go back to the palace with you, at least, not yet."

Isaac saw that Jake was wavering, so he assisted with their explanation. "There's a war on. We're going to enlist in the Pangean military. We've seen what those Ursians are capable of. I won't let such a thing happen again if I can help it. Besides, Jake lost our passage papers during the battle. Military service may be our only way of getting out of all the immigration lines being formed."

Jake said, "I didn't lose them. It was Craig-"

Isaac's stone-heavy eyes stopped Jake. Isaac looked back at Ilene and gritted his mouth and eyelids shut to keep his spare sobs and tears dormant.

Jake concluded their presentation to her. "Ilene..." he moved closer to her. "Marlene did amazing work raising you. No," he corrected himself, "that's not right. Calling it a 'work' would suggest that it was just some job done merely for wages. Raising you was her purpose and passion in life. Because in you, I see all of her heart and love. Please send me a message when you discover the day of her funeral. I wish to be in attendance... that is if the invite still stands..."

Isaac looked curiously at Jake. Then, Ilene hugged them both. "Thank you. Thank you both for being so good to me. Farewell, my friends."

Jake made one last joke. "So... that's a yes then, right?"

So, by order of Queen Barda, Ilene was returned to her life of luxury befitting a princess. A carriage was arranged for her so that she could leave the milling crowds of lost Princeberg. Ilene rode in the carriage up a series of vertical paths. Her parents rode ahead of her, still on their horses. The sight of the green hills kissing the fading gold of the sky made her feel at home again more than anything.

The serene light in the sky evoked in her thoughts of days when visits to Rodinia marked a return to what she considered her second home. It also signaled days when Marlene would play more with her than at the constant schoolhouse and den of discipline that the maid created out of the palace in Pangea. For in Rodinia they went out on adventurous hikes, swam in various ponds, and admired the end of every mountain cliff.

When night was cast over the world, they arrived at the royal estate itself- a three-story mansion located in the hidden confines of trees under the side of a mountain. None of her happy experiences were made manifest to Ilene again. There was no testing of the opening alcove's echo made by her maid in jest- only the hallow creak of the doors by a somber servant. No smell of Marlene's fine cooking graced the kitchen. Its smell faded away, never to be renewed. No rival to race up the stairs or through the halls ever challenged Ilene. No one asked if she wanted some milk or a story when she was left to sleep in her old room.

For a while she could not move from the spot in which she entered. Long after the sound of the closed door faded, she remained still. Ilene looked upon her lush bed. She stared out her window to see the countryside along with the lake at the foot of the mountain. Her closet on the other end of the room was left open from the last time that she was at Rodinia.

Every cabinet was a bookcase or a place to see herself in the mirror. Each one was fenced by stuffed animals. Ilene couldn't move because, in her heart, she knew that these comforts meant nothing without the arms of her friend wrapping around her.

Ilene knew that the moment her weary flesh touched the bed's softness she would break down at its touch, forced further to remember Marlene. But fatigue took Ilene, and she placed her body down into her bed. She didn't care that the blood and dust all about her would yield an unending stain to the sheets.

She surprisingly prevented an extreme episode of crying with but a single sniff. Ilene wondered if this meant that she could carry on without Marlene, or if she was starting to lose her loving devotion to her too quickly. But before she could complete that challenging thought, she was fully immersed in sleep as night fell.

A new thought woke her up. She suddenly remembered something. Marlene's room!

She got herself up. Through the darkness of the halls, she knew every step that she needed to take by memory. As quick as her sudden waking thought, she was back in her old maid's room- smaller, scarcer, but full of nostalgic memories too. It seemed to have been unused since last Marlene was there- given the small fogs of dust.

Ilene came here often after nightmares to sleep with Marlene. Mother Barda once lectured little Ilene for this. When Ilene's room was found empty one morning, the queen thought the princess was missing. "I thought that you were lost or kidnapped, daughter! How dare you waste the resources of the guards and staff like that!"

Some things never change. Ilene admired the small bed tucked away in the corner. Marlene told Ilene many funny stories like the sloth in the Kenorland jungles who lost a magic acorn. Ilene felt more relaxed just thinking of Marlene curled next to her, whispering the tale softly into her ear.

Yet Ilene was not in search of such memories as that. She was looking for something more. It wasn't hard to find. Beyond the bed, there was only one cabinet for clothes and a writing desk. It almost felt like her room back in Princeberg when she thought about it.

On the writing desk was an open journal. Little Ilene tried to look at it about a year ago when she first saw it. Marlene happened by and slammed it shut.

"What have I told you about people's property, Ilene?"

"Oh, I'm sorry, Marlene. I thought that it was a new story book. Is that your diary?"

"It is **my** personal property, and you can't even look at such things without the owner's permission. Is that clear, little miss?"

"It is. Yes. Although now you have me too curious. But out of love for you I shall not be tempted into reading about your secret desires to kill me with an axe. Now then, do you fancy some lunch?"

This jesting relaxed Marlene into a pleasant afternoon. Afterward, the whole incident was all but forgotten.

Until now, Ilene thought. *Now, out of that same love, Marlene: I must read your secrets so that I may better preserve your memory. May Alpha forgive my breach of your privacy, but I don't want any part of you to be lost to the void. Never...*

Ilene opened the book. She went quickly to the last entry. It was dated during the middle of this year, a month before the Ursian trip.

"Mansion seems clean enough. We'll be off tomorrow to Pangea for a few weeks prep for the wedding in Ur. Soldiers must be commissioned by the government, and I must get Ilene her needed trip supplies too. Alas, the work of the military and the work of wedding planners is never done."

"I do so look forward to Ilene's wedding. It is the most important step in one's adulthood. I wish her all the happiness. How I wish I could've found such a sweet ending with Jake. How happy we would've been together. Just when I think that I'm over it, the sappy sadness for losing him gets at me again. It's been, what, Marlene? Almost 10 years? Yes. Of course."

"But it still bothers me- what could have been. Perhaps the jesters in Ur are even funnier, sweeter, and kinder than dear Jake was. But I doubt it. Well, I must be off! Hope I don't forget anything. Ilene still needs help packing more books! I swear if that spoiled girl doesn't want to bring her entire collection! NOTE: Don't forget to pack this diary later!"

Ilene laughed happy tears at Marlene's forgetting of the diary. Reading it, it was as if the maid were back- writing her witticisms beyond death.

Even years later, she loved Jake still. This would make him happy. Or would it make him sadder? She was unsure.

I wonder if this diary has any entries from back when they were together.

She flipped back to the first page. Over 20 years ago! Praise Alpha for Marlene's inhumanly small handwriting. She could fit *The Holy Volume* on a napkin if she were tasked to. Ilene looked for a mention of Jake, no doubt during the secret period of their relations. Just when Ilene thought that maybe Marlene left the subject out for fear of discovery, she landed on something. About 18 years ago.

"Had the most mortifying but blessed day. I swear that I'm not a klutz! Everyone makes mistakes, but mine get the most attention it seems. I was serving King Jericho soup and I tripped, and it fell upon him! The scalding heat made him scream. As fast as lightning, the soldiers aimed guns upon me. One would think that I was trying to assassinate him. It was all straightened out and he forgave me."

"The queen gave me a hateful eyeful during the whole of the incident. I was dismissed to my house duties for the day. Later tonight, Jake came by the kitchen as I was finishing up my own soup dinner. That impetuous scoundrel! I knew that he knew from the moment that I saw his smarmy smile."

"'Trying to assassinate our dear leader again, are you? What evil witch's brew are you concocting? Spicy Curry? Clam Chowder? Gumbo?'"

"I nearly beat him away with my spoon. He licked it instead. Then his eyes got so- ugh! I'm so weak! Told him not to sneak kisses like that (though it was really I who started it, shame on me)."

"'We could be found out,' I said."

"'So?' he said."

"I'm beginning to think that the thrill of getting banished, lashed, or even worse for his affairs with me turns him on more than anything- especially when I have to re-explain it to him in a hushed tone as he brushes his skin on mine."

"'Well,' he said after I explained this again, though we both damn well knew the risks, 'I promise not to tell anyone if you promise to fix up an extra bowl for me.'"

"'I dunno. Bribery might not look so good on your list of crimes.'"

"I was happy to make some soup for him of course. How I love to trade jest for jest with that dear man. But: horror! I accidentally spilled his bowl on him as I did the king! He laid into me in that same moment."

"'Why, bless my britches! I'm on par with royalty! I've been anointed with the same holy soup as his majesty!'"

"We laughed and laughed. We couldn't help it. We didn't care who heard after we lost control. It was as if we had the Pangean palace all to ourselves. Aye. The king and queen of mirth- that's us. How we are blessed!"

"Might've laughed so hard that I told him that I loved him. He stopped. He blushed. I laughed even harder. He kissed me again! Well, at least we didn't wake anyone. So blessed..."

Ilene smiled at the fortune of happening upon the story that Jake told her. It touched her heart to see how happy they were together. Knowing how horribly it all ended... she had to read more.

She flipped ahead about a year until she found what she was looking for.

"The queen was bound to find me out eventually. I could only fake sickness for so long."

Ilene thought that maybe this wasn't what she was looking for. She wanted to see where the queen discovered their affair, not an instance of faking illness to get off work. She was about to skim on when she began to get curious as to why Marlene was feigning poor health in the first place.

"She knocked on my door today. I let her in. What could I do? Deny her? I put myself back into bed, covering myself. I had one last desperate ploy."

"'I'm still very contagious, your majesty. I wouldn't get too close. Was there anything you-?'"

"She effortlessly peeled the sheets off me- my pregnant stomach revealed unto her."

Ilene was in shock. It... couldn't be... She had to read on.

"She seemed to stare at me for an eternity. I could only cry, lost to her mercy."

"'Who?' she finally asked."

"I couldn't help but instead reply by asking what's she going to do to us."

"'Who?' she asked even more firmly."

"I didn't want to give Jake up. I didn't want him to get hurt, or to lose him- even if it meant a thousand lashes for me."

"'Please,' I begged, 'don't make me tell. I knew that the consequences for intercourse in the palace would be steep. I'll take whatever he'd get- double even! Just don't hurt him. I'll do anything!'"

"She stared on at me. She seemed to be thinking."

"'Here's what's going to happen: you will carry the child to birth. You may name it, care for it, even love it. But the child will be known to all as my heir. No one will know the truth but us. Then I'll leave your tramp alone. But such relations stop as of now. If I get wind of such foolishness again, or I once more see you held up from work by pregnancy... you will drink the bitter water to terminate the next child and be banished alongside your mate. Understood?'"

"Her words hung in my ear. My child- it was going to belong to her. No one can know- for Jake's sake. Oh, Alpha... forgive me..."

Ilene's mind echoed everything that she just read. The conclusions that her thoughts linked together were startling. *It can't be...*

She flipped on.

"I'll name her Ilene-"

No.

She flipped on.

"She's growing up so fast. Yet she's so spoiled. I swear I'll slip up in front of her someday."

She flipped on.

No.

"How I wish she knew how much her real mother loves her."

She flipped on.

No.

"Barda could never really love her like a daughter. But as her true mother-"

No!

"I can."

Ilene crushed the pages between her trembling fingers in agony. Her head curled over the desk. It shook erratically with each burning tear.

"Marlene," she sobbed, "Not her... not my... no..."

EPILOGUE: WHAT NOW?

She still couldn't end the flipping, even after all but tearing the pages apart. She couldn't stop.

She whimpered to herself. *Why was Jake still exiled? How did my... friend get banished?*

"Piano practice was interrupted today by **him**- the jester. He played it off smoothly. He performed some bit of comedy as he hopped into our practice while saying that it's too early for piano, pretending some fear that we'd wake the parents even though we always played softly. He told little Ilene to instead go play the drums on the trees outside or on the guard's armor."

"With her giggles and young look to my face for approval, I let her off."

"'And as for you,' he said, 'we got some alone time to catch up on.'"

"I couldn't. I got up. 'Not today, Jake. I can't let Ilene out of my sight. We've much to do today... schooling, etiquette, a dinner ball in Rodinia to prep for-'"

"'Tut-tut,' he said, 'Time enough for that. The soldiers will protect her out there. I wasn't even joking when I made wise about your being up too early. One day it's piano at 9, then 8, now 7? What's next? 6? 5? At this rate, you'll be up before any of our troops.'"

"I didn't say anything. I picked up Ilene's music sheet and tried to walk calmly from the room."

"'I'm beginning to think that you're avoiding me.'"

"'No, Jake, I-'"

"There was no going back."

"'I just- there's so much work now with Ilene. I-'"

"'I get it. I've noticed that you've slowly phased me out these past few years. Perhaps we can't keep this up. How can we hide our thing together when you've got their kid to take care of? I guess the kid needs **someone** to care for her. She couldn't ask for a better guardian than you. Ah, well. Anyway: I'll get out of your way.'"

"His sad, but understanding face broke me. I told him to wait. I looked out the window to see little Ilene, our little girl. She **was** safe with the palace guards- playing drums on the armor of her sworn protectors. It was still early. What could one visit with sweet, silly Jake hurt?"

Ilene grimly flipped on, knowing of all the pain to come. She landed.

"Alpha, damn my backsliding! I've lost him to my lust- forever! Discovery of my lost corset was found in Jake's room. Bless him- he continually insisted to his arresters, 'I swear. Those are mine!'"

"Several beatings were issued. They made all of the staff watch in the throne room. I couldn't show one flinch as his black eyes bled out."

"The queen's edict: 'Tell us who she was, or you will be exiled. You will lose the benefits of your station as royal jester. Confess and you will both only be lashed with your positions intact. **Now** who was she?'"

"Jake shook his head. Though his eyes were shut black, he looked right at me."

"'You guys are going to feel awfully silly when I break out my corset collection.'"

"'Enough foolishness. Take him to his quarters to pack his belongings. He is to be off the grounds by sunset.'"

"His brothers followed after him, saying that they're with him. At least he wasn't alone."

"'At this time,' said the queen, 'I offer the woman a chance to step forward if she truly wishes to be with the jester. She cannot fornicate under our palace roof. It is an abominable shame. We, the king, staff, and I must not only be held up as examples of Alphite holiness, but we all have a child to raise together as the heir to our kingdom's legacy. Don't presume that your lusts are more important than the kingdom... nor her. Step forward now and be with the jester. Only forsake your place with us and dear Ilene. Stay, and this disgusting display will end. Only then will I mercifully allow you a place at our side. Who will it be? Ilene or the jester?'"

"She knew. She was clearly talking to me. She knew that Jake was the only one. She knew that choosing between him or little Ilene would end it. Alpha, help me, I almost ran off with him and his brothers at that moment. But then my eyes fell to those small, innocent little pupils on Ilene sitting in her smaller throne next to the queen's- so afraid, so confused about why they hurt her dear jester. I couldn't. I couldn't leave my daughter. O forgive me, Alpha!"

"Further tempting cruelty by Barda: she sent me to his room with one last quick meal before his exile. He seemed almost finished packing when I went in."

"'The guards outside my door aren't getting too impatient, are they? I offered them the chance to help me pack.'"

"Ever the joker, I thought. I could only sadly chuckle and put his sandwich and milk down. Before I could think of the proper goodbye that wouldn't out us, he suddenly collapsed his tear bleeding face on to my neck."

"'I-I'm so sorry, Marlene! I should have been more careful!' he whispered with sharp sobs. 'If I ever dreamed that this could've happened, I'd never- I-oh...' he groaned..."

"I told him to calm down. 'Dear Jake'... I found myself saying, 'It's all right, Jake. No tears, okay? It's not your fault. You hear me, now? **Not** your fault... Bad things like this just can't help but happen. Making yourself ashamed of it all won't help either of us.'"

"This seemed to stop his crying. For once I can't recall who first initiated our kiss. But it being the last, it was definitely the sweetest. Part of me hoped that the guards **would** get impatient and happen upon us. Then we'd both be exiled, and we could stay together like this. Then I remembered Ilene and I broke myself off from him... forever."

"I walked out of Jake's room, out of Jake's life, and I never looked back."

So, there it was. Marlene was Ilene's true mother. Every breath felt heavier. She didn't know what to do with the truth. Scream it to the heavens? Confront Barda with this? How could she explain this to Jake? Could she even go on knowing that her

419

true mother was gone before she truly knew her?

All she could do was take the diary back to her room. She hid it under her mattress until she could figure out what was to be done. All that was left was to find sleep, except only worry for the future was all that could be found.

Sometime later, three knocks cried out. The first knock went unnoticed, just as sleep was starting to take her. The second was like a gunshot as Ilene sprang up and ran to the door while the third knock sounded. Ilene opened the door. The Pangean knight that led her rescue stood before her, still encased in his full armor.

"May I come in?"

Ilene nodded nervously. As he marched inside, he stated, "I do hope that I'm not intruding, but I have an urgent matter to discuss with you."

Before he could elaborate, he instructed Ilene to close the door. "Here is the world that you now live in, Ilene, whether you like it or not. Pangean intelligence has reason to believe that the Ursians will continue to spread the rumor that you are the Goddess, Omega-Incarnate, come to bring judgement day. This will allow the highly religious nation to have many foreign followers and allies in the growing war. We're already making efforts to counteract this by sending out some of our own Alphite priests as missionaries. Likewise, it is easy to deduce that they are planning a full-scale invasion of Rodinia with you, and your parents, as the prime targets. Some scouts have reported that such attacks have already begun in Pangea itself."

Ilene could only ask, "Why are you telling me all of this? I'm not a soldier."

The armored man sighed. "In days of old, the leaders of countries would fight alongside their people during war. Now, to avoid the loss of such officials, they sit on their thrones and 'monitor' the battles. It seems that the tradition will be revived soon. There have been sightings of Empress Lida herself on one of the Ursian ships."

Ilene's blood went thick with frosted zeal at the mention of her name.

"During our return trip to Rodinia, I shared a smoke with your jester. He told me of all that you've been through- the loss of your maid, and his brother. What struck me most about his story was how both deaths affected you. He said: 'She seemed so helpless, as if she thought that she could've done something, but she couldn't.' He also believes that you may be responsible for the death of an Ursian lieutenant who killed his brother. Is this true? Tell me... did it feel good to get revenge?"

Ilene saw Marl again. His serene face dissolved happily away again upon hearing that he had killed the man who murdered his son.

"Yes," she said boldly.

The knight moved closer. "Then I offer you the opportunity to train in secret under me so that you may fight by your country's side and defeat Ur."

"What exactly is in it for you?"

"Because I want revenge on all of Ur too."

He removed his helmet.

"MARIUS?"

It was the shipmate from her first journey to Ur.

"What do you say, Ilene?"

END OF BOOK ONE

ACKNOWLEDGEMENT

Special thanks to my family who has encouraged me throughout the years- especially my parents (Paul and Lisa Tucker).

HUGE thank you to Jason Thornsberry for the amazaing artwork! Find more of his incredible art on Facebook, Instagram, and TikTok!

Shout out to my pet bird, Gandalf, for helping me with the editing.

A hearty Alphite salute to those who helped #SpreadtheRumor online, by word-of-mouth, and via local media. May Alpha bless you for your service to the Ursian Empire.

And to my readers. Thank you SO much for reading my book! All of you have helped my greatest dream come true! Now go chase yours! You can do anything you set your mind to.

ABOUT THE AUTHOR

Cody R. Tucker

Cody was born in Lima, Ohio (March 31st, 1992). He is a graduate of Wright State University. There, he achieved a Bachelor's in English with an emphasis in Creative Writing. He is the author of the "Omega" trilogy of fantasy novels. He lives in Ohio with his pet bird (and assistant editor) Gandalf. They got more novels cooking. Stay tuned!

BOOKS IN THIS SERIES

The Omega Trilogy

BOOKS BY THIS AUTHOR

The Omega Rumor

The Omega War

COMING SOON

Omega's Fall

COMING SOON

Made in the USA
Middletown, DE
09 September 2024

60072493R00245